Praise for the Believe Series

"As grandparents of fifty grandchildren, we heartily endorse the *Believe and You're There* series. Parents and grandparents, gather your children around you and discover the scriptures again as they come alive in the *Believe and You're There* series."

—STEPHEN AND SANDRA COVEY
Stephen Covey is the bestselling author of *7 Habits of Highly Effective People*

"Bravo! This series is a treasure! You pray that your children will fall in love with and get lost in the scriptures just as they are discovering the wonder of reading. This series does it. Two thumbs way, way up!"

—MACK AND REBECCA WILBERG
Mack Wilberg is the music director of the Mormon Tabernacle Choir

"This series is a powerful tool for helping children learn to liken the scriptures to themselves. Helping children experience the scriptural stories from their point of view is genius."

—ED AND PATRICIA PINEGAR
Ed Pinegar is the bestselling author of *Raising the Bar*

"We only wish these wonderful books had been available when we were raising our own children. How we look forward to sharing them with all our grandchildren!"

—STEPHEN AND JANET ROBINSON
Stephen Robinson is the bestselling author of *Believing Christ*

"The *Believe and You're There* series taps into the popular genre of fantasy and imagination in a wonderful way. Today's children will be drawn into the reality of events described in the scriptures. Ever true to the scriptural accounts, the authors have crafted delightful stories that will surely awaken children's vivid imaginations while teaching truths that will often sound familiar."

—TRUMAN AND ANN MADSEN
Truman Madsen is the bestselling author of *Joseph Smith, the Prophet*

"My dad and I read *At the Miracles of Jesus* together. First I'd read a chapter, and then he would. Now we're reading the next book. He says he feels the Spirit when we read. So do I."

—CASEY J., AGE 9

"My mom likes me to read before bed. I used to hate it, but the *Believe* books make reading fun and exciting. And they make you feel good inside, too."

—KADEN T., AGE 10

"Reading the *Believe* series with my tweens and my teens has been a big spiritual boost in our home—even for me! It always leaves me peaceful and more certain about what I believe."

—GLADYS A., AGE 43

"I love how Katie, Matthew, and Peter are connected to each other and to their grandma. These stories link children to their families, their ancestors, and on to the Savior. I heartily recommend them for any child, parent, or grandparent."

—ANNE S., AGE 50
Mother of ten, grandmother of nine (and counting)

When Ammon Was a Missionary

Books in the *Believe and You're There* series

Believe and You're There

When Ammon Was a Missionary

Book 6

ALICE W. JOHNSON & ALLISON H. WARNER

DESERET
BOOK

Salt Lake City, Utah

Library of Congress Cataloging-in-Publication Data
Johnson, Alice W.
  Believe and you're there when Ammon was a missionary / Alice W.
Johnson and Allison H. Warner ; illustrated by Jerry Harston and Casey Nelson.
    p. cm.
  Summary: After stepping through Grandma's new painting, Katie, Matthew, and Peter find themselves near the fields of King Lamoni, the Lamanite ruler. The children learn that loving service is the best form of missionary work.
  ISBN 978-1-60641-247-3 (paperbound)
  1. Ammon (Book of Mormon figure)—Juvenile fiction. 2. Book of Mormon stories. 3. Children's stories, American. I. Warner, Allison H. II. Harston, Jerry, ill. III. Nelson, Casey (Casey Shane), 1973– ill. IV. Title.
  BX8627.4.A6J64 2010
  289.3'22—dc22   2009042216

Printed in the United States of America
R. R. Donnelley and Sons, Crawfordsville, IN

10   9   8   7   6   5   4   3   2   1

Believe in the wonder,
Believe if you dare,
Believe in your heart,
Just believe . . . and you're there!

Contents

Chapter One

Starry, Starry Night

"That's easy for you to say," Katie replied to her taunting brothers, as she, Matthew, and Peter lay in sleeping bags in Grandma's backyard. The stars gleamed in the late summer night sky overhead. "You try it with one of your friends first, and let me know how it goes!"

Matthew cleared his throat and gulped at his sister's retort, his eyes sweeping the immense panorama above him. "Well, hmmm . . ."

"That's what I thought!" Katie said, feeling victorious. "It's not so easy when the shoe is on the other foot, is it, Matthew?" She spotted the North Star twinkling extra brightly above them, anchoring the Big Dipper and pointing to the Little Dipper.

"I guess not," he had to admit. "But there has to be a way. After all, missionaries do it all the time."

"That's different! They talk to people they don't even know. Aubrey is my friend, and that's the way I want it to stay," Katie explained. Aubrey and Katie had become good friends when Aubrey's family moved in across the street. Now, they both were going to start junior high next week, and they couldn't wait.

"Well, if she is really a friend, why don't you want to tell her about the gospel?" Matthew asked Katie.

"I want to tell her, but . . ." Katie hesitated.

"But what?" he asked.

"Sometimes it changes everything. Like, what if she doesn't want to hear?" Katie answered him.

Matthew nodded his head slowly. He had to admit she had a point. But how was anyone going to know how wonderful the gospel was if everyone kept it a secret?

"Okay," he said, empathizing with Katie, "I see what you're saying." But standing his ground, he added, "But there has to be a way!"

"Hey, look right up there!" Peter interjected, pointing excitedly at the night sky. "That's Pegasus! He carried lightning bolts for Zeus." Clearly, Peter had been learning about Greek myths and how constellations were named after the ancient imaginary characters in them.

Katie and Matthew looked up into the sky as Peter pointed out the stars that made up the constellation called Pegasus. As they tried to pick out the shape of a horse made by the stars, Peter announced confidently, "I wouldn't have any trouble telling one of my friends about the gospel."

Katie laughed. "I'll bet you wouldn't, little brother." Peter was fearless about talking to people. It was one of his best qualities. Right now, Katie wished she had a little more of his bravado.

"You're right, Matthew," she said, picking up their conversation again. "There just has to be a way to share the gospel without making Aubrey uncomfortable. But what is it?" Katie spoke as if she were thinking out loud.

"Look over there to the left," Peter pointed again. "That's Scorpius, the scorpion. He killed the great hunter, Orion. Only you can't see Orion in the sky until wintertime."

"How do you know so much about the stars anyway?" Matthew asked, clearly impressed.

"Don't you remember learning about those things when you were a Cub Scout?" Peter asked, scanning the sky for more constellations. "You know, Katie, if it were me, I'd just ask my friend right out, 'What do you know about The Church of Jesus Christ of Latter-day Saints?' Then I'd say, 'Do you want to learn more about it because I'd love to tell you!'"

Matthew smiled to himself. "You are quite a guy, Peter. You're a little crazy, but you get right to the point. I wish I could be more like that. I think I'd have to take it slow. I'd want to get to know the person first, and what he thinks about God and serious stuff like that. And then I would decide how to approach him."

"I've thought that maybe I could invite Aubrey to come to a church activity with me. Maybe she'd like it and would want to know more about the gospel on her own," Katie said hopefully.

"See that band of light that looks like a misty cloud? That's the Milky Way," Peter said, continuing his astronomy lesson. "That's our galaxy," he added, pointing toward the expanse of light arching in the heavens over them.

"Peter, I don't think you are listening to a word I'm saying," Katie challenged her brother.

"Why do you say that?" he asked, surprised at his sister's frustrated tone.

"Well, here I am trying to figure out what to do, and all you can talk about is the Milky Way and constellations and things like that," she countered.

"I guess you're right," Peter conceded, "but how can I lie here with all of those stars up there and not think about how amazing they are?"

"Yeah, but what about me and my problem?" Katie pushed out her bottom lip and uncharacteristically started a very convincing pout.

"Oh, come on, Sis! While I've been looking at the stars, I've been listening to everything you've said, and I've been thinking," Peter reassured her.

"So have you come up with any good ideas?" Matthew asked, curious to hear Peter's response.

"Maybe . . . well, here's what I've come up with. The Milky Way is made up of all kinds of stars, right? Some of them are really old, and some of them are young. Some shine brighter than others, some are close and some are far . . ."

"Okay, okay, we get the picture. What are you getting at?" Katie interrupted, sounding a little antsy.

"Here's my point," Peter responded. "Stars are kind of like people. All of us are different from each other, too—just like stars. And since there are lots of different kinds of people, there must be lots of different ways to tell them about the gospel. My way is to just tell people straight out. And Matthew wants to get to know people first and think about the best way to approach them. It seems to me that your way, Sis, might be to first be a good friend to the person—just like you already are—and then show her what the gospel is all about just by how you live it. Remember how you made chocolate-chip cookies to welcome Aubrey to the neighborhood? And then you helped Aubrey and her mom organize their garage after they were moved in. It seems like you're a good example of a Latter-day Saint for Aubrey already."

Katie's eyes widened in wonder with every word her little brother uttered. "Peter, I am inspired by what you're saying! You really have been thinking, haven't you?"

"I guess so." Peter smiled bashfully.

"I'll just have to summon up my courage and figure out a way to talk to Aubrey," Katie mumbled as she closed her heavy eyelids.

"Speaking of courage, do you know who had a lot of courage?" Peter asked, and then answered his own question. "It was Hercules. See his constellation right over there? He was sent on twelve labors for

Zeus. On the first one, he killed the Nemean lion. Then, let's see . . . what was his second big task?"

That was the last thing Katie and Matthew heard. Sleep overcame them, and they nodded off peacefully beneath the magical stars of the Milky Way.

Chapter Two

More Than Coincidence

The next morning as Katie gazed up at the craggy crests cutting into the emerging morning sky, she remembered Aubrey, recently moved from Texas, saying that she felt the tall peaks surrounding their small, protected valley were going to fall down on her. Katie was chuckling silently at the memory when the familiar slap of Grandma's screen door jolted her back to the present. "Good morning, everyone!" Grandma greeted them cheerily.

"It's too bad the boys aren't awake yet," she said loudly to Katie, as she surveyed the two motionless sleeping bags on the lawn. "I suppose you and I will simply have to eat the hot waffles by ourselves."

Without missing a beat, Matthew and Peter jumped up and raced each other to the kitchen.

A short time later, Matthew munched happily on a strip of savory bacon as he asked, "Grandma, is your new painting ready?"

"Well! What with the waffles and all, I thought you'd forgotten about my new painting," Grandma teased.

"Are you kidding?" Peter asked, his mouth dropping open. "How could we forget that?"

"Well, you happen to be in luck, kids. There's a brand new painting sitting on the easel in the art cottage right now!" Grandma beamed as she delivered the good news.

"Right now? Let's go!" Peter chugged down the last of his orange juice and headed for the door.

"Not so fast," Grandma stopped him with a smile. "Katie and I have to finish our waffles first. But if you're really in a hurry, you could start the dishes," Grandma suggested, thoroughly amused.

Katie and Grandma cleverly timed their breakfast to be finished just as the dishes were completed. As they put the last forkfuls of food in their mouths, they were whisked out the back door by two very eager boys.

Hurrying along the flagstone path, Peter and Matthew danced excitedly, circling around Grandma and Katie, chanting, "Believe, believe, believe! Believe, believe, believe!"

They arrived at the cottage door, the boys breathless and Katie and Grandma laughing. "All that's left is for me to open this door," Grandma said, as she reached in her pocket, produced the key, and unlocked the door to the magical world of the art cottage. "Let's hear that password, kids. That is, if you have enough breath left to get it out."

Still jostling and laughing, the children chanted in unison the mysterious poem Grandma had inscribed in the front of their journals:

"Believe in the wonder,

Believe if you dare,

Believe in your hearts,"

And then, after taking a big breath, they all shouted with gleeful, giggling abandon,

"Just believe . . . and you're there!"

Still laughing, the children flopped down on the pillows in front of the easel, and Grandma sank thankfully into her rocking chair.

"You were certainly up late last night, children," Grandma said, as she settled herself. "You must have been discussing something very interesting."

"Oh, we were," Peter spoke enthusiastically. "I

was telling Matthew and Katie all about the constellations and how they got their names." Then his voice dropped a bit, and he sounded thoughtful and earnest. "And we were working on a problem. Katie has this new friend, Aubrey, who just moved in across our street. We were trying to help Katie get up the courage to tell Aubrey about the gospel."

"You might say we were figuring out how to be missionaries," Matthew explained.

"I'd say that's quite a coincidence, when you consider my new painting and the story we're going to read today. But then, I've always believed that some things are more than coincidence," Grandma mused, with a knowing smile on her face. "When you talk about missionaries, you surely have to think of Ammon, a great missionary from the Book of Mormon."

"Yeah!" Peter declared, his eyes lighting up. "He's the one who cut off the arms!"

Katie grimaced. "Why do you have to bring up that part?"

"Let's get the story straight from the beginning, shall we, kids?" Grandma picked up her Book of Mormon and began turning its pages.

"Aren't you going to show us the painting?" Peter asked, the suspense nearly killing him.

"All in good time, my boy." Grandma smiled down at her impatient grandson. "Let's see . . . here we are. Ammon was one of the four sons of good King Mosiah. But in his youth, he was not so good himself. Ammon and his brothers and their friend, Alma the Younger, went about trying to destroy the Church and threatening the believers."

"I know! And an angel appeared to them, and his voice sounded like thunder, and it shook the ground, and they fell down to the ground like they were dead," Matthew said excitedly.

"Yes, that's right," Grandma said. "And then . . ." she went on.

"Oh no, you're not going to tell the whole thing, are you? We'll be here for days!" Peter said with dismay.

Grandma laughed. "Why don't I give you a very short version that will set the stage for the painting, and then we'll uncover it. Will that work, my impatient Peter?"

"Okay, okay," Peter agreed.

"Here goes, then." Grandma talked briskly. "After the angel came, Alma, Ammon, and his brothers realized how bad they had been. They repented of all they had done and tried to make things better for the Church and its members. Now their father, Mosiah, was the king, and he was getting old. He was going to turn over the kingdom to his sons. Ammon would have been the new king. But instead of accepting their father's offer, they decided to be missionaries instead. They loved the gospel now, and they wanted to bring souls to Christ. They went to different places to preach the word of God. And Ammon," Grandma took a deep breath, "went to the land of Ishmael. Did everyone follow that?" The children nodded emphatically.

"All right, Peter," Grandma addressed the anxious boy. "The moment has come! Why don't you uncover the painting, and we'll get to our story?"

Peter sprang to his feet and whisked the sheet off the painting. The scene Grandma had painted was of a green, grassy pasture, dotted with dozens of grazing sheep, tended by several shepherds. Behind the pasture was a large, primitive-looking city with adobe homes built into the terraced hills. Perched right in the city's center was a sprawling, grand building shaped like a pyramid. A pathway cut along the

hillside from the huge building to the low, lush pastureland.

Peter flashed an impish smile at his brother and sister and flopped back on his pillow. "Go ahead, Grandma, we're all ears," he said, confident that a new adventure was about to unfold.

"I know this is not usual, but today I would like to start with a song I learned from my grand-mother." Grandma began to sing in her sweet wob-bly voice:

I can share the gospel while still in tender youth,
Telling others all about its plain and precious truth.
But sometimes I am worried they might not want to hear
About the restoration of the church I hold so dear.
Service and friendship and courage in my heart
Are just the missionary tools to help me do my part.
For if I help but one soul hold fast the iron rod,
How great shall be the joy I feel when I return to God.

As Grandma finished, Katie couldn't help thinking that the story of Ammon just might hold the answer to her Aubrey problem.

Chapter Three

"We Come in Peace"

Grandma picked up her Book of Mormon, adjusted her reading glasses, and began reading aloud. "'And as Ammon entered the land of Ishmael, the Lamanites took him and bound him, as was their custom to bind all the Nephites who fell into their hands, and carry them before the king.'"

Katie, Matthew, and Peter sat poised on their pillows, prepared to leave the art cottage at the slightest movement in the painting.

Grandma read on. "'And thus Ammon was carried before the king who was over the land of Ishmael; and his name was Lamoni; and he was a descendant of Ishmael.'"

"Eeee!" A little squeaking sound escaped Katie's lips as she caught sight of one of the king's shepherds strolling slowly with the sheep along the path that led from the king's stables to the pastures.

A grin spread across Peter's excited face, and he rubbed his hands together in anticipation of the children's impending departure.

"'And after [Ammon] had been in the service of the king three days, as he was with the Lamanitish servants going forth . . .'" Grandma continued reading, but not one of her three grandchildren heard a word she read.

Keeping their eyes glued to the canvas on the easel, they silently linked hands. Peter thrust his hand into the painting, and . . . WHOOSH! The air swirled forcefully around the children, lifting them easily from their soft pillows in the art cottage, carrying them through the air for a short moment, and depositing them safely in the land of Ishmael. The journey seemed to take but an instant.

"That was quick!" Peter declared, gasping for breath as the dusty air settled around them.

"I'll say!" Matthew agreed. "What a ride!"

"I didn't even have time to take a breath!" Katie exhaled loudly and slowly as she turned around to inspect their surroundings. They had landed in a small clearing, sheltered by thick green bushes and tall trees. Overhead, a beautiful sky made a blue backdrop for the rich, green vegetation. Shining through the leaves, radiant beams of sunlight created intricate shadow patterns on the ground beneath them.

A well-worn dirt path cut right through the middle of the grassy clearing. One end of the clearing opened to reveal dozens of white sheep in the green pasture beyond, which sloped down to a wide, slow river. Through the trees at the other end of the clearing, the city was visible, with its low dwellings and the imposing building.

"Look how big that building is!" Peter marveled, awestruck at the sheer size of the structure.

"I'm pretty sure that is Lamoni's palace," Matthew reasoned sensibly.

"I'd have to agree, and those must be his flocks over there," Katie concluded.

As they stood inspecting the view, they heard the snap of twigs and the crackle of leaves. They realized too late that someone was running toward the clearing where they stood. A panicked look crossed Katie's face, and she stood frozen, her eyes searching for a place to hide. But there was no time. A brown-skinned, dark-haired boy about Matthew's age burst into the clearing before any of them could move a muscle.

"Oh, no," Matthew muttered under his breath, "now what?"

He didn't have to wait long to find out. The boy, who was as startled as the three children, let out a loud whoop. Then, turning on them, he expertly twirled the staff he carried in his hand, bringing it to rest on Matthew's chest and demanding, "Who are you?"

Matthew opened his mouth, but couldn't speak. He looked to Katie, and, from the look on her face, Matthew feared she was going to cry—or faint. He fumbled for her hand, ready to escape at a moment's notice. He could feel that she was shaking all over.

All of a sudden, before Matthew could grab his hand, Peter piped up cheerily, "Hey, that was cool. Do you know any more karate?"

Moving his staff to Peter's chest, the boy's eyes narrowed, and he repeated his demand, this time

more forcefully, "Who are you, and what are you doing here?"

Suddenly Matthew noticed that, although the Lamanite boy's words sounded brave, the staff he held to Peter's chest was quivering. Perhaps, Matthew thought, the boy was as frightened as they were.

Peter responded, "I'm Peter." And then, imitating his favorite animated movie character, he added emphatically, "We come in peace."

"You come in peace?" the boy asked hopefully.

Finding his voice, Matthew jumped in. "Yes, we do. We come in peace."

The Lamanite boy lowered his staff slowly, obviously more relaxed, but still a little cautious. He asked again, this time more kindly, "And why are you here?"

"We wanted to see the king's sheep and visit your beautiful city," Matthew answered simply, gesturing first to the pastures and then to the nearby town.

"Are you Nephites?" the boy asked.

"No, we're Americans. We come from up north of here," Peter said proudly.

"I am very relieved," the boy said thankfully. "When I saw your light hair, I was afraid you were Nephites, coming to do us harm. I've never heard of

Americans, but as long as you are not Nephites . . . and you do seem nice . . . I am sorry if I scared you with my staff." He looked meaningfully at Katie as he apologized.

"Oh, don't worry," she laughed, "I'm just fine." Katie's voice sounded high and nervous, and she was not entirely convincing.

"Forgive me, please. My name is Gid. I am the son of Mishgar."

"I'm Katie, and these are my brothers, Matthew and Peter." Then she added haltingly, "We are the children of Walter."

Gid seemed to accept this readily, and he smiled in forthright friendship as he said, "I am on my way to fetch something for my father. He is in the pastures down by the river with the king's sheep. Would you like to come with me?"

"Yes, of course we would." Peter accepted the invitation immediately.

"We do have one problem." Gid furrowed his brow and ran his finger through his dark hair.

"What's that?" Matthew asked.

"Well, we are Lamanites here. You can tell by our dark skin and hair. Your skin is much too light. People might think you are Nephites, like I did.

Then they would bind you and take you to prison," Gid explained, clearly concerned.

"I see the problem," Matthew said, holding his fair-skinned arm next to Gid's brown one.

"I have an idea," Peter said, scooping up some of the rich, dark dirt covering the ground. It was so heavy and moist, it felt almost like clay. "Let's rub some of this dirt on our skin." He covered his face and arms with the reddish-brown loam and then started on his legs. When he finished, he looked to Gid for his approval.

Gid inspected him from top to bottom and nodded. "Yes," he said. "I think that will work very nicely."

Katie and Matthew scooped up big handfuls of dirt and transformed themselves into Lamanites, too. "Hmm," Gid said as he walked around them, inspecting them carefully. "Just one more thing," he said, taking the wide sash from his waist. "Katie, your hair is the most unusual color I have ever seen. It's the color of gold. We must cover it." Gid placed the sash on Katie's head, spreading it carefully to cover her hair, and then tied it on top in a large, firm knot.

When he was finished, he took one more long,

careful look at the three of them. Satisfied at last, he nodded and announced, "Come, my Lamanite friends. Let us be off!"

Chapter Four

A Friend to the King

The four children began walking toward the city in high spirits. Gid was proud of his flourishing hometown, and he was looking forward to pointing out the interesting sights to his new friends.

Katie and Peter walked in front of Matthew and Gid, who had quickly struck up a ready friendship.

"My father works for the king," Gid informed all his visitors. "He is the chief of all the keepers of the king's flocks."

"I knew a shepherd once," Peter exclaimed. "He lived near Bethlehem."

"That must be far away from here. I have never heard of it," Gid responded.

"Oh, yes. It is very far away," Matthew jumped right in, preventing Peter from saying more. "It is so far away that we have only been there once."

Katie joined the rescue, quickly changing the subject. "Does your father like being a shepherd?" she inquired of Gid.

"Yes, but it can be dangerous. When he takes the sheep to drink at the waters of Sebus, sometimes robbers come and scatter the flocks. Then, before the sheep can be gathered, the robbers sneak away with a few."

"Why is that so dangerous for the shepherds? Do the robbers try to hurt them?" Katie asked.

"No, that is not the problem. The king gets very angry with the shepherds when the sheep they are watching get scattered and stolen. He has even ordered that some shepherds be killed as punishment," Gid explained solemnly.

"Gid! Gid! There you are!" someone yelled frantically, approaching the children from behind.

They all turned to see a man running toward them as fast as he could go.

"Father!" Gid answered, his voice filled with concern. "What is it? What has happened?"

The panting man paused, doubled over with his hands on his knees, breathless from running. Between gasps, he wheezed, "The sheep . . . waters of Sebus . . . Ammon . . . arms. Can't stop now . . . ," he continued, motioning for them to follow. "Must tell the king . . . come!"

"Come on!" Gid dashed off to catch up with his father. "Follow me," he called to the three bewildered children.

Peter took off, keeping Gid in his sights. Matthew grabbed Katie by the hand and followed behind, running to keep up.

"Matthew, are we going where I think we're going?" Katie managed to ask.

"You mean the palace?" Matthew asked, not slowing down.

"Uh-huh," Katie half-moaned her response.

"That's what I'm thinking," he replied.

"Oh, no!" This time she wailed loudly, stopping

29

in her tracks. "Don't tell me we are going to have to see all those arms!"

"We can't worry about that now, Sis! We're going to lose the others if we don't hurry up." Matthew grabbed Katie's hand and sprinted around a corner, which opened up into a small marketplace. Matthew spied Peter and Gid just as they disappeared through a large, stone archway on the other side of the market.

"Come on, Sis, we're almost there," Matthew encouraged Katie, as he dragged her through the marketplace, darting in and out of the stands and people.

As they passed through the arch, they found themselves in a grand plaza, right in the center of the city. At the far end of the plaza, the mammoth palace towered above them. It was a sprawling, pyramid-shaped structure, made up of many smaller buildings on different levels. The walls were decorated with rich, colorful paintings and elaborate carvings. Stone stairs led up the center of the structure, interrupted by a smaller plaza halfway to the top. The stairs continued from the small plaza to the uppermost part of the palace. This highest level was flat, protected from the blazing sun by a large canopy held aloft by four ornate, wooden posts.

"There they are!" Katie called out, spotting the others at the base of the palace stairs.

They caught up to Mishgar and the boys. Mishgar and his fellow servants were gathered there, talking excitedly. Several of the servants carried bulky bundles covered with large pieces of leather.

"There you are!" Peter cried, giving Matthew a big bear hug. "We lost you in the crowd."

"We were right behind you," Matthew said, "but someone slowed me down a bit." He gestured with his head toward his big sister, rolling his eyes just a bit.

"What are those men carrying?" Katie asked nervously.

Peter grimaced. "Those are the arms that Ammon chopped off of the Lamanite robbers."

"You just stay right over here." Matthew put himself between Katie and the men with the arms.

Mishgar hurried back to the children. "Come, Gid. We shepherds are going into King Lamoni's court to tell him of Ammon's bravery. You can come, if you like."

"These are my new friends, Father. They are called Matthew, Katie, and Peter," Gid said, gesturing to each child in turn. "May they come in too?"

"Sure, sure," said Mishgar, distracted by the thought of telling the king what had happened. "You and your friends stand at the back of the court and be very quiet," Mishgar instructed. Solemnly and silently, the four children nodded their understanding.

The servants led the way into the palace and its throne room, and each in turn laid his bundle in front of the king's throne.

From the back of the large chamber, the children stood quietly, awestruck by the commanding presence of the king and his many attendants. The king sat at the front of the huge chamber on his raised, rich-looking throne, flanked on either side by servants and advisors.

But it was the king himself, clothed in exotic, royal attire, at whom the children couldn't stop staring. A jaguar-skin skirt hung from his waist, held in place by a belt made of shiny silver chains adorned with the long, pointy teeth of wild animals. A netted jade collar was fastened around his neck, and a colorful headdress with plumes of blue and green quetzal feathers sat upon his head. Mishgar and the other servants knelt at his feet.

"Stand forth and testify concerning this matter," King Lamoni commanded the servants.

As chief shepherd, Mishgar spoke first. Then each shepherd, in turn, told of the things which he had seen at the waters of Sebus. It seemed that a group of thieves, whooping and charging wildly, had come to frighten and scatter the sheep. But the newest shepherd, Ammon, just three days on the job, calmly told the other shepherds to gather the flocks. Then he faced the marauding enemy alone.

First, he killed six men using his sling. Then the robbers, angry with Ammon for slaying their brethren, went after him with their swords. Mishgar described what happened next. "Every time a man lifted his club to smite Ammon, Ammon smote off his arms with his sword. He withstood the enemies' blows by smiting their arms with the edge of his sword, and he caused them to flee by the strength of his arm."

The king was astonished and said, "Surely, this is more than a man. Behold, is not this the Great Spirit who doth send such great punishments upon this people, because of their murders?"

Mishgar answered, "Whether he be the Great Spirit or a man, we know not. . . . We know that he is a friend to the king. And now, O king, we do not believe that a man has such great power, for we know he cannot be slain."

When King Lamoni heard these words, he said, "Now I know that it is the Great Spirit; and he has come down at this time to preserve your lives, that I might not slay you as I did your brethren."

"What does he mean by 'the Great Spirit'?" Peter asked Gid in a low whisper.

"To us, the Great Spirit is God. I think the king is afraid that he has done wrong in the past to kill his servants when sheep were lost or stolen. And he fears that the Great Spirit has come down to stop him from doing it again," Gid replied.

"I guess his conscience is getting the better of him," Katie commented.

Everyone was quiet, waiting for the king to go on. The king shifted from one side to the other in his seat. Finally he asked, "Where is this man that has such great power?"

"As you commanded earlier in the day, he is feeding your horses and preparing your chariots to take you to tonight's feast at your father's house," Mishgar replied.

The king was amazed by this news. First,

Ammon had risked his own life to save the sheep—and he had defeated the robbers all by himself. And now, instead of expecting a hero's welcome, he was out in the stables tending to the horses!

The astonished king said to all in his court, "Surely there has not been any servant among all my servants that has been so faithful as this man; for even he doth remember all my commandments to execute them. Now I surely know that this is the Great Spirit, and I would desire him that he come in unto me, but I durst not." He sank back in his seat and closed his eyes, deep in thought.

"I think the king really wants to ask Ammon to come to him, but he's worried about what Ammon will think of him," Katie murmured softly in Matthew's ear.

"Isn't that how we all are sometimes? We want to be close to Heavenly Father, but we're afraid to ask Him to be near because we're not perfect yet," Matthew answered Katie with the very kind of insight she had come to expect from her thoughtful brother.

"It's funny," she replied to Matthew. "Even though Lamoni is a king, he's a lot like the rest of us, isn't he?"

Chapter Five

"I Am a Man"

As he had been instructed earlier that morning, Ammon now worked steadily in the stables to prepare the horses and chariots for King Lamoni's upcoming journey. While the king's court was marveling at Ammon's miraculous feats, Ammon worked away until he was satisfied that everything was in order. Only then did he prepare himself to be presented in the king's court.

Ammon climbed the stairs to the palace and strode with calm assurance across the central courtyard toward the royal chamber. He paused before entering. The noble men and women of the court were outfitted in extravagant plumed headdresses, luxurious animal skins, and beaded shawls. All their finery seemed a stark contrast to Ammon's humble shepherd's clothing. But Ammon knew the Lord was with him. With quiet dignity, he approached the throne.

The king was still deeply troubled by the way he had treated his servants in the past. Furthermore, the possibility that Ammon was indeed the Great Spirit worried him greatly. His heart was heavy, and his very appearance seemed changed from the last time Ammon had been in his presence.

Ammon interpreted the change as displeasure, and he turned to leave Lamoni's presence. Lamoni motioned to one of his servants, who called after Ammon, "Rabbanah."

Peter nudged Gid and whispered, "What does 'rabbanah' mean?"

Gid whispered back, "It means 'great and powerful king.'"

"Oh." Peter nodded his understanding, although he thought it was interesting that a humble shepherd was called "great king" right in front of Lamoni, perched on a grand throne in a magnificent palace.

"Rabbanah," the servant continued, "the king desireth thee to stay."

Ammon stopped and turned, squared his shoulders, and stepped forward to face the king.

Respectfully, he asked, "What wilt thou that I should do for thee, O king?"

Lamoni sat in total silence for an hour—a whole hour! He seemed too troubled to speak. No one in the throne room dared move. Even Peter was unusually still. Ammon waited patiently for the king's answer. Sensing that a mighty struggle was taking place in the king's heart, Ammon prompted him again, asking, "What desirest thou of me?"

Still, Lamoni gave no answer.

Filled with the Spirit, Ammon perceived the thoughts of the king. He stepped forward and addressed the silent king once more. "Is it because thou hast heard that I defended thy servants and thy flocks, and slew seven of their brethren with the sling and with the sword, and smote off the arms of others, in order to defend thy flocks and thy servants; behold, is it this that causeth thy marvelings?"

And then Ammon answered the king's most burning question with this simple, clear statement: "Behold, I am a man, and am thy servant; therefore, whatsoever thou desirest which is right, that will I do."

In wonder and surprise, the king opened his

mouth and asked Ammon, "Who art thou? Art thou that Great Spirit, who knows all things?"

Ammon said simply, "I am not."

Still unable to grasp how Ammon could know what he was thinking, the astonished king questioned him again. "How knowest thou the thoughts of my heart? Thou mayest speak boldly, and tell me concerning these things; and also tell me by what power ye slew and smote off the arms of my brethren that scattered my flocks—and now, if thou wilt tell me concerning these things, whatsoever thou desirest I will give unto thee."

Filled with the spirit of missionary work, Ammon replied, "Wilt thou hearken unto my words, if I tell thee by what power I do these things? And this is the thing that I desire of thee."

The king answered, "Yea, I will believe all thy words."

Ammon continued with boldness, "Believest thou that there is a God?"

The king looked puzzled and answered, "I do not know what that meaneth."

"Believest thou that there is a Great Spirit?" Ammon asked.

"Yea," the king said.

"This is God," Ammon explained, and then asked, "Believest thou that this Great Spirit, who is God, created all things which are in heaven and in the earth?"

Lamoni nodded. "Yea, I believe that he created all things which are in the earth." Then he admitted, "But I do not know the heavens."

"The heavens," Ammon went on, "is a place where God dwells and all his holy angels."

"Is it above the earth?" asked Lamoni.

"Yea, and he looketh down upon all the children of men; and he knows all the thoughts and intents of the heart; for by his hand were they all created from the beginning."

King Lamoni said, "I believe all these things which thou hast spoken. Art thou sent from God?"

Ammon replied, "I am a man; and man in the beginning was created after the image of God, and I am called by his Holy Spirit to teach these things unto this people, that they may be brought to a knowledge of that which is just and true; and a portion of that Spirit dwelleth in me, which giveth me knowledge, and also power according to my faith and desires which are in God."

Then Ammon taught King Lamoni and his

servants. He began at the creation of the world. He taught them all that the prophets had spoken, and he laid before them all that was contained in the holy scriptures. He taught them of their ancestors, Lehi and Ishmael, who had left Jerusalem, and of their journey in the wilderness. He told them of the hardships that Lehi and his family had experienced. He gave an account of the rebellion of Laman and Lemuel and the sons of Ishmael. Then he told of the records that had been kept from the time that Lehi left Jerusalem to the present time.

Ammon went on to teach them all about the plan of redemption, the plan prepared before the world began. He told them about Jesus Christ, who was soon to come to live on earth, and how He would suffer for our sins so that all repentant people could be redeemed and return to live with God in glory.

Lamoni and all in the court listened intently to what Ammon taught, and they believed his words. When Ammon finished, the king, realizing his need to be redeemed, cried out to the Lord, "O Lord, have mercy; according to thy abundant mercy which thou hast had upon the people of Nephi, have upon me, and my people." When Lamoni had uttered these words, he collapsed, falling forward onto the ground.

His terrified servants rushed forward, surrounding him. "Quickly, get some water," one shouted.

One servant removed Lamoni's headdress and laid the king's head upon his cape. "King, my king, wake up, wake up!" he called frantically, lightly striking the king's cheeks to rouse him. But all the servant's efforts were in vain. Lamoni remained still and lifeless on the floor.

Panic broke out in the chamber. Some servants cried out, "He's dead! The king is dead!"

"No! It cannot be!" others wailed.

In the back corner of the chamber, Gid, Matthew, Peter, and Katie huddled close together to escape the escalating chaos.

Gid, his heart beating fast, looked around the room for Mishgar. "Where is my father?" he asked, his voice full of concern.

"There he is," said Peter, pointing. Mishgar hovered over the king, pressing a flask of water to his lips, hoping for him to swallow some. But it was no use. Lamoni lay unmoving on the cold stone floor.

"Stand back," one of the king's servants ordered. "We must take him unto the queen."

A stunned silence filled the crowded chamber. The king, it seemed, was dead. The people of his court looked on, horrified, as Lamoni's loyal servants came forward, lifted the king's lifeless body to their shoulders, and solemnly carried it away.

Chapter Six

"He Doth Not Stink"

The moment the king's body left the royal chamber, pandemonium broke out. As the panic rose, Mishgar fought his way through the distraught courtiers to find his son, Gid, and Gid's three friends, now pressed into the back corner of the chamber.

"Come quickly," he said, taking Gid's hand. "There is such chaos here, we will be much safer if we return home and wait for news there."

Following Mishgar and Gid, the children were carried along by the crowds fleeing the palace in fear. The streets were filled with frantic, frightened people. Matthew tried to stay close to Mishgar and Gid, but amidst all the confusion, he lost sight of his Lamanite friends.

"Where have they gone?" Katie moaned desperately.

"They were just up ahead, but . . . but I can't see them just now," Matthew replied, sounding nearly as desperate.

"Oh, no," Katie wailed again. "What if we can't find them? Then what are we going to do?"

Matthew took her hand and pulled her through the crowd behind him. Maybe they could make it back to the quiet clearing where they had landed, he thought to himself.

"Wait for me!" Peter called, afraid he'd be left behind. He grabbed Katie's hand. The children were now connected, and instantly the turmoil that surrounded them became silence. Weightless, they were carried swiftly through space and time to the safety and serenity of the art cottage.

Just as they had left her, Grandma sat in her rocker, calmly reading aloud the account of Lamoni from the scriptures. Her voice was soothing and tranquil. "'And it came to pass that his servants took him and carried him in unto his wife, and laid him upon a bed.'"

Katie quickly looked over at Matthew and Peter, worried they might still be dressed in their Lamanite tunics. Thankfully, the boys were in the same T-shirts and jeans as before, but Peter's cheek was smudged with dirt.

"Peter, your cheek," she whispered and pointed, so Grandma wouldn't hear.

He grabbed the bottom of his shirt and quickly wiped the dirt off.

"Thanks," he said, smiling at Katie gratefully. But when he caught sight of his sister, his eyes got big, and he pointed wildly at her head. Katie's hands shot up, where she discovered Gid's red sash still covering her hair.

"Thanks," she mouthed

silently, as she hastily unwound the sash and tied it around her waist.

"That was close," Matthew murmured softly.

"I'll say!" Katie mouthed, letting out a big breath. She checked to see if Grandma noticed anything, but Grandma read on unfazed, engrossed in the fate of Lamoni.

"'And he lay as if he were dead for the space of two days and two nights; and his wife, and his sons, and his daughters mourned over him, after the manner of the Lamanites, greatly lamenting his loss.'"

"So, is the king really dead or not?" Peter interrupted Grandma.

"Well, everyone thinks he is, don't they?" Grandma replied.

"He looked pretty dead to me," Peter announced confidently.

"Oh, really?" Grandma looked quizzically at her grandson.

"What an imagination you have, buddy," Matthew said, laughing nervously and patting Peter on the back. "Why don't we let Grandma finish the story?"

"Okay, go on, Grandma," Peter encouraged her. "I promise I'll be quiet."

"'Good idea!" Katie said, giving him a stern look. This wasn't the first time Peter had nearly spilled the beans about their time travels.

"'And it came to pass,'" Grandma went on, "'that after two days and two nights they were about to take his body and lay it in a sepulchre . . .'"

"A what?" Peter couldn't help asking Katie.

"It's a tomb, remember?" Katie whispered. "Keep listening."

All the time Grandma was reading, the painting on the easel remained still and lifeless. There had been no sign of movement since they had returned. Surely, Katie thought, this couldn't be the end of their adventure!

"Grandma, could you fast forward a little? I can't wait to hear what happens." Impatient Peter was practically pleading.

"Well, let's see. The queen calls for Ammon and he goes to her."

"I remember this part," Matthew jumped in. "The king lay on his bed for two days, and most people thought he should be buried."

"Oh, yeah," Katie remembered, giggling. "They said that the king 'stinketh.' It says so right in the scriptures! But the queen thinks they're all wrong. She says, 'To me, he doth not stink.'"

"That was her way of saying she didn't think her husband was really dead, right, Grandma?" Matthew asked.

"Right," Grandma agreed. "She said to Ammon, 'The servants of my husband have made it known unto me that thou art a prophet of a holy God, and that thou hast power to do many mighty works in his name; therefore, if this is the case, I would that ye should go in and see my husband.'"

Then Grandma posed an important question. "Now, children, why do you think the queen wanted Ammon to go see the king?"

"Well," Matthew was the first one to answer, "I think she was hoping that Ammon could wake him up."

"That's what I think, too, Matthew. But Ammon knew that Lamoni was under the power of God. This is how the scriptures describe what was happening to Lamoni: 'The dark veil of unbelief was being cast away from his mind, and . . . the light of the glory of God . . . lit up in his soul, . . . and he was carried away in God.' Ammon knew that this is what was happening, so after he went in to see the king, he said to the queen: 'He is not dead, but he sleepeth in God, and on the morrow he shall rise again; therefore bury him not.'"

"The queen must have been so relieved!" Katie exclaimed.

"I'll say—if she believed Ammon, that is. Did she, Grandma? Did she believe him?" Peter asked.

"Good question, Peter. Let's keep reading, shall we?" Grandma replied. "'Ammon said unto her: Believest thou this? And she said unto him: I have had no witness save thy word, and the word of our servants; nevertheless I believe that it shall be according as thou hast said.

"'And Ammon said unto her: Blessed art thou because of thy exceeding faith; I say unto thee, woman, there has not been such great faith among all the people of the Nephites. And it came to pass that she watched over the bed of her husband, from that time even until that time on the morrow which Ammon had appointed that he should rise. And it came to pass that he arose, according to the words of Ammon.'"

"Wow! I guess that proved that Ammon really was a prophet of God!" Peter exulted.

"And that the queen was right to have such great faith in what he said," Katie pointed out.

Katie turned to study the painting once again. To her amazement, this time the painting was alive with tiny figures running toward the palace.

"Matthew, look," she whispered, nudging him.

"I see it, Sis," he whispered back.

As they watched, scores of people thronged the palace steps, moving about as if they were talking excitedly.

"Let's go see what's happening," she whispered, undoing the sash from around her waist and quickly tying it over her hair.

Peter noticed the moving people in the painting, too. His eager eyes came alive. "Oh boy, can we go?" he mouthed, with a glance toward Grandma, who was still engrossed in the scriptures.

Quietly, all three children arose as one. Matthew's face shone with anticipation, and he offered one hand to his brother. Peter took hold of it, and Katie took the other, as Peter thrust his free hand right into the painting. Just as had happened before, the air began swirling around them, lifting them off the ground . . . and in the blink of an eye, Grandma and the art cottage were gone. In what felt like no time at all, the children came to rest, unnoticed, on the crowded steps of Lamoni's palace. They found themselves surrounded by dozens of Lamanites, discussing with each other, in wonder, the amazing events of the day.

Chapter Seven

The Spirit of the Lord

As they stood on the steps of the palace, in the midst of the teeming multitude, the children heard talk of Lamoni's miraculous awakening rippling through the crowd. Small groups of people bunched together, marveling at what had taken place. "He lives! The king has come back!" people exclaimed in wonder.

Even as the good news spread, some in the crowd came from the royal chamber, now telling a new tale—this one not so happy. Confusion quickly rolled through the bewildered throng.

"The king has collapsed again," the cry went out, "and this time, the queen has collapsed with him."

Gasps of disbelief filled the air. "The queen?" a woman whimpered somewhere behind them. "Who will be next?"

"What of Ammon?" another cried. "Where is he?"

"He, too, has fallen to the ground, and all the king's servants with him," a loud voice in the crowd answered back.

"Come on! Let's get a better look," Peter urged Matthew and Katie, and he disappeared into the dense crowd.

"Peter!" Matthew called after him. "Wait for us!" But undaunted, Peter forged ahead.

"It's no use, Sis," Matthew said shaking his head. "Come on, we'll just have to go in there and get him."

"Another adventure, compliments of our little brother," Katie muttered, grabbing Matthew's hand as he was swallowed by the crowd.

Inside the royal chamber, the crowd was even thicker. "Excuse us, excuse us," Matthew repeated again and again, as they inched toward the throne.

Finally, they pushed through the last of the people surrounding the king. In front of them, Lamoni lay again on the cold stone floor, with the queen, his servants, and Ammon lying near him.

Nearby, Peter stood with the crowd surrounding him. He waved them over. "Hey guys, look!" he said, pointing to the scene before them. "They all look like they're dead, but they're really not!"

"Peter, Katie, Matthew." Someone was softly calling their names. "Over here!"

That could only mean one thing! Gid must be here! They spotted Gid and his father making their way toward them along the perimeter of crowd. Gid waved and flashed them an enormous smile.

Katie smiled back. "It makes me feel so much better to know they are here," she said, relief washing over her.

Mishgar and Gid slid in beside the children, greeting them with warm hand clasps and pats on the back. Then the questions flew.

"Where have you been? I haven't seen you for three days. Have you heard what has happened?" Gid asked.

"We have heard some of it, but why is everyone lying on the ground?" Peter questioned him.

"You should have been here!" Gid began. "The king miraculously awakened after three days, just as Ammon said he would. As he arose, he stretched out his hand to the queen, and declared, 'Blessed be the name of God, and blessed art thou.' Then he went on to testify with great power, 'For as sure as thou livest, behold, I have seen my Redeemer; . . . and he shall redeem all mankind who believe on his name.'"

"You should have seen his face as he spoke. It was filled with pure joy—greater joy than I have ever witnessed," Mishgar added. "The joy seemed to overwhelm him, and he sank to the ground again, just as he did before."

"He saw Jesus," Katie said reverently, awed by the thought of it.

"Just hearing that gives me goose bumps all over," Matthew shivered. "It makes me so happy!"

"Now you know how the queen must have felt, because she was overcome like Lamoni, and she fell to the floor, too," Gid went on. Then looking Matthew in the eye, he said softly, "I felt such a powerful feeling here," he gestured to his heart, "a feeling I have never felt before."

Matthew rested his hand on Gid's shoulder. "That must be the Spirit of the Lord," he explained.

"Then Ammon must have felt it, too. After the king and queen were overcome, Ammon fell to his knees and offered a prayer to God," Mishgar went on. "He thanked God for pouring out his Spirit upon the Lamanites. Then he collapsed to the ground, too."

"What about all the servants? What happened to them?" Peter asked.

"All of them began to pray to God with all their might, until one by one they were all overcome with the Spirit, and each of them fell to the ground, too," Gid went on.

"Every single one of them?" Katie asked.

"All but one. Her name is Abish. She is a servant to the queen," Mishgar explained.

"Why was she still standing?" Matthew was curious.

"Abish already knew about Ammon's God. She already believed in this Redeemer that visited the king," Gid said.

"But how did she learn about the Redeemer?" Matthew asked.

"Apparently, her father had a remarkable vision— maybe something like the king had while he was overcome for three days," Mishgar said.

"It must have been a really powerful experience if it convinced his daughter to believe, too," Katie observed.

"Yes," Mishgar agreed thoughtfully, "it must have been."

"Where is Abish now?" Matthew asked.

"She felt the power of God when Lamoni told the court what he had seen—just like I did," Mishgar explained. "She recognized the joy in Lamoni's face. She said it was the same joy she had felt when she first heard about her father's vision. So she ran from house to house to tell everyone about what had happened. She wanted everyone to come, to see and feel

what was happening here. She wanted all of us to feel the power of God and believe in Him, too."

"So that's why there are so many people coming to the palace," Matthew reasoned.

"Judging from the size of this crowd, I guess the news has spread," Gid observed.

As the chamber filled to overflowing, alarm spread among the gathering people as they saw the king and queen lying on the ground, surrounded by their servants. All the bodies lying on the stone floor appeared to be dead. Shouts of anger and fear echoed all around.

"This great evil has come upon the king and his household because he allowed a Nephite to come among us. He should have known better!" shouted a man standing near Peter.

Then, from the far side of the chamber, another man declared emphatically, "The king brought this calamity upon himself! Had he not killed the servants whose flocks were scattered at the waters of Sebus, surely this would not have happened."

Suddenly, a cry went up from a gang of unkempt, wild-looking men, rapidly making their way to where the king and the others lay upon the ground.

The crowd parted as the leader of the gang forced his way through, followed by his men.

Emboldened by the accusations he had heard, he shouted, "This man," and he pointed right at Ammon, "killed my friends at Sebus. He will not go unpunished!"

Another man in the gang rushed forward, his hand firmly gripping the sword on his belt. "You killed my brother!" he yelled at Ammon, who still lay as if dead. Then the man advanced menacingly, until he stood right over Ammon. The crowd gasped as he drew his sword with a flourish.

Terrified, Katie cowered behind Matthew, burying her face in her hands. "Oh, no," she wailed, "I can't bear to watch."

"Now I will take vengeance on you," the enraged man bellowed, swinging his sword high above his head, his arm now fully extended. He let out a spine-tingling scream and lunged toward Ammon, ready to strike. Then without warning, the scream turned to silence. The sword fell from the man's grasp, clanging noisily to the floor, and he crumpled to the floor, his body limp, still, and lifeless.

Chapter Eight

Of Testimony and Changing Hearts

Silence—stunned silence—filled the royal chamber. In the space of a mere instant, the man who wanted to kill Ammon had been struck dead by an unseen force, right at Ammon's feet. And Ammon still lay unmoving, completely undisturbed! A terrible fear came upon the multitude when they saw the fate of the man now dead on the floor.

A fellow shepherd grabbed Mishgar's arm. "Mishgar, what is the meaning of all this? Where does this great power come from?"

"I have seen only what you have seen," Mishgar replied. But the feelings in his heart were another matter altogether. How was he to make sense of the powerful witness he felt in his soul?

Whispers began to ripple through the crowd, and

a nearby woman declared, "Ammon is the Great Spirit, I know it." Others around her weren't so sure.

"He can't be the Great Spirit," a man near her argued. "But he must have been sent by the Great Spirit." And so the rumblings in the crowd started to swell, and on every side heated debates raged about Ammon and who he was.

Above the rest a bellow was heard. "He is not the Great Spirit. He is a monster!" The crowd roared their approval.

"He was sent here from the Nephites to torment us and cause all manner of mischief," another accuser hollered.

"We must send him back to where he came from. We don't want his kind here!" Another roar of approval went up.

"We have done wrong, and the Great Spirit has sent Ammon to correct us. We need to repent," one man insisted forcefully.

Several people in the crowd turned on him, and another man stepped forward, a sinister look on his face. "How can you say we are the ones that need to repent? This Nephite brought with him these calamities. He alone caused the destruction of so many of our brethren!" Now the crowd was an angry mob, roiling with rage.

"Are you getting a little worried?" Katie whispered to Matthew.

"A little, but if we stay close to Mishgar, I think we will be all right," Matthew answered, with more confidence than he felt. "It couldn't hurt to say a prayer though," he added.

"I already have," Katie assured Matthew.

The quarreling mounted with each passing moment. Katie was afraid a fight might break out, and someone would get hurt or killed.

Suddenly, a Lamanite woman broke through the perimeter of the crowd and stood next to the prostrate king. Gid leaned over to Matthew. "Look! That is Abish. She has returned."

Abish looked around at all the people making terrible accusations and threatening each other. It was too much for her to bear, and her face crumpled with sadness. She began to weep openly.

Then, kneeling next to the queen, Abish took her by the hand as if to raise her from the ground. The moment Abish touched her hand, the queen rose to her feet and cried in a loud voice, "O blessed Jesus, who has saved me from an awful hell! O blessed

God, have mercy on this people!" She clasped her hands with joy and continued speaking, now in strange words. "I can't tell what she is saying," Katie said. "Can you understand her?"

Matthew shook his head. "Not a word," he replied. From the puzzled looks on the faces of the onlookers, it was clear that they didn't understand the queen, either.

Then the queen went over to Lamoni, and as she took him by the hand, he arose. Filled with power and conviction, he began calling the people in the chamber to repentance. Stunned by the change in their king, many in the chamber listened intently, with softened hearts and willing ears.

"My people," the king said, "we are the sons and daughters of Ishmael, who came up out of Jerusalem with Father Lehi. Ours is a noble heritage."

"He looks different," Gid whispered to Matthew.

"He is different," Matthew said. "His heart has been changed. Now he believes in God, and in His Son, Jesus Christ. He has been converted to the true gospel."

"How would that make him so different?" Gid asked.

"Listen, and you'll see," Matthew assured him.

"I have learned of the scriptures, the records kept from Father Adam to Lehi, and from Lehi down to the present time," Lamoni continued. "But most important, I have learned of the Savior, and of His redeeming love, whereby we can be reunited with God. This knowledge fills my soul with joy."

Moved by the king's words, Gid turned to Mishgar in earnest. "How can we feel that joy, Father?"

"I am uncertain, son. Let us listen. Perhaps we will learn," Mishgar answered.

The king continued testifying, "All this is possible because of the Redeemer, Jesus Christ. He will come to the earth and suffer for our sins, that if we repent, we will be forgiven, and God will remember our sins no more. I know this is true, for I have seen Him. I believe on the name of Jesus Christ. And behold, He will redeem all who believe on His name."

The testimony of the king—the king who was once known for cruelty and brutality, but was now repentant and humble—touched those who listened. And many believed his words and were converted, too.

"Hey," Peter nudged Matthew, "why are some of the people leaving?"

"I guess some don't believe what Lamoni is saying," he told Peter sadly.

"How can they not feel that it is true?" Peter asked, dismayed by Matthew's conclusion.

"I don't know, buddy, but it seems like that is how it always is," Matthew explained. "Some people choose to open their hearts to the gospel, and some people refuse. Heavenly Father always lets us choose for ourselves."

"Look!" Katie exclaimed. "It's Ammon! He is standing up, too!"

Indeed he was. And Ammon, the missionary, began teaching the multitude with great power and authority. As he spoke, each of Lamoni's servants stood, too, and each bore testimony of what he had experienced.

"My heart has been changed, and I am filled with the exquisite joy of the gospel of Jesus Christ," one servant declared.

"It is the same with me," said another. "And I have no more desire to do evil." Each servant spoke earnestly and reverently.

One, a shepherd, came toward Mishgar and knelt as he testified to the gathered crowd. But he seemed to be talking especially to Mishgar as he declared, "I have seen an angel, and he talked to me, just as I am talking to you. He taught me of God and of His righteousness."

Matthew looked on, awed by the Spirit of God, which seemed to fill the chamber. "Do you feel that?" Matthew asked Gid in a low voice.

When Gid did not answer, Matthew turned and discovered his Lamanite friend wrapped in Mishgar's loving arms. As father and son shared their new-found joy in the gospel of Jesus Christ, their embrace grew even stronger. And, as they stood cheek to cheek, tears of gratitude and happiness flowed freely down their faces.

Chapter Nine

The Power of God

The sun hung just over the horizon, casting a golden glow on the city. Rays of fading sunlight filtered across the evening sky, coloring the clouds with warm shades of orange and yellow and pink. Reluctantly, the crowds who were summoned to the palace by Abish's earnest pleadings made their way home before nightfall.

"In all my days, I have never seen and heard such marvelous things as I have today. How I wish Mother had been with us," Mishgar lamented.

"Let us tell her when we get home, shall we, Father?" Gid comforted him.

"Yes, son, we shall," Mishgar smiled, "but first I must check on the animals at the king's stables. With four extra sets of hands, the work will go much faster.

Will you help me?" Mishgar asked the children, with a hopeful look.

"Are there horses?" Peter inquired.

"Yes, lots of horses," Gid replied.

"Then let's go!" Peter replied eagerly.

Katie nudged Matthew, "We ought to leave soon, don't you think?" Matthew nodded, and announced to Gid and Mishgar, "We would love to help, but afterward we will have to start for home. Our family is expecting us."

"We'll hurry then," Mishgar promised. "Come this way." They all walked along the narrow, twisting streets until they came to the outskirts of the city. Mishgar led them to a large, low building with a set of thick wooden doors. He lifted the heavy metal latch, swung wide the doors, and entered.

They were in the king's stables. Rows of stalls lined the enclosure. Each stall held one of the king's horses. Peter could hardly contain his excitement. He had never seen so many strong, beautiful horses, and he wasted no time greeting each one.

A servant was pitching fresh hay into the feeding troughs at the front of each stall.

"Sam," Mishgar called to him, "where are the rest of the men?"

"They are not here. My daughter came to tell us that Abish, the queen's servant, was summoning everyone to the palace. Apparently Abish claimed that God was at work there, and that everyone should go and see the miracles He wrought," Sam explained. "Without a word, the other servants dropped their tools and ran straight to the palace."

"So why are you still here?" Mishgar asked. "Didn't you want to go, too?"

"Yes," Sam said, "but someone had to stay behind to care for the animals."

Humbled by Sam's selflessness, Mishgar quickly picked up a discarded pitchfork and began pitching hay right alongside him.

"You do not need to help here," Sam protested. "After all, you are the chief shepherd. Surely you have more important things to do."

Mishgar stopped, put a hand on each of Sam's shoulders, and spoke to him sincerely. "We serve the same king, Sam. I am pleased to work at your side until the work is done." Mishgar couldn't help remembering Ammon's faithful service to the king.

Mishgar and Sam worked in silence, until Sam had the courage to ask, "Mishgar, did it all happen the way Abish said it did? Were the king and queen really lying on the floor, overcome by the Spirit of God?"

Mishgar leaned on his pitchfork and nodded his head, "Yes, my friend. It happened just as she said it did. Abish knew it was the power of God that had come upon them. She was sure that if the people would come and see, they would believe in the power of God, too."

"It took great courage for her to make known that she had believed in God for many years, and then to persuade the whole city to come and witness God at work," Sam said with admiration in his voice.

"Yes, it did," Mishgar agreed. "Because of her courage, many of the people who went to the royal chamber now believe in God and in his gospel."

"Mishgar, are you one of those people? Do you believe in God?" Sam was beseeching Mishgar with real intent.

Katie, Matthew, and Peter, who had been listening carefully to this conversation, held their breaths.

"Yes, Sam, I do," Mishgar responded, his voice filled with emotion. "Today, when one of the servants of the court awakened, he knelt, looked in my eyes, and testified that he had seen an angel."

"He saw an angel?" Sam could hardly believe it.

"Yes, he did. All of them did—the king, the queen, and all the servants who were overcome. As this servant testified to me, I felt I could see deep into his soul. And I knew he spoke the truth. As I heard his words, I felt God's power flow through every part of my body, until I was completely filled with his Spirit."

As Mishgar testified to Sam, he was again filled

with the Spirit of God, just as before. How he wanted Sam to feel it, too! Mishgar met Sam's sincere gaze, and declared, "It is true, Sam. What the servant said is true. There is a God. And His Son, Jesus Christ, is coming soon to the earth to redeem us all."

As Sam listened to Mishgar's testimony, he felt the power of God's spirit flow into his body, just as Mishgar had described. "I believe your words, Mishgar. No, it is more than that. I know," he said, his voice choked with tears. "I know that what you have told me is true. God lives, and His Son, our Redeemer, shall save us all."

"You feel it, too, Sam. You feel it, too." And Mishgar embraced his fellow believer warmly. "We shall talk more later," Mishgar assured Sam, "but now I must get home to my wife. I want to share with her all I have seen and heard. Good-bye, Sam, until tomorrow. Come, children," Mishgar beckoned to his son, and his son's three friends—two young boys and a girl with her hair swathed in a long, red scarf.

Outside the stable, Matthew asked Gid, "Which way to the clearing where we first met you?"

"Take this road to the corner, turn right into a wide pathway and follow it for a time. You will soon come to the clearing," Gid said, pointing the way. Then he asked, "Will you ever be back, Matthew? I think you and I could be really good friends."

"Maybe we will be back someday, but America is far away." *You have no idea just how far,* Matthew thought to himself.

"Good-bye, then, and God be with you, my new friend," Gid replied, clasping Matthew's hand in a warm handshake.

Mishgar slipped his arm around his son's shoulder, and father and son walked happily together toward their home and their new life—a life filled with the power of God.

The sun slipped behind the hills as the children made their way to the edge of the city and down the shepherds' path to the clearing where they had first arrived.

"I guess it's time to go," Katie said wistfully. She took Gid's sash off of her head and carefully hung it over a branch, where Gid would be sure to find it when he came through with the king's sheep.

She offered one hand to Matthew and the other to Peter. Just before taking hold, the children took a long look around them. To one side of the clearing, sheep grazed safely, no marauding robbers in sight.

To the other side, the city could be seen, the king's palace rising majestically at its center.

This was the palace where Ammon, the missionary, fearlessly preached the gospel in all its glory. And this was the palace where King Lamoni would now rule in righteousness, guided by the matchless power of God.

Chapter Ten

How Great Shall Be Your Joy

As always, when the children returned, Grandma was sitting in her rocking chair reading, as if nothing unusual had happened.

"'And it came to pass that there were many that did believe in their words; and as many as did believe were baptized; and they became a righteous people, and they did establish a church among them . . .'"

"So that's what happened to Gid and Mishgar!" Peter blurted out.

"Who?" Grandma asked.

Matthew elbowed Peter in the ribs. "Why don't we let Grandma finish the chapter, buddy?"

"Oh, fine!" Peter grabbed his side where he had been poked and made a face at his brother.

Thankfully, Katie stepped in. "Hey, Peter, come sit here by me." Peter slid over next to Katie, and the big sister slipped her arm around her younger brother. "Go on, Grandma," she urged, "we're listening."

"'And thus the work of the Lord did commence among the Lamanites; thus the Lord did begin to pour out his Spirit upon them; and we see that his arm is extended to all people who will repent and believe on his name.'"

"Well, that is quite a story, isn't it?" Grandma said, as if she could hardly take it all in. "What did you think of that?"

"I think that is the most exciting one we've seen yet!" Peter replied enthusiastically.

"I think you mean the most exciting one we've *heard,* don't you, Peter?" Katie coached her brother with a knowing wink.

"Right! The most exciting one we've heard," Peter quickly corrected himself.

"What made it so exciting to you?" Grandma asked. "Matthew, you go first."

"Well," Matthew thought for a moment, and then answered, "I suppose it would have to be when Lamoni, the queen, Ammon, and all the servants woke up and started testifying about what they had seen. It was amazing! I never thought about what it would be like to talk to an angel before. But it must have been wonderful, because you could tell that all those people were changed forever."

"Man! I wish I could change for even one day!" Peter said.

Grandma laughed. "I know just how you feel. It is hard to change for good, isn't it? But when you feel—let's see how they say it in the scriptures—yes, here it is, when you feel 'the power of God,' it's easier. At least it is for me."

"I think the power of God is another way to describe the Holy Ghost," Matthew offered thoughtfully. "When I feel the Holy Ghost in my heart, it's easier for me to do the right thing, too, Grandma."

"You have learned some valuable lessons, my boy," Grandma said, touched by Matthew's understanding. She turned to Peter. "How about you, Peter? What did you learn?"

"Well, first off, I learned that Ammon was superstrong, like when he cut off the robbers' arms. But he didn't just have strong muscles. He was strong because God was helping him."

"Very good," Grandma sounded impressed. "Anything else?"

"Well, I learned that when you serve people, they like you better. And you like them better, too."

"Really." Grandma was interested. "How so, Peter?"

"Just think what would have happened if Ammon hadn't served Lamoni. First, Ammon wouldn't have been there to save the king's sheep. Then, Lamoni would never have listened to what Ammon had to say, and he wouldn't have learned about the gospel," Peter said.

Grandma glowed. She loved to hear her grand-children's insights. She always learned something new—and important—from them.

"All right, Katie, my girl, how about you?"

Katie didn't even have to think. "I learned the most from Abish."

"Yes, that is one of my favorite parts too," Grandma nodded. "What is it you learned, dear?"

"She was faithful, and courageous, and loyal. It made me think about my friend, Aubrey. I want to tell her about the gospel, but I've been afraid to do it because . . ." Her voice trailed off.

"Because what?" Grandma prompted her.

"I didn't want things to change between us. But now I think I can see how to do it." Katie sounded happy and determined.

"Let's hear it, Sis," Matthew encouraged her.

"Okay, last night you said the way you'd go about sharing the gospel is to get to know someone first and then tell them about God," Katie began.

"That's right," Matthew agreed.

"Well, I've done that part. Aubrey is becoming one of my dearest friends," Katie said.

"And you said you thought it would help to serve her, right?" Matthew reminded his sister.

"Right, and I've done that, too. Aubrey knows she can count on me whenever she needs me," she said.

"Now all you need is some courage!" Peter piped up.

"That's just what I was thinking." Katie was glad that Peter had cut right to the chase. "I need courage, just like you, little brother." She ruffled Peter's hair with a smile. "Courage, mixed with faith. That's a good recipe for getting the job done, don't you think?"

"Sounds good to me," Grandma said.

"When I saw how happy Lamoni and the queen and their servants were, I knew I couldn't deny Aubrey the chance to have that happiness too."

"That's just how I felt too." Grandma said closing her eyes, a hint of a smile crossing her lips. The children sat up straight and looked quizzically at each other, wondering what exactly Grandma meant. But Grandma just rocked back and forth in her chair, lost in thought.

Had Grandma been to Lamoni's palace too? None of her grandchildren knew how to ask. They waited patiently until the smile faded from Grandma's face, and her eyes flickered open.

"Oh, yes, darlings! You're here," she said, almost as if she had forgotten their presence. "I was just thinking about how wonderful it must be to hear the gospel for the first time, and to feel the Holy Ghost witness that it's true."

"I never thought of it that way, Grandma. My testimony has grown little by little, because I have been taught all the way along, by my parents, my teachers, and . . . of course, you," Matthew said thoughtfully.

Then Peter remembered the power of the king, the queen, and all the servants testifying together. "Yeah! I think it helps to be taught by lots of believers, sometimes. Hey!" A light went on for Peter. "Why don't we invite Aubrey and her family to family home evening? That way we all could teach the gospel, and Katie won't have to go it alone. Besides,"

About the Authors

Alice W. Johnson, a published author and composer, is a featured speaker for youth groups, adult firesides, and women's seminars. A former executive in a worldwide strategy consulting company, and then in a leadership training firm, Alice is now a homemaker living in Eagle, Idaho, with her husband and their four young children.

Allison H. Warner gained her early experience living with her family in countries around the world. Returning to the United States as a young woman, she began her vocation as an actress and writer, developing and performing in such productions as *The Farley Family Reunion.* She and her husband reside in Provo, Utah, where they are raising two active boys.

About the Illustrators

Jerry Harston held a degree in graphic design and illustrated more than thirty children's books. He received many honors for his art, and his clients included numerous Fortune 500 corporations. Jerry passed away in December 2009.

Casey Nelson grew up the oldest of eight children in a Navy family, so they moved quite often during her childhood. Graduating with a degree in illustration, she taught figure drawing in the illustration department at Brigham Young University, worked as an artist for video games, and performed in an improvisational comedy troupe. Casey is employed by the Walt Disney Company as a cinematic artist for their video games.

now he looked a little impish, "we could all have some fun at the same time!"

"Peter, you always have a way of getting right down to it, don't you? I'll see if they can come this Monday night," Katie said gratefully.

"I thought you were too scared," Matthew teased his sister.

"Not anymore! I can't wait to be the Lord's missionary, just like Ammon and Abish," Katie proclaimed confidently.

"You start writing in your journals, and I'll go get lunch ready," Grandma said, as she tiptoed through her grandchildren, who had sprawled on the art cottage floor, their journals before them.

As Grandma walked down the flagstone path, she thought of her three young missionaries, busily writing in their journals. The song her grandmother taught her came again to her mind, and she sang as she walked:

For if I help but one soul hold fast the iron rod,
How great shall be the joy I feel when I return to God.

"Yes, dear children," Grandma thought, as she smiled from ear to ear. "How great shall be your joy!"

Hazardous Waste Site Management: Water Quality Issues

Report on a Colloquium Sponsored
by the Water Science and Technology Board

February 19–20, 1987

Colloquium 3 of a Series

Water Science and Technology Board
Commission on Engineering and Technical Systems
Commission on Physical Sciences, Mathematics, and Resources
National Research Council

NATIONAL ACADEMY PRESS
Washington, D.C. 1988

rec'd 1/9/89

National Academy Press • 2101 Constitution Avenue, N.W. • Washington, D. C. 20418

Library of Congress Cataloging-in-Publication Data

Hazardous waste site management: water quality issues: report on a colloquium / sponsored by the Water Science and Technology Board.
   p. cm.
   Bibliography: p.
   Includes index.
   ISBN 0-309-03790-5
   1. Hazardous waste sites—United States—Congresses. 2. Water quality management—United States—Congresses. I. National Research Council (U.S.). Water Science and Technology Board.
TD811.5.H435 1987
363.7' 28—dc 19   87-31311

PROVOCATEURS

JOAN BERKOWITZ, Risk Science International, Washington, D.C.

WILLIAM CIBULAS, Agency for Toxic Substances and Disease Registry, Atlanta, Georgia

NORBERT DEE, U.S. Environmental Protection Agency, Washington, D.C.

LEO M. EISEL, Wright Water Engineers, Denver, Colorado

JOEL HIRSCHHORN, Office of Technology Assessment, Washington, D.C.

DAVID W. MILLER, Geraghty & Miller, Inc., Plainview, New York

ISHWAR P. MURARKA, Electric Power Research Institute, Palo Alto, California

TOBY PAGE, Brown University

COLLOQUIUM COORDINATORS

SHEILA D. DAVID, *Program Officer*
CAROLE B. CARSTATER, *Program Assistant*
JEANNE AQUILINO, *Production Assistant*

Preface

In 1985 the Water Science and Technology Board (WSTB) inaugurated a colloquium series, "Emerging Issues in Water Science and Technology," to focus debate and the attention of the scientific and engineering community on important issues in the field. *Drought Management and Its Impact on Public Water Systems*, the report of the first colloquium, was published in March 1986, followed by the report of the second colloquium, *National Water Quality Monitoring and Assessment*, in February 1987. The third colloquium, held on February 19–20, 1987, addressed the emerging scientific, engineering, and institutional issues associated with setting cleanup levels at hazardous waste sites, a major public policy question that is often articulated as "How clean is clean?"

The nation's regulatory agencies are faced with the difficult task of defining target cleanup levels for contaminated soil or ground water. A number of approaches have been used: setting cleanup levels at background, allowing some level of contamination to remain, and taking no action whatsoever. Regulatory agencies must also determine the level of resources required to reduce or eliminate risk to humans and the environment, an effort that involves the use of a variety of scientific and technical tools in making these risk management decisions and the addressing of a number of nonquantitative societal issues. These tasks have important implications for both the health risks of the American population and the cost of remediation at the diverse sites currently being evaluated to determine the nature and extent of contamination. As a result, the setting of target cleanup levels for these sites is quite controversial.

WSTB's third colloquium, entitled "Hazardous Waste Site Management: Water Quality Issues," provided a forum in which to consider the current limits of the available scientific and technical data base and to identify and debate the nonquantitative issues from the differing perspectives of the affected parties.

A steering committee of board members, working closely with WSTB staff, created and organized the colloquium format. Nine papers were presented by recognized experts affiliated with federal and state regulatory agencies, environmental and citizens groups, and industries that generate, store, or dispose of hazardous waste. The presenters included scientists and regulators involved in setting cleanup levels, as well as the affected parties.

The preparation of the papers was carefully monitored by the steering committee through the review of preliminary outlines and manuscripts in progress. Provocateurs were selected to stimulate debate and discussion after the authors presented highlights from their papers. The 60 attendees participated actively in various workshops that evaluated the roles of hydrogeology, engineering, and risk assessment/toxicology, and discussed alternative regulatory strategies for setting cleanup levels at hazardous waste sites. Written summaries from the workshops are presented in this report along with statements made by the provocateurs during the question-and-answer periods.

The report has two major sections: an overview and the background papers by individual authors. The colloquium chairman, Michael Kavanaugh, prepared the overview based on a review of the background papers and consideration of the presentations and workshop discussions. The entire report has been read by a group other than the authors, but only the overview has been subjected to the report review criteria established by the National Research Council's Report Review Committee. The background papers have been reviewed for factual correctness. To preserve the individual perspectives encouraged by the steering committee as part of the colloquium format, however, the conclusions, recommendations, and findings arrived at in the background papers have not been exposed to the intensive evaluation undergone by the overview.

The WSTB gratefully acknowledges the generous contributions of time and expertise of the colloquium participants. Special thanks are extended to those who made formal presentations, acted as provocateurs to stimulate discussion, or served as rapporteurs in guiding the workshops. It is hoped that the discussions presented here will stimulate new ideas and research and generate action by those involved in the complex water quality issues raised in the remediation of hazardous waste sites.

Contents

xi

Overview

One of the most controversial and difficult decisions facing public policymakers and regulatory agencies responsible for the remediation of contamination at hazardous waste sites is the definition of cleanup levels for environmental media found to contain toxic or hazardous materials. Since the passage of the Comprehensive Environmental Response, Compensation, and Liability Act (CERCLA) in 1980, this issue has demanded an ever-increasing level of effort by all participating parties, including affected community groups, environmental organizations, generators, remediation contractors, environmental lawyers, and regulatory agencies at all levels.

The stakes in this debate are high. Human health is at risk. The cost of the remedial measures required to achieve background levels or other conservative cleanup levels for a given contaminant could exceed the industry's, and eventually the public's, capacity to fund. In some cases, no existing technologies can achieve these low levels. On the other hand, setting less stringent cleanup levels based on practicality or cost-effectiveness could result in solutions that cause unanticipated harm to human health and lead to costly legal battles between governmental agencies and impacted or interested parties—most notably various environmental organizations and citizens groups.

Given the contentious nature of this issue and the critical role played by water science and technology, the Water Science and Technology Board (WSTB) selected as the topic for its third colloquium the question of setting water quality goals at hazardous waste sites. The colloquium's objective was to evaluate whether the scientific, technical, and regulatory methods currently used for setting cleanup levels are adequate, and, if they are not, to suggest areas for improvements. Within the limits of the available time and resources for WSTB colloquia, this was an ambitious undertaking. It required, first, that the current procedures used throughout the United States be discussed critically, and second, that the scientific bases for the decision process be presented and critically assessed. These requirements formed the basis of the format used in the 1 $\frac{1}{2}$-day meeting.

Three speakers were asked to address current approaches used by regulatory agencies—and the U.S. Department of Defense (DOD)—in addressing water quality cleanup levels. The views of impacted parties regarding the adequacy of these approaches were also presented by representatives from water utility, industry, and environmental groups. Finally, two speakers were asked to assess the adequacy of two key scientific areas that play a major role in specifying cleanup levels, namely, ground water modeling and risk assessment. Each issue paper was followed by a formal critique, and workshops were held to assess the scientific and technical bases used in the standard-setting process (the workshops addressed engineering, hydrogeology, risk assessment, and regulatory strategies).

The recent passage of the Superfund Amendments and Reauthorization Act (SARA) in November 1986 has increased the importance of this colloquium. Whereas the number of sites known or expected to contaminate ground water grows rapidly, the number of sites at which hazards have been eliminated remains low. Of the approximately 23,000 potential sites listed by the U.S. Environmental Protection Agency (EPA), approximately 900 are currently (1987) listed or proposed for listing on the National Priority List (NPL). According to J. Winston Porter, EPA's assistant administrator for solid waste and emergency response, speaking at a recent conference in Washington, D.C. (November 1986), decisions on remedial action, and, implicitly, decisions on acceptable cleanup levels in affected media have been made at approximately 130 of these sites. In addition to NPL sites, there are nearly 7,000 treatment, storage, and disposal facilities regulated under the Resource Conservation and Recovery Act (RCRA), 911 operating

DOD facilities, more than 15,000 presumably nonhazardous land-fills, and perhaps hundreds of thousands of leaking underground storage tanks from which contamination of soil, ground water, or surface waters may have occurred or may be about to occur.

Thus, the backlog of sites at which remediation will be required is large, and the selection of cleanup levels will be a major focus of federal, state, and local regulatory agencies for many years to come. The impact of this process on the ultimate costs of hazardous waste site remediation is uncertain. As of 1986, EPA estimated that remedial actions at an NPL site cost an average of $8.6 million. With the passage of SARA, these costs are expected to increase. Section 121 of that law stressed the importance of selecting permanent remedies to the maximum extent practicable. The cleanup levels specified for ground water at Superfund sites must be based on applicable or relevant and appropriate requirements (ARARs) provided by other federal environmental statutes such as the Clean Water Act and the Safe Drinking Water Act. Of particular significance was the requirement that maximum contaminant level goals, which are designated by EPA's Office of Drinking Water (ODW), must be achieved by any remedial action, provided such goals are technically feasible when cost is taken into consideration. Based on a memorandum of understanding between ODW and EPA's Office of Emergency and Remedial Response, it now appears that maximum contaminant levels will be the ARARs used for site remediation.

Prior to the passage of SARA, the resolution of conflicts over the most appropriate remedial action at Superfund sites was handled on a case-by-case basis. State regulatory agencies have followed a similar strategy. Implicit in the decisions reached on appropriate remediation programs was the setting of target cleanup levels for affected environmental media. Prior to SARA the various forms of legal settlements between regulatory agencies and responsible parties reached at Superfund sites illustrated the diversity of methods used and the lack of consistent guidelines. The types of agreements included the following:

- cash "buy-outs," in which responsible parties agreed to pay a certain amount to regulatory agencies for the relief of future liability, without regard to specific cleanup levels;
- agreements to conduct specific remediation activities, without designated cleanup levels;

- the specification of "requisite" remedial technologies to eliminate hazards to human health and the environment;
- open-ended commitments to do "whatever is necessary" to protect human health; and
- agreements to remediate until specified cleanup levels are achieved.

Only in the latter case have environmental criteria or standards been used explicitly to select the remedial alternative. This lack of a consistent method for setting target cleanup levels was a primary concern of EPA and impacted parties, and it led to the explicit language on this issue in Section 121 of SARA.

Section 121 was an important and controversial attempt to produce uniformity in the remediation process according to explicit criteria and standards. But has Section 121 provided explicit and unequivocal guidance to EPA and other regulatory agencies for setting cleanup levels at Superfund hazardous waste sites? A review of the papers presented at this colloquium would suggest that it has not. In addition, many non-NPL sites throughout the nation also require the setting of cleanup levels, and EPA protocol as outlined in Section 121 of SARA may not always be followed or be applicable to all sites.

Three major issues emerged from the colloquium regarding cleanup level setting. First, the point of compliance at which ARARs should be applied must be resolved. Impacted parties (water utilities, environmental groups) generally support compliance at the edge of the waste management unit or site of release, while generators argue for a point of compliance at property boundaries or at the point of impact (e.g., a downgradient water well).

Second, the appropriate level of risk and the acceptable target levels must be selected. As expected, impacted parties support very conservative risk management decisions, with explicit support for cleanup levels corresponding to at least the one-in-a-million incremental cancer risk level for known or suspected human and animal carcinogens. Private industry and other generators (e.g., DOD), on the other hand, stress a comparative risk approach and argue that 1 in 100,000 (10^{-5}) or 1 in 10,000 (10^{-4}) is a more practical and cost-effective target level that still adequately protects human health and the environment.

Finally, the colloquium participants raised the issue of the adequacy of our current data base for making both risk analyses and risk management decisions. There is considerable uncertainty that has not yet been quantified in all of the scientific techniques required for a quantitative resolution of the cleanup level dilemma. Exposure assessment using current models of contaminant transport in affected media (primarily unsaturated or saturated soil) is constrained by the lack of data on the fate of contaminants. The effectiveness of many remedial technologies to achieve very low levels of contamination in soils or ground water is poorly understood. In addition, the toxicologic data base and the methods used to estimate chronic risks at low levels of human exposure to contaminants are highly uncertain. Despite these shortcomings the risk management process implied in the debate over cleanup levels will continue to rely on informed judgments based on the existing scientific and technological data base. The colloquium provided a useful overview and a critique of the strategies that might be used to proceed in this uncertain process.

OVERVIEW OF PAPERS

As Richard Dowd, the keynote speaker, clearly indicated, setting cleanup levels at hazardous waste sites reflects many of the same issues that have confronted regulators for the past 15 years. Decisions must be made in spite of severe limitations on the accuracy of predictions regarding the impacts of these decisions.

Regulators must choose safety factors to account for this level of uncertainty. In contrast to the regulatory issues of the 1970s, however, the focus of regulation has shifted to the control of toxic materials with unverifiable potential long-term chronic effects. This fact places a greater burden on the science of quantitative risk assessment, which relies in turn on the accuracy of predictions regarding the fate of recalcitrant or poorly degradable organic contaminants in the subsurface environment—a highly complex environment, when compared to surface waters or the lower atmosphere.

Drawing on his experience with the implementation of the Clean Air Act, Dowd stressed the importance of developing methods for setting standards at hazardous waste sites that use the best available scientific knowledge, that can be verified by current means of measurement, and that use safety factors or logical conservative assumptions. He urged the commitment to a rational standard-setting methodology, anchored in reality and good science. This is without question a desirable goal; yet the application of these principles in the current environment of intense public concern over real or perceived hazards will be difficult.

Current Methods

Halina S. Brown's paper, which reviewed the approaches used by five governmental agencies for setting cleanup levels, suggested that Dowd's concerns are being addressed in several instances. Brown provided a succinct and useful summary of methods proposed or actually used by EPA, the U.S. Army, the California Department of Health Services (DHS), the Washington State Department of Ecology (WDOE), and the New Jersey Department of Environmental Protection (NJDEP). With the exception of the U.S. Army method, each of these approaches is currently used (DHS, WDOE, NJDEP) or will be used (EPA) to establish target cleanup levels at both NPL and non-NPL sites. Generally, these methods are rational; that is, they use procedures that are based on our current scientific understanding of contaminant fates and human exposures, they attempt to provide safety factors that explicitly address the areas of limited knowledge, and they are linked to regulatory requirements established under other federal environmental statutes.

In essence, the methods are attempts to define a risk assessment procedure for selecting cleanup levels, with the common goal of protecting human health and the environment. Although the methods differ in their details, which are clearly described in Brown's paper, the unambiguous application of any of the methods is inhibited by a number of common problem areas:

- media-specific numerical criteria for many contaminants are lacking;
- numerical criteria (e.g., standards, water quality criteria) developed for other federal statutes may not be applicable to hazardous waste sites;
- the extrapolation of toxicologic data obtained from animal experiments is highly uncertain and not verifiable;
- multiple contaminants are treated as having additive effects rather than multiplicative effects; and

- the assumption of equilibrium partitioning between media is very conservative and usually does not match reality.

In addition to these shortcomings, it should be noted that none of the methods addresses the issue of quality control of the techniques (primarily solute transport models) used to estimate contaminant movement. Large uncertainties must be expected, depending on the type of model used, the complexities of the media being modeled, and the amount and quality of the data available. Furthermore, as discussed by the colloquium participants, the unambiguous definition of the contaminant concentration is lacking, given the three-dimensional nature of the subsurface environment and the expected concentration fluctuations with time. Despite the passage of SARA, continuing disagreements among the opposing parties in these issues can be expected, along with a high potential for litigation.

Although the writers of SARA had hoped to define an objective and uniform method for setting ground water cleanup levels, as discussed in Linda Greer's paper, the overview of the decision process presented in the paper written by Edwin Barth, William Hanson, and Elizabeth Shaw of EPA suggests that a case-by-case approach will still be used in reaching a record of decision for the remedial action at each site. Whereas target cleanup levels must be selected from applicable or relevant requirements, the final determination of the cleanup levels rests on the "appropriateness" of the requirement, taking into account such imprecise concepts as fund balancing, technical feasibility, and cost-effectiveness. Barth and coauthors stress the importance of evaluating alternatives that meet a range of ground water protection goals, within various time periods. In addition, because of uncertainties in the efficacy of the technologies used for ground water cleanup, the authors recommend flexibility in the decision process to permit alternative remediation strategies, should monitoring indicate that the selected remedy will not achieve the selected goals. This "reopener" recommendation, however, although logical on technical grounds, could further complicate and delay the decisionmaking process for the selection of a remedy.

The method developed by the DHS, as described by David Leu and Paul Hadley, encompasses many elements of the proposed EPA method, but it takes a more conservative position regarding the range of alternatives that should be evaluated during the decision process. Any proposed remedial alternative must, at a minimum, meet the specified target goal, designated as an applied action level (AAL), for each contaminant or mixture of contaminants in each medium of concern. Although no mention is made of technical feasibility or cost-effectiveness, the DHS decision tree method ultimately rests on EPA's feasibility study process as described in the agency's guidance documents. There appears to be no relief from the difficult value judgments required by the risk management process.

Views of Impacted Parties

Based on other provisions of SARA that stress the involvement of citizens and community groups in the decision process, the success or failure of any approach to specify acceptable target cleanup levels will depend heavily on the opinions of impacted parties. The remarks by Ronald Esau, representing an impacted water utility with 60 percent of its water supply source at risk from accidental industrial releases of organic contaminants, and Linda Greer, from the Environmental Defense Fund, an influential national environmental organization, indicate that support for cleanup levels less stringent than background or a low risk level of 10^{-6} appears unlikely from these groups.

Such a posture can also be expected from other water utilities. Their real fear is that the distribution to consumers of contaminated ground water that meets all ARARs might lead to toxic tort cases, with large costs to the consumers rather than to the parties responsible for the contamination.

Linda Greer presented the environmental community's position on the selection of ARARs for ground water cleanup (using existing detection limits) and on the definition of the point of compliance. Although this position is a desirable goal for impacted parties, according to many colloquium participants, technical feasibility and fund balancing issues make these goals unattainable.

One party directly impacted by this decision process is industry. As Thomas Hellman pointed out, remediation costs could escalate dramatically if overly conservative standards are imposed at hazardous waste sites. The cost for remediation of 1,800 potential NPL sites could increase to $81 billion, compared to the $8.5 billion cost currently estimated by EPA.

Hellman indicated that the number of sites to be remediated

is likely to decrease if costs escalate, and excessive delays are also to be expected. In addition, he raised the specter of unforeseen but clearly negative consequences for the economic viability of industry. Whether or not this is a substantive issue would require more extensive analysis.

The Status of the Technical Information Base

Risk management decisions associated with setting cleanup levels at hazardous waste sites rest on three broad scientific and technical disciplines: hydrogeology, risk assessment, and remedial engineering. The adequacy of our current knowledge in these areas was the focus of the final two papers in the colloquium and the subsequent workshops, although the time available was insufficient to address thoroughly the complex scientific and technical issues involved in evaluating the adequacy of existing methods for setting cleanup levels. In each broad area, models are available to assess the fate (hydrogeology, engineering) and potential impact (risk assessment) of many hazardous chemicals on humans and the environment, but there are widely divergent levels of certainty in the projected results.

Although the three broad areas overlap divergent scientific disciplines, the deficiencies identified in the papers by James Davidson and P. S. C. Rao, by Robert Tardiff, and in the work groups, were remarkably similar. Among these deficiencies or shortcomings are the following:

- models (solute transport, risk extrapolation, performance of remedial technologies) do not account for all of the processes affecting the fate and impact of the contaminants;
- the models lack accuracy when confronted with a high degree of heterogeneity (complex hydrogeology, multiple contaminants, two-phase flow, variable susceptibility in populations);
- data requirements to ensure high levels of confidence in the accuracy of predicted results are prohibitively expensive and sometimes, in the case of risk assessment, impossible to obtain (we cannot test a million mice, much less test the chronic impacts of contaminants on humans); and
- all analytical methodologies suffer from a lack of knowledge on the fundamental processes underlying observed phenomena (biotic and abiotic fate of organic contaminants, biology of carcinogenesis, contaminant adsorption on soil).

These deficiencies produce levels of uncertainty that have not been well defined to date in the remediation process. Despite these uncertainties, however, all participants clearly preferred the use of the existing technical information base in the decision process rather than a reliance on arbitrary or poorly documented decisions.

SUMMARY

The process of setting cleanup levels at hazardous waste sites poses new challenges to the regulators, the regulatory community, and the impacted parties, when compared to the implementation of other environmental statutes. Although all participants in the debate over the details of the risk assessment/risk management process desire an objective, tractable method for setting cleanup levels, numerous obstacles make this goal difficult to achieve.

All of the participants in the colloquium were in agreement on the importance of using the best available scientific and technical knowledge in the decision process. Although the techniques employed in hydrogeology, risk assessment, and remedial engineering are deficient in many aspects, they provide essential bases for informed decisionmaking in the face of great uncertainty. Indeed, the approaches proposed by EPA and other regulatory agencies cannot avoid the difficult value judgments that are implicitly required when large areas of uncertainty exist in the technical information base.

It was apparent from the discussions held during the colloquium that there has been progress toward a unified approach to setting cleanup levels at hazardous waste sites. Further advances in our understanding of the basic mechanisms of contaminant fate and the impact of contaminants on humans and the environment are urgently needed, however. Technologists must continue to strive to educate the public about the potential hazards at sites and the risks associated with alternative remediation strategies. Perhaps the continued debate on the "How clean is clean?" issue will lead to a successful balancing of the conflicting demands of affected parties and result in environmental protection at a cost commensurate with the reduction in actual risks. It is the hope of all of the colloquium participants that this document will be a useful benchmark in that debate.

MICHAEL KAVANAUGH, *Chairman*

Issue Papers and Provocateurs' Comments

1

Setting Environmental Standards for Hazardous Waste Sites: A Break from the Past or a Continuum?

RICHARD M. DOWD

Keynote addresses are an environmental hazard; they constantly present the danger of boring the audience into somnolence before the real proceedings get under way. After I examined the program for this symposium and read some of the thoughtful papers prepared for our discussion, I became particularly apprehensive about triggering such a reaction this afternoon. Certainly, as a practicing scientist, I would be much more comfortable reporting to you on, for instance, my findings on a comparison of recent ground water investigations involving the effects of well casing materials on monitoring results.

But the more I thought about the general direction of this program's papers, in light of my own experiences with standard setting in various environmental media and regulatory programs over the past 15 years, the more I began to believe that our discussions here actually represent one point in a continuum. The standard-setting art has evolved over these 15 years, but we still face an uncanny sense of merely running in place when we look at some of the issues that still bedevil us. I would like to describe some milestones in the evolution of this art and one principle in particular that I believe our experience has demonstrated to be bedrock.

Let me start by trying to put the setting of standards for hazardous waste sites into something of a historical context. I would be the first to label my brief account of standard setting as a revisionist history of the evolution of environmental rule making

13

over the past 17-odd years. Like many people, I would date the modern era of environmental regulation as starting around 1970 with the passage of the National Environmental Policy Act and the Clean Air Act. I further believe, as many of you may, that there are some differences in the way we did things routinely before 1977 and the way we have done things routinely since that time.

In those early years of modern environmental regulation the emphasis was on what we tend to call conventional pollutants, those chemicals that were then known to make up the bulk of wastes disposed of from stacks or pipes and discharged into the air or water. In that time, the approach to setting standards for the most part used the concept of thresholds. The concept was useful, particularly in dealing with ways to regulate these bulk contaminants that cause or contribute to the types of human illness that were generally associated with these conventional pollutants. This concept of threshold levels below which these substances were "safe" was built into the language of the legislation and in turn drove the regulations. In both of the 1970s air and water laws, we thought we knew enough to determine the danger levels and to establish a threshold above which damage occurred—to people and to ecological systems—and below which damage did not occur. We also believed, and the legislation iterated, that beyond that threshold we needed to provide a certain margin of safety. With such a margin, if there were a mistake in our estimate of the threshold or if the standard were slightly exceeded, we would still be out of the damage range.

During these years, some of the most intensive debate occurred over how large these margins of safety ought to be and what they should take into account. Even as recently as 1980, when debate was raging over the revision of the photochemical oxidant (ozone) air standard, a major part of that argument was the size of the margin of safety, as well as where the threshold was. In general, in setting those early standards the threshold concept had value in addressing health concerns, but it did not routinely allow ecological or other values, including aesthetic concerns, to be addressed. For example, visibility was regarded as a secondary value, as was materials damage, and these concerns were therefore termed "welfare" effects and addressed through the so-called "secondary standards." And although the legislation mandated the setting of these secondary standards, it put little emphasis on achieving or enforcing them. As a result, many of the secondary standards have essentially been scrapped or have just not been enforced.

Yet part of this neglect or downgrading is a result, it seems to me, of our inadequate knowledge in those areas. We had very little baseline data with which to work and a very limited understanding of some basic ecological processes. Our monitoring systems were almost nil—and some of us might argue that they have not been all that much improved today—and our modeling capabilities were in their infancy. In only a few cases did we know how to judge effects on ecological systems. We did know, for example, that dissolved oxygen affects aquatic life, and the water law set a goal of "swimmable, fishable" water quality. Thus, there was a dissolved oxygen standard, with a threshold that was set to prevent fish from dying. But dealing with other waterborne pollutants proved far more troublesome, and, in fact, the committees writing the 1972 legislation essentially threw up their hands over the difficulty of directly relating the concentrations of contaminants in water to human health or to ecological values. Essentially, the approach adopted in the law mandated a technology-based standard. Thereafter, attempts were made to relate such standards to water quality parameters on a quantitative basis.

Most standards, then, in this first wave of environmental regulation, focused on the stack or on the outfall. They reflected attempts to set a number based on a threshold and required environmental managers to control the stack or outfall emissions to meet the numbers. Other environmental legislation followed a similar approach. For example, the federal pesticide statute that made EPA, rather than the U.S. Department of Agriculture, responsible for setting acceptable limits on pesticide residues in food incorporated this threshold concept under the term "tolerance."

Even during this phase of regulatory development, however, there were elements that foreshadowed the regulatory approach of the post-1977 period. The nascent cancer policy that EPA first published in 1975 was a preview of coming attempts to quantify, weigh, and balance—a process that has since evolved into what we could basically call the "postthreshold concept" age of regulation. More and more, we began to deal with what we generically refer to as toxics. This focus—on substances different in nature, concentration, and behavior from the conventional bulk pollutants—has itself been driven, in many cases, by advances in analytical chemistry and the improvement in the sensitivity of our methods, developments that have driven detection limits lower and lower. The shift in focus has also been fueled by changes in biological experimentation: the number of long-term studies on rodents and other mammals to determine whether or not substances are carcinogenic has burgeoned since the early 1970s. We began to collect a data base that previously had been nonexistent, and this new body of information has led to major changes in the way we look at the issues and, consequently, to an evolution in standard setting.

The first important legislative embodiment of this change was reflected in the passage of the Toxic Substances Control Act in 1976. This legislation was spurred by public concern over the discovery of suites of chemicals that were present—often in unknown levels—in soil, air, and water across the country in the mid-1970s. Not only were the concentrations of these chemicals often unknown; in many cases, their effects were also a question. And because so many of these substances were so widely prevalent and so integral a part of our industrialized society, concern about them led to a substantial increase in the use of different forms of quantitative risk assessment. In particular, when dealing with known or suspected carcinogens, risk assessments became an indispensable tool because of the (appropriate) consensus that there may not be thresholds in these instances; that risk may exist at any level, no matter how low; and that there is no strong basis for assuming—with a few exceptions—that the human body recovers from exposure to environmental carcinogens. If, therefore, the possibility of risk cannot be allowed to drive standards to zero—because existence of the carcinogens in question is deemed necessary or inevitable—then the only alternative is either to determine some nonzero value for acceptable risk or at least a level at which the benefits of such an exposure or risk outweigh the costs. This conclusion has led to growing efforts to focus on long-term chronic effects and a corresponding increase in research on and the application of quantitative risk assessment.

In recent years—since 1980—public concerns over hazardous wastes have overtaken the earlier focus on conventional pollutants and moved to an almost exclusive preoccupation with the presence of toxic chemicals and the possibility that even trace concentrations can cause long-term chronic health damage. Such fears have, to some degree, led to a call for restrictions even on minute concentrations that may, in fact, be irrelevant to human exposure and therefore to human health risk.

To some extent, demand for the development of such stringent standards reflects a worthy premise: that already bad situations should not be made worse and should, in principle at least, be cleaned up. And there is where the rub sets in for the standard maker.

Obviously, we can take a worst-case analysis, apply it to an unrealistic extreme, and set a standard designed either to prevent or to "cure" it. But before we say that this is a bad idea—or a good one, for that matter—we should consider some of the elements involved in setting any standard. Theoretically, at least, the standard setter must, at a minimum, take three categories of knowledge into account:

1. the effects of whatever substance is of concern, whether these be carcinogenic, mutagenic, acute or chronic, long or short term; and the levels at which these effects can occur, either the reference dose or threshold, or a zero level;

2. the concentrations at which the substance is present in whatever media are of concern (in the case of hazardous wastes, these media are generally ground water and soils); and

3. how the material is transported and transformed as it moves to and from its site.

As we look at our knowledge base regarding contamination at hazardous waste sites, we find that, in comparison to our base for air and water standard setting in the pre-1977 period, we know very much less than was then the case in almost all of these categories, particularly ground water. Our intellectual capital is thin.

If, for the sake of discussion, one accepts my broad revisionist history of regulatory standard setting, can any useful comparisons be drawn from it about the differences between then and now in formulating sensible standards? Today we are dealing with much smaller quantities or concentrations of substances than in previous times; we have much less knowledge about effects at these small levels than we previously had about effects of higher concentrations of other pollutants; and we are tending to look toward chronic and long-term effects rather than acute, short-term effects. One other notable difference should be explicitly mentioned: we are often routinely attempting to deal with multiple chemicals, in multiple media, through multiple routes of transport and exposure. Even a cursory review of the papers prepared for this symposium highlights these characteristics of contemporary standard setting.

I do not intend in these remarks to address the details of how standards should be set. Many of the colloquium's participants have studied this issue in far more depth than I have and have been developing promising methodologies to generate sensible values. But I have recently been considering some of the principles that must underlie any standard-setting efforts if the results are to mean or achieve anything in the real world, and it is that thinking that I would like to share here.

For any standard to be valid, I suggest that it must have an objective, a meaningful range of application, and a realistic means or measure for verifying its success. These criteria apply, I believe, to standards in any field, whether it be (for example) education, consumer safety, or environmental protection. It is this third criterion of verification—and its underlying assumption of what I call a "commitment to truth"—that is the focus of the rest of my remarks.

In dealing with standards designed to protect health, there is necessarily a concern with ensuring adequacy, and conservatism is often invoked as a necessary principle. Indeed, the objective of a health standard ought to include the provision of a desired level of protection, and, accordingly, margins of safety and ranges of application could be larger or smaller, depending on the degree of protection deemed adequate. But where conservatism cannot be invoked as a principle, in my view, is in the area of measurement, of verification. Here, in trying to assess truth, we cannot afford to wear either rose-colored or dark glasses. Without a commitment to unadorned truth on the part of all involved in standard setting or evaluation, standards will end up as mere exercises that do not encourage increased knowledge—which itself could lead to the reevaluation of existing standards—and perhaps therefore not even to improved protection.

In this regard, we can learn something from some of the preceding efforts in standard setting in the more traditional areas. Here, too, we were initially compelled to act, to select numerical values and limits, in the face of incomplete knowledge about pollutant effects, levels, and transport routes and mechanisms. Because we could not use inadequate knowledge as an excuse for delay, we were forced to develop predictive tools—for example, models to assist in relating emissions at the stack level to atmospheric conditions some distance away, and eventually to concentrations that people outside property lines would breathe. Thus, in the air quality area, the need to establish ambient air quality standards— both to satisfy the legislative control scheme and to incorporate our then-current knowledge of thresholds—led inevitably to a need to develop good air quality dispersion models based on and encouraging an understanding of the transport and transformation of chemicals in the atmosphere.

Despite the fact that the application of air dispersion modeling, as it has developed, reflects a tendency to require the use of models that predict the worst cases—the most severe meteorology coupled with the highest emissions—the truth of the models themselves can be tested, and these worst cases can be verified. Monitoring can determine whether the models predict accurately or inaccurately. There have been considerable debate and controversy over whether or not one of the criteria for model validity that is often used—consistency between accepted models and newly developed models—is necessary. But in any event, there has never been any question that the models need to be logically consistent, that they need to be tested and verified, and that there ought to be a real relationship between predictions and actual atmospheric conditions in the world about us. Likewise, in determining human exposure—and therefore risk—monitoring must be representative of the contamination that exists where people breathe. In fact, some monitoring programs have been challenged, successfully, on the basis that they do not realistically test the air to which people are exposed.

Among other things, this commitment to truth has led to a substantial improvement in our knowledge base of the physics and chemistry of the atmosphere and the movement and transformation of pollutants. Of course, we do not know everything, but we have begun the process of knowing in a much more vigorous way than we did in 1970.

The lessons learned in the often difficult process of developing air quality models to verify standards can be applied in the case of hazardous waste standard setting. It is my concern that if standards are set in this area without ensuring that the measures adopted for their validation incorporate a commitment to truth similar to that we are building into verification processes for other standards, the resulting lack of relationship to real-world conditions will make it difficult for scientists and engineers to contribute to sensible decisionmaking in a regulatory agency. Without developing appropriate methodologies—be they for modeling or for monitoring systems—to formulate and test our hazardous waste standard setting, our efforts will not embody the commitment to truth, to verification, to testing against the real world that I am advocating.

In areas like hazardous wastes, in which we are faced with inadequate knowledge, tight timetables for taking action, and heightened public concern that we act to protect human health adequately, it is tempting to respond by establishing worst-case conditions, however unrealistic, and regulating "against" them. Take, as one example, the attempt to establish a methodology for delisting wastes at a hazardous site. EPA devised a methodology and model that assumed that 100 percent of a given chemical for a site would leach into the ground water. At the same time, because the model—rightly—dealt with multimedia effects, the model makers wanted to incorporate any volatilization of the chemical into the air. The model they devised simultaneously assumed that 100 percent of the chemical leached into the ground water, and 100 percent of the chemical also volatilized into the air. The results of these two exercises were to be compared against existing air and water standards. But this simultaneous 100 percent behavior is not logically consistent; it cannot reflect the real world, it does not incorporate a commitment to truth, and it will not lead to any improvement in science or in technology to deal with hazardous waste sites. The assumptions are so excessively conservative as to be logically impossible.

My argument here is not against conservatism; I repeat my belief that conservatism is an appropriate policy in standard setting and in model development. It is an acceptable, even necessary, part of the political process to establish a level or a standard or a number that is more protective than the minimum. But that is not the same as constructing a model that, because of its conservatism, because of the illogical assumptions that are built into it, can never be validated under real-world conditions.

In my view, there is never justification for not holding to the principle of using the real world as our ultimate measure. We may not always satisfy the test of absolute consistency with real-world conditions, either because of our lack of knowledge or through flaws in our standard-setting processes. Those processes must, however, allow for correction. Only a problem so overwhelming that mitigation cannot wait would, in my view, justify our abandoning efforts to make standards conform to reality.

Does the seriousness of the dangers posed by hazardous waste sites satisfy this criterion for abandoning "realistic" standard setting? I believe not. In support of this belief, I would like to cite a newly completed evaluation by EPA of the relative risks associated with 31 different environmental hazards in terms of four concerns: cancer risks, noncancer risks, ecological effects, and welfare effects. The relative ranking for the risks associated with hazardous waste sites was low to medium, pretty much right in the middle of EPA programs. Although details of this ranking could be debated, it seems clear that hazardous waste sites are not an overwhelming risk compared with other areas of concern.

I do not mean to suggest that a commitment to truth needs to stand in the way of standard setting. I am fully aware that political pressure and public concern often require, properly, action by regulatory agencies even in the absence of full knowledge. However, the absence of knowledge and an understanding of uncertainties is not the same as ignoring knowledge.

Our understanding of the movement of trace chemicals (sometimes in quantities that make "trace" a misnomer) will undoubtedly increase. As long as we are committed to using the best of that understanding in our standard-setting processes, as long as we are prepared to revise our view of the world as we learn, the standard-setting process will be healthy and defensible.

There are many incentives to improved understanding: increased regulatory attention, public concern, and large potential costs (environmental, human health, and economic). But in all of this we cannot delude ourselves: if we do not see the "real" world, we cannot solve "real" problems.

As Polonius, that ultimate bore, provoker of drowsiness—and purveyor of truth—says in *Hamlet*, "To thine own self be true, and it must follow, as the night the day, thou canst not then be false to any man."

2
Establishing and Meeting Ground Water Protection Goals in the Superfund Program

EDWIN F. BARTH III, WILLIAM HANSON, AND
ELIZABETH A. SHAW

Decisions on contaminated ground water at uncontrolled hazardous waste sites are complicated because of complex fate and transport patterns. The process being developed will guide remedial project managers and other decisionmakers concerned with ground water remedial actions at Superfund sites so that a consistent ground water evaluation and decision approach is applied to all such sites.

APPLICABLE OR RELEVANT AND APPROPRIATE REQUIREMENTS

Under the National Contingency Plan (NCP) (*Federal Register*, 1985), remedial actions at Superfund sites shall meet or exceed all applicable or relevant and appropriate federal requirements and consider other pertinent federal criteria, advisories, and guidances and state standards. Federal requirements that may be applicable, relevant, or appropriate to Superfund ground water actions are included in the Resource Conservation and Recovery Act (RCRA) Subpart F regulations. Determinations of ground water protection

---

This paper was first presented at the 7th National Conference on Management of Uncontrolled Hazardous Waste Sites, Washington, D.C., December 1-3, 1986. It was prepared prior to the Superfund Amendments and Reauthorization Act. The concept presented in this paper may be modified following the promulgation of the revised National Contingency Plan.

levels under both RCRA (as alternate concentration levels) and Superfund may be based on a site-specific risk assessment.

The Safe Drinking Water Act and the Clean Water Act resulted in the development of maximum concentration levels (MCLs), maximum concentration level goals (MCLGs), health advisories, and water quality criteria for the protection of public health, all of which are evaluated for ground water protection levels in the Superfund program. EPA's ground water protection strategy (U.S. EPA, Office of Ground-Water Protection, 1984) is an important component of Superfund's ground water approach. The strategy says that ground water should be protected differentially based on characteristics of vulnerability, use, and value. Special ground water (Class I) is highly vulnerable to contamination because of the hydrological characteristics of the areas in which it occurs. It is characterized by either of the following: the ground water is irreplaceable, in that no reasonable alternative source of drinking water is available to substantial populations; or the ground water is ecologically vital, providing the base flow for a particularly sensitive ecological system that, if polluted, would destroy a unique habitat.

Current-use ground water (Class IIA) and potential-use ground water (Class IIB) that are sources of drinking water (or have other beneficial uses) include all non-Class I ground water that is currently used or is potentially available for drinking water or other beneficial use.

Ground water not considered to be a potential source of drinking water and of limited beneficial use (Class III) is nonusable ground water that is highly saline—that is, with total dissolved solids (TDS) levels over 10,000 milligrams per liter (mg/l)—or that is otherwise contaminated beyond levels that allow cleanup using methods reasonably employed in public water treatment systems. This condition must not be the result of a single waste site but rather the result of a wide range of sources. Class III is further separated by the degree of interconnection with adjacent water. Class IIIA is highly to moderately interconnected and is thus most relevant to Superfund. Class IIIB ground water has a low degree of interconnection and typically occurs at greater depths. As will be explained in this paper, the Superfund program will use these ground water characteristics in the evaluation of alternative response actions.

DEVELOPMENT OF GROUND WATER ALTERNATIVES

In general, source control measures should facilitate the achievement of long-term remediation objectives and goals for ground water. EPA's guidance document for feasibility studies under the Comprehensive Environmental Response, Compensation, and Liability Act (CERCLA) (U.S. EPA, 1985a) calls for the development, screening, and detailed evaluation of alternatives proposed for remedial actions. For ground water contamination problems, this process involves the development of a limited number of remediation alternatives to be presented to the decision-maker.

The performance goal of each ground water alternative should be expressed in terms of a cleanup concentration (in the ground water) and a time period for the restoration for all locations in the area of attainment. Performance goals in terms of ground water concentrations may be available as MCLs, proposed MCLs, or more stringent state standards. If these are not available, concentrations may be derived from health-based criteria such as excess unit carcinogenic risk (UCR) or referenced dose values. Other potentially approved standards include health advisories or water quality criteria or both. Health-based criteria may also be developed if no standards, advisories, or criteria are available. (The reader is referred to the Superfund Public Health Evaluation Manual [U.S. EPA, 1985b] for information on developing health-based criteria.) Restoration time periods may range from very rapid (1 to 5 years) to relatively extended (perhaps several decades).

If ground water with the characteristics of Class I or Class II is contaminated with known or suspected carcinogens, the program suggests the development of a limited number of ground water protection goals be developed that vary between 10^{-4} UCR and 10^{-7} UCR and vary between restoration time periods. A point-of-departure alternative for initial decision evaluation should be developed at a 10^{-6} UCR with a limited restoration time period. For noncarcinogens, alternatives should be developed that meet chronic or acute threshold levels in varying restoration periods.

In situations in which the plume is not in close proximity to a receiving body of water, plume containment measures (e.g., gradient control) should also be evaluated, which will eventually result in a 10^{-4} UCR and 10^{-7} UCR for carcinogen levels in the ground water. Other alternatives (a limited number, possibly

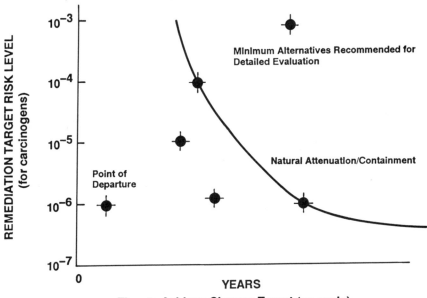

FIGURE 2-1 Suggested alternatives to be developed for ground water contaminated with carcinogens.

two or three) should also be developed around the point of departure. (Figure 2-1 presents a conceptual risk/restoration time plot of these suggested alternatives for carcinogens contaminating ground water with the characteristics of Class I or Class II.) The alternatives will then be evaluated to compare the trade-offs between the cleanup level, the time it takes to achieve the level, and the cost of the action.

DECISION ANALYSIS

The decision as to which remedial action alternative to select and implement depends on many factors. Those factors relating to the concentration level for carcinogens in the ground water include other health risks borne by the affected population and population sensitivities.

For example, at the Reilly Tar Superfund site (U.S. EPA, 1984), the population had been exposed to contaminated ground water for an indeterminable period of time, which influenced the decision to use a "more protective" lower concentration level. Similarly, a more protective lower concentration level may be evaluated if the exposed population is unusually sensitive to the contaminants. Acute and chronic levels for noncarcinogens are threshold values and therefore are not influenced by these two factors.

Factors that influence the restoration time period for ground water contaminated with carcinogens and noncarcinogens are as follows:

- feasibility of providing an alternative water supply;
- current use of ground water;
- potential need for ground water;
- effectiveness and reliability of institutional controls; and
- ability to monitor and control the movement of contaminants in ground water.

The existence of other drinking water sources of sufficient quality and yield, sources that are readily available and that may be used as an alternative water supply, reduces the importance of rapid restoration of the contaminated ground water. On the other hand, where a demand for drinking water from ground water is likely in the future and other potential sources are not sufficient, those remedies that achieve more rapid restoration should be favored.

The effectiveness and reliability of institutional controls to prevent the use of contaminated ground water for drinking water purposes should also be evaluated. If these controls clearly are not effective, rapid restoration may be necessary.

In some circumstances, complex flow patterns increase the potential for unanticipated migration pathways and may reduce the effectiveness of remedial action. In these situations, remedial actions that will rapidly restore ground water, such as extensive source control and high-rate pumping, should be emphasized.

Other factors that should be considered in determining the appropriate ground water protection goals for carcinogens and noncarcinogens include limiting the extent of the contamination, its impact on environmental receptors, the technical practicability of implementing the alternative, and the alternative's cost.

Limited increases in concentration may be evaluated if the expanded area of ground water contamination is relatively small, the period of degradation is short, and the ultimate discharge of the plume has no significant effect on surface waters.

The technical practicability of each alternative must also be evaluated in light of the contaminant characteristics and applicable hydrogeological conditions, which may not allow the effective implementation of the alternative to clean up the ground water. Environmental receptors should be taken into account when evaluating the appropriate cleanup concentration levels and time period.

Finally, under the NCP, response actions must be cost-effective. Therefore, a careful evaluation of capital outlays and the operation and maintenance costs associated with each alternative must be considered and compared to those of each of the other alternatives. Ground water remediation time frames may be extended if the agency decides that the costs to meet performance goals in 1 to 5 years are extraordinarily high and as long as institutional controls will be effective for the additional period.

Figure 2-2 presents general ground water goal areas associated with the ground water characteristics on the risk/restoration plot for carcinogens. The decisionmaker should first evaluate the point-of-departure remedy and then move to other general areas on the plot as influenced by the ground water's characteristics. The reader should be cautioned that the general areas delineated on the plot are not rigid.

FLEXIBLE DECISION PROCESS

Complex fate and transport mechanisms of contaminated ground water often make it difficult to predict accurately the performance of ground water remedial action. Therefore, the remedial process must be flexible, allowing changes in the remedy based on the performance of several years of operation.

To illustrate this principle, Figure 2-3 presents three possible situations that may occur after several years of a ground water response action. In the first scenario (Case 3A), the target concentration will be reached within the desired time period. In the second scenario (Case 3B), the target concentration will be reached somewhat later than the desired time period. In the final scenario (Case 3C), the target concentration will not be reached in a foreseeable time period.

A performance feedback concept has been incorporated into

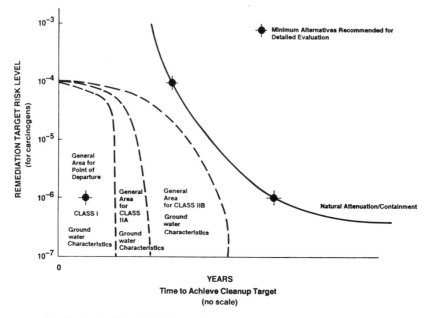

FIGURE 2-2　　Performance range for ground water remedial alternatives.

the decision process so that in situations in which the performance goal will not be met (e.g., in Case 3B and Case 3C) the decisions may be reevaluated based on actual experience. If the remedial action is not meeting expectations, the decisionmaker should decide the extent to which further or different action is necessary and appropriate to protect human health and the environment. Figure 2-4 illustrates this evaluation process. Should it be determined that it is not practicable to restore the ground water to the initial cleanup goal level, an exception to the NCP could be demonstrated, based on extraordinary costs or the technical impracticability of meeting applicable or relevant and appropriate federal requirements.

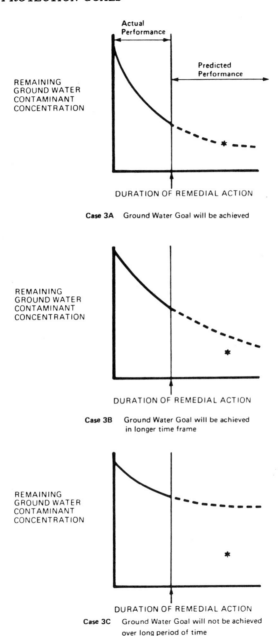

FIGURE 2-3 Possible restoration scenarios when evaluating performance data.

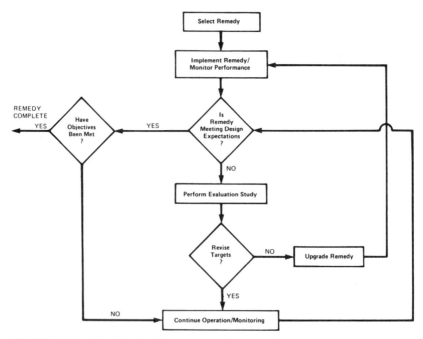

FIGURE 2-4   Flexible decision process for ground water remedial actions.

REFERENCES

Federal Register. 1985. November 20.

U.S. Environmental Protection Agency (EPA). 1984. Record of Decision— Reilly Tar Site. Washington, D.C.

U.S. EPA. 1985a. Guidance on Remedial Investigations Under CERCLA. Prepared for Hazard Waste Engineering Research Laboratory, Office of Emergency and Remedial Response, and Office of Waste Programs Enforcement. Washington, D.C., and Cincinnati, Ohio. June.

U.S. EPA. 1985b. Superfund Public Health Evaluation Manual. Draft Office of Emergency and Remedial Response. OERR. Washington, D.C. December.

U.S. EPA, Office of Ground-Water Protection. 1984. Ground-Water Protection Strategy. Washington, D.C. August.

PROVOCATEUR'S COMMENTS
Joel Hirschhorn

The preceding paper does not give me a lot of opportunity to be critical in a sense because it is a general framework, with which I find myself in agreement. It is a technically rational framework. One point I find myself in particular agreement with, which was not stressed in the presentation but is in the paper, is the use of classification systems, particularly for aquifers. As Superfund grows (we are talking about thousands of sites), it becomes necessary to move away, in my opinion, from a logic that says that every site is unique. Although every site may be unique, just in the same way that every person is unique, that does not mean that you cannot use classification systems to help manage a very complex and large number of sites. So I applaud the use of a classification system—in this case, for aquifers.

There are a couple of issues that have not been fleshed out in the presentation. First, it is going to be increasingly necessary to deal with multiple exposures by the government or whatever authority is dealing with cleanups and performing risk assessments. People have to pay more attention to the exposures that citizens are getting from various sources. In other words, if you do a risk assessment and you say, here is the exposure from a particular contaminated water supply, you cannot neglect the fact that the same population is being exposed to the same, similar, or different chemicals from other roots of exposure, including other cleanups. We have seen situations in which half a dozen cleanups are going on, stuff is going into a river that is becoming the drinking water supply downstream, and none of this has been factored into the risk assessment. I feel that this is a fundamental fallacy and limitation of what we see going on in risk assessment. A lot of levels of exposure that might be deemed acceptable on a case-by-case basis are certainly not acceptable in a cumulative sense.

A very interesting point in this paper is the framework, which is something, again, I agree with. We have talked about it for years, and it does not get much attention in the "How clean is clean?" issue. It is a completely different logic that is predicated on the idea that the starting point should be the issue of the future use of a natural resource. What will be the future use of a piece of land or a body of water? It is the future use in particular that will determine exposures, and from there you can deal with risk. If we talk about the future use of a natural resource as the primary factor, then there are a lot of policy implications because in the United States the use of water and land is fundamentally a local and state decision, not a federal one. I think we have created a monster with the Superfund program—that is, a great deal of federal authority (because the federal government provides a lot of the money); yet if we apply this logic of dealing with the future use of natural resources, you would have to shift decisionmaking to a local level. Now, I personally think that is desirable; shift the burden to the people who have to live with that resource to decide how clean is clean and to deal with the institutional problems of ensuring future use. We have a long history of dealing with deeds, deed restrictions, and things like that. Historically, Love Canal was an example not of a failure of industry or technology but a failure of institutional control on the future use of land. If you look at chemical codes, the authorities, the limitations on the use of that land, you will find that it was government, local government authorities, who in fact simply forgot about what was told to them and went ahead and used the natural resource in an inappropriate way—and that was the real cause, historically, of Love Canal. I think we have to deal more with this issue of the future use of natural resource and to think of it as a departure point in the assessments of cleanup goals. It happens to be what is done in the United Kingdom, and I find that their cleanup program is much more cost-effective and sensible than ours.

Superfund, in my view, is probably going to be an incredible waste of money because we have a great deal of underreaction and a great deal of overreaction. It is a system that is not optimized in any engineering sense. One other fact that is buried in the framework discussed in the paper is the real problem: it sounds fine, in terms of generalities, to talk about cleanup goals driving what will happen, but in fact, what really happens in the system is that technology and money dictate how much cleanup is done. I do not think we ought to ignore the fact that there are opportunities in this framework presented by EPA to have people decide on the level of cleanup simply on the basis of what available technology can do or what bureaucrats have decided is an appropriate amount of money for a site. My interpretation of how Superfund really works is that somebody decides this site is worth about $10 million; now, go out and tell me how to spend $10 million, and that is the amount of cleanup you get. I am not so sure that this is going to change in the more eloquent framework presented here.

Finally, my last point is that any framework in any technical methodology ought to be sensitive to implementation issues. Just as giving a loaded gun to a child does not make any sense, giving risk assessment to people without adequate information and adequately trained people to use it is also folly. Creating a Superfund program at an $8 billion spending level without adequate information, adequate technology, and adequately trained people is another folly, analogous to giving a loaded gun to a child. I wish we would talk more about how we can implement these frameworks, how we can implement the use of risk assessment; and if we cannot implement it now or in 5 to 10 years, are you willing to talk about making a commitment to delay action until we get the information or the technology or the trained people? If you want to wait, then what is the interim strategy and what are the interim framework and methodologies to be used? For the most part, what I see are long-term methodologies and a lack of implementation ability now.

3

Some Approaches to Setting Cleanup Goals at Hazardous Waste Sites

HALINA SZEJNWALD BROWN

During the past decade the assessment and cleanup of hazardous waste sites has come to occupy a prominent position in the activities of federal, state, and local governments. Currently, EPA estimates over 23,000 potential sites nationwide and over 850 on the Superfund national priority list. In Massachusetts alone, there are about 400 confirmed hazardous waste sites, of which 21 are on the Superfund list.

Cleanup of these sites raises a vexing question: How clean is clean enough? The question is neither new nor unique to hazardous waste sites. Yet compared to direct emissions of toxic materials into water or air, soil contamination presents a significantly more complex problem. As illustrated in Figure 3-1, human and nonhuman exposure to soil contaminants can occur through a variety of pathways. Also, because hazardous waste sites usually contain large numbers of toxic substances with a wide combined spectrum of adverse effects, cleanup standards must be sensitive to this multiple route/multiple agent exposure pattern. Finally, specific circumstances of human intake of the substances through multiple media are difficult to predict or measure.

Determining the extent of cleanup of hazardous waste sites can be approached using one of two general methods: absolute or relative. The absolute approach is based on the assumption that we can define acceptable concentrations of hazardous materials in the environmental media from which no significant risk of adverse

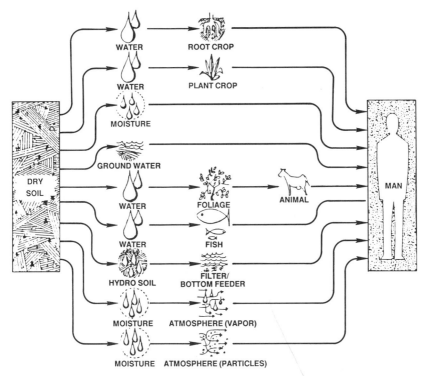

FIGURE 3-1 Pollutant pathways from soil to man. SOURCE: Dacre et al. (1980).

effects to humans and the environment would be expected. For toxic effects to humans that have a threshold, this level would be somewhere below the expected threshold for the population at risk. For nonthreshold effects such as cancer, the definition of "clean" is often linked to some acceptable or, as some (Kasperson, 1983) argue, tolerable risk level.

The common feature of absolute approaches is their search for universally acceptable numbers (i.e., standards, guidelines, and criteria). Once established, these numbers drive the cleanup process because they, in effect, define the term "clean."

In contrast to the absolute, standard-based approach to managing environmental pollution, the relative approach defines "clean" for each particular situation. It may be driven by technology, costs, comparison with other current and historical hazards, or risk/benefit analysis, or it may be expressed as a percentage reduction of a hazardous material (for example, 99.99 percent). In essence, an acceptable level of contamination is defined as that associated with the most acceptable option in a particular decision problem. Hence, the acceptable level is defined for each situation through the risk management process rather than used as an absolute goal for hazard management.

It has been argued (Fischhoff et al., 1981) that the absolute approach to acceptable risk (or, by analogy, to "How clean is clean?") is simplistic and unworkable in most situations and that the issue should be viewed as a decision problem, unique for each specific situation. Despite the criticism, however, the standard-based approach has been consistently the favored one for risk managers. There are several reasons for this:

- Once a standard is adopted, its application is simple and noncontroversial.
- It is easy to justify and defend in court.
- It provides a means of communication among all the technical and nontechnical participants of the risk management process on both sides of the issue.
- It *appears* to be an objective process grounded in scientific analysis and free of value judgments.
- It relieves policymakers from the cumbersome burden of dealing with uncertainty and from being charged with imposing their own values and beliefs on society.
- It simplifies the problem by automatically determining the goals of risk management activities.
- It reflects a recurrent hope that we will find a scientific method for objectively resolving the problem of "How clean is clean?"

The purpose of this paper is to review five currently used approaches to determining "How clean is clean?" at hazardous waste sites. The paper focuses on the general concepts that are used as well as on specific methods. The work of the following agencies is reviewed: U.S. Environmental Protection Agency, U.S. Army, California Department of Health Services, Washington State Department of Ecology, and the New Jersey Department of Environmental Protection.

THE EPA SUPERFUND PUBLIC HEALTH
EVALUATION MANUAL

General Concepts

This document is a comprehensive manual for site assessment and the establishment of cleanup goals. Conceptually, the EPA methodology is similar to that of California in its view of the environmental migration of chemicals, the role of chemical analysis and dispersion modeling in determining media-specific concentrations of chemicals, and the reliance on toxicity-based criteria to determine cleanup levels. There are, however, differences between the two methodologies. One notable difference is that California concerns itself with all chemicals found at a site, whereas the EPA manual recommends the use of indicator compounds, chosen on the basis of minimum effective dose (MED) for toxic effects, carcinogenic potency, environmental mobility, and persistence.

The following terminology is used in the EPA manual.

Critical Toxicity Value

This is a property of toxic substances that reflects the quantitative relationship between daily dose and magnitude of adverse effect of that substance. Three types of critical toxicity values are used:

- *Acceptable intake for subchronic exposure* (AIS). The highest human intake of a chemical, expressed as milligrams per kilogram (mg/kg) × day, that does not cause adverse effects when exposure is short-term (but not acute). This AIS is usually based on subchronic animal studies.
- *Acceptable intake for chronic exposure* (AIC). The highest human intake of a chemical, expressed as mg/kg × day, that does not cause adverse effects when exposure is long term. The AIC is usually based on chronic animal studies.
- *Carcinogenic potency factor.* A measure of carcinogenic potency of a chemical, derived from animal data. It corresponds to a lifetime cancer risk per unit dose $(mg/kg \times day)^{-1}$.

Estimated Daily Intake

This is a daily dose of a substance by a specified route of

exposure under some particular exposure conditions related to the site. Two types of estimated daily intake values are used:

- *Subchronic daily intake* (SDI). The projected human intake of a chemical averaged over a short period of time, expressed as mg/kg × day. The SDI is calculated by multiplying the peak short-term concentration (STC) in an exposure medium by the human intake factor for that medium and by the body weight factor.
- *Chronic daily intake* (CDI). The projected human intake of a chemical averaged over 70 years, expressed as mg/kg × day. The CDI is calculated by multiplying the peak long-term concentration (LTC) in an exposure medium by the human intake factor for that medium and by the body weight factor.

Critical toxicity values are derived from studies on animals or observations made in human epidemiologic studies. Each is specific for the route of exposure specified in the experiment on which it is based. Thus, AIS (oral) is different from AIS (inhalation), and they cannot be used interchangeably. Acceptable intake values and carcinogenic potency index are properties of a substance administered under specified conditions and are therefore applicable at any site for any exposure scenario. Estimated chronic and subchronic daily intakes (SDI and CDI) are calculated for a particular site and reflect conditions at that site as well as the estimated route, magnitude, and duration of human exposure.

Derivation of Acceptable Intakes for Subchronic and Chronic Exposure

A distinction is made between chemicals that produce carcinogenic effects and those that do not. Acceptable intake values are calculated only for compounds that do not exhibit carcinogenic properties.

The evaluation manual is not specific on details of the derivations of the AISs and AICs beyond the fact that they are derived from no observed adverse effect levels (NOAELs) and that the protection of sensitive members of the population is considered. Based on that information, it is reasonable to assume that AISs and AICs are derived from quantitative toxicity data by applying uncertainty factors to experimentally derived NOAELs.

Estimation of Daily Intake

The methodology is based on the assumption that human exposure to toxic materials present at the site can originate from the following media: air, ground water, surface water, soil, and contaminated fish. Human intake of toxicants from these media can occur through ingestion, inhalation, and skin absorption. Although soil as a medium and skin as a route of absorption are acknowledged, the methodology does not specify how human intake should be calculated for these. Instead, the manual recommends that the agency be contacted on a case-by-case basis when intake from soil and through skin (or both) is expected to be significant.

Human intake is estimated separately for each indicator compound/route of exposure/duration of exposure/population exposed. Duration of exposure is divided into chronic and subchronic. Thus, for a particular population, SDI and CDI are estimated for each chemical X and route Y using the general formulas:

$$\text{SDI}_{X,Y} \; (\text{mg/kg} \times \text{day}) = \text{STC}_{X,Y} \times \text{human intake factor}_Y$$

and

$$\text{CDI}_{X,Y} \; (\text{mg/kg} \times \text{day}) = \text{LTC}_{X,Y} \times \text{human intake factor}_Y,$$

where $\text{SDI}_{X,Y}$ and $\text{CDI}_{X,Y}$ are subchronic and chronic daily intakes of chemical X by route Y; $\text{STC}_{X,Y}$ and $\text{LTC}_{X,Y}$ are short- and long-term concentrations of chemical X in a medium associated with route of exposure Y; and the human intake factor of the medium is associated with route of exposure Y. This is illustrated below for two routes and three media:

$$\text{SDI}_{X,\text{inhal}} = \text{STC}_{X,\text{air}} \times \text{human intake factor}_{\text{air}},$$
$$\text{CDI}_{X,\text{inhal}} = \text{LTC}_{X,\text{air}} \times \text{human intake factor}_{\text{air}},$$

and

$$\text{SDI}_{X,\text{oral}} = \text{STC}_{X,\text{water}} \times \text{human intake factor}_{\text{water}}$$
$$+ \text{STC}_{X,\text{fish}} \times \text{human intake factor}_{\text{fish}}.$$

These examples show that for each route of exposure to a chemical, the total human daily intake is a sum of the daily intakes from all media by the same route. The additivity applies only to the same population exposed at the same time and for approximately the same duration (chronic versus subchronic).

For carcinogenic substances, CDI values are also used to calculate lifetime carcinogenic risk, according to the formula:

$$\text{Lifetime risk}_{X,Y} = \text{CDI}_{X,Y} \times \text{carcinogenic potency factor}_{X,Y}.$$

The value of lifetime risk is later used to determine cleanup levels for the site.

Daily intake values for chronic and subchronic exposure, as well as carcinogenic risk, are calculated for specific exposure conditions and are therefore specific for each site.

Exposure to Multiple Chemicals by Multiple Routes

Noncarcinogenic Effects

The methodology assumes that the effects of simultaneous exposure to several chemicals that cause *the same type* of toxicity are additive. Therefore, total daily intake of each chemical must be adjusted to meet the acceptable intake level. This is shown in the following:

$$\sum_{i=1}^{m} \frac{\text{CDI (route)}_i}{\text{AIC (route)}_i} \leq 1$$

$$\sum_{i=1}^{m} \frac{\text{SDI (route)}_i}{\text{AIS (route)}_i} \leq 1,$$

where i is the substance number. Once again, the acceptable intakes for chronic and subchronic exposures are specific for the duration of exposure and the route of exposure (oral or inhalation).

The methodology also assumes that the effects of exposure to a particular substance through several exposure routes are additive, as shown in the following:

$$\sum_{j=1}^{n} \frac{\text{CDI (subst)}_j}{\text{AIC (subst)}_j} \leq 1$$

$$\sum_{j=1}^{n} \frac{\text{SDI (subst)}_j}{\text{AIS (subst)}_j} \leq 1,$$

where j is a route number.

The overall hazard index for multiple routes of exposure to multiple chemicals with similar toxic effects can be expressed as a sum of hazard indices for each route. Thus, for chronic exposure:

$$\text{Hazard index} = \sum_{i=1}^{m} \sum_{j=1}^{n} \text{CDI}_{ij}/\text{AIC}_{ij}.$$

No significant adverse effects would be expected in the population if the hazard index does not exceed 1 (hazard index $\leq$ 1).

Carcinogenic Effects

The assumption of additivity is also applied to compounds producing carcinogenic effects. For multiple carcinogenic compounds absorbed through a specific route, the total risk is:

$$\text{Cancer risk for route } Y = \sum_{i=1}^{m} \text{CDI}_{Yi} \times \text{carcinogenic potency factor}_{Yi}.$$

Likewise, the risks from multiple routes of exposure to substance X are additive:

$$\text{Cancer risk for substance } X = \sum_{j=1}^{n} \text{CDI}_{jX}$$
$$\times \text{ carcinogenic potency factor}_{jX}.$$

The total carcinogenic risk for multiple substances and multiple routes is:

$$\text{Cancer risk} = \sum_{i=1}^{m} \sum_{j=1}^{n} \text{CDI}_{ij} \times \text{ carcinogenic potency factor}_{ij}.$$

Only chronic, 70-year exposure duration conditions are used for calculating cancer risks.

Cleanup Criteria

Site Assessment

Site assessment involves the following steps:

Step 1.   Selection of indicator compounds.

Step 2.   Estimation of concentrations of indicator compounds in environmental media at the points of maximum human exposure, both for short and long periods of time (STC and LTC).

Step 3.   Comparison of STCs and LTCs in specific media with environmental criteria such as drinking water standards and guidelines, ambient air standards, and water quality criteria. The assessment stops here if standards/guidelines are available for *all* indicator compounds. Otherwise, the process proceeds to Step 4.

Step 4.   This step involves the most comprehensive health assessment. Estimated human daily intakes (SDIs and CDIs) of indicator compounds are estimated for each substance/route of exposure/duration combination. Cancer risks associated with SDIs and CDIs are also calculated. Also in this step the hazard index for multiple routes of exposure is calculated. Step 4 requires knowledge of critical toxicity values such as acceptable intake for subchronic exposure (AIS) and carcinogenic potency factors.

Target Levels

The goal of a cleanup is to meet target levels for indicator compounds. Target levels are defined differently for compounds with and without environmental standards. For a target concentration for compound with a standard, an acceptable target concentration is one that does not exceed the specific standard for that medium (requirements). Target concentrations for compounds without standards are divided into two categories: potential carcinogens and chemicals with noncarcinogenic toxic effects.

For potential carcinogens, cleanup levels should maintain cancer risk in the range from 10^{-4} to 10^{-7} for a lifetime exposure, with 10^{-6} as the desirable target risk level. This is a total risk for a particular population. The target concentration is that concentration that will produce chronic daily intake associated with this range of risks. If only one carcinogenic substance is present, the target concentration is calculated using the formula:

$$\text{Target concentration (medium)} = \frac{\text{target chronic daily intake}}{\text{intake factor (medium)}},$$

$$\text{Target concentration (medium)} = \frac{\text{acceptable cancer risk}}{\text{potency factor} \times \text{intake factor (medium)}}.$$

For multiple routes/multiple agents, the target chronic daily intake (and therefore the target concentrations) can be apportioned between media and chemicals in any combination as long as the total cancer risk is within the 10^{-4} to 10^{-7} range.

For chemicals with noncarcinogenic toxic effects, the target concentration is defined as that at which (1) chronic daily intake does not exceed the acceptable intake for chronic exposure for individual substances/routes; and/or (2) the hazard index for multiple routes/multiple substances exposures does not exceed unity; that is,

$$CDI \text{ (subst, route)} \leq AIC \text{ (subst, route)},$$

$$\text{Hazard index} \leq 1.$$

As with carcinogenic substances, for multiple exposures the concentrations of individual substances in specific media can be apportioned in any way as long as the two conditions are met.

CALIFORNIA SITE MITIGATION DECISION TREE

General Concepts

This document provides state decision makers with a standardized approach to setting site-specific cleanup levels. It is based on the assumption that a toxicant deposited in the soil will be distributed among the environmental media in accordance with its chemical and physical properties as well as the properties of the media (air, soil, surface water, and ground water). It further assumes that the biologic receptors (humans and terrestrial and aquatic biota) will be exposed through contact with one or more of these media. The system relies on environmental monitoring and predictive formulas and models to estimate the actual concentrations of toxic agents in each medium. The emphasis is on defining acceptable concentrations of toxic materials in environmental media at points of contact with the biologic receptors. Three terms are essential to understanding the system:

- *The maximum exposure level* (MEL) is a daily dose (mg/day) of a substance that is not expected to produce adverse health effects in a 70-kg adult chronic exposure.

- *The applied action level* (AAL) is a concentration of a substance in a particular medium that, when exceeded, presents a significant risk of adverse impact to a biologic receptor. AALs drive the cleanup process for a site.

- *The cleanup level* is a site-specific criterion that a remedial action would have to satisfy in order to keep exposure at the biologic receptor level at or below the AAL.

The maximum exposure level provides the toxicologic basis for the derivation of AALs and is substance specific. AALs are derived from the MEL and calculated for each medium (water, air, soil) using the average daily human exposure level to that medium as their basis. Like MELs, AALs are substance and species specific. Thus, for a particular agent, human AAL (soil) is different from human AAL (air) or AAL (water). Likewise, human AAL (water) is most likely different from aquatic AAL (water). In essence, AALs define "How clean is clean?"

Derivation of MELs for Humans

For the purpose of developing MELs and AALs, toxic substances are divided into two groups: (1) threshold agents, which produce effects for which there is a threshold; and (2) nonthreshold agents, which produce effects for which no threshold level can be assumed, such as cancer, mutations, and genotoxic or teratogenic effects.

Threshold Substances

The following sources of quantitative and/or qualitative data on the toxic properties of substances are recommended, in a descending order of preference: human or animal toxicity data, drinking water standards and guidelines, and occupational exposure limits, which are used by the American Conference of Governmental Industrial Hygienists to determine threshold limit values (TLVs). These undergo internal review by professional staff before being used as the basis for MEL derivation.

From human or animal toxicologic dose-response curves. The derivation of MELs from toxicologic dose-response curves follows a classic method of acceptable daily intake (ADI) derivation, which is illustrated in the following formula:

TABLE 3-1 Uncertainty Factors Used for the Derivation of Maximum Exposure Limits (MELs)

Uncertainty Factor	Basis for MELs
10	Large controlled epidemiological studies
10 or 100	Occupational standards--this range of uncertainty factors accommodates the background behind the various occupational standards
100	NOAELs derived from chronic animal studies
1,000	NOAELs extrapolated from subacute animal studies
100,000	NOAELs extrapolated from acute animal studies

NOAEL = no observed adverse effect level.

$$\text{MEL (mg/day)} = \frac{\text{NOAEL (mg/kg} \times \text{day)} \times \text{adult body weight (kg)}}{\text{uncertainty factor}},$$

where NOAEL is a no observed adverse effect level and body weight is 70 kg for an adult.

The NOAEL can be derived either from human epidemiologic data, which are preferable but rarely available, or from animal laboratory data. As shown in Table 3-1, different uncertainty factors are assigned, according to the source of the data.

From occupational TLVs. MELs are derived from occupational TLVs according to the formula:

$$\text{MEL (mg/day)} =$$

$$\frac{\text{TLV (mg/m}^3) \times 20 \text{ m}^3/\text{day} \times 8 \text{ hr} \times 5 \text{ days} \times 47 \text{ years}}{\text{uncertainty factor} \times 24 \text{ hr} \times 7 \text{ days} \times 72 \text{ years}}.$$

As shown here the 8 hours per day/5 days per week occupational limit for 47 years of exposure is extrapolated to a 24 hours per day/7 days per week for 70 years environmental exposure. The uncertainty factor is 10 or 100, depending on the uncertainty associated with a particular occupational limit.

Nonthreshold Substances

For nonthreshold agents, the MEL is defined as the level of exposure that ensures an incremental maximum excess risk (above background risk) of affecting one individual in a million, on a lifetime exposure. Thus, for these agents the acceptable level is derived from an estimated quantitative risk and is equated with an individual lifetime excess risk of one in a million (10^{-6}). The quantitative risk assessment is performed in-house using a multistage linearized model for low-dose extrapolation and a 95 percent upper bound of dose-response data. The methodology relies on the system developed by the International Agency for Research on Cancer (IARC) to classify carcinogenic properties of substances. In the California system, all substances classified by IARC as "probable" or "possible" human carcinogens are treated as nonthreshold agents (carcinogens).

Derivation of AALs

Acceptable action levels for each medium are derived from MELs using the following formula:

$$\text{AAL (medium)} = \frac{\text{MEL}}{\text{intake factor}} \times \text{PF},$$

where the intake factor is the average daily intake of the medium. The pharmocokinetic factor (PF) is an adjustment factor to account for differences in absorption, distribution, and elimination between the different routes of exposure.

For air and water, AALs are calculated as follows:

$$\text{AAL (water)} = \frac{\text{MEL (mg/day)}}{2 \text{ l/day}} \times \text{PF},$$

$$\text{AAL (air)} = \frac{\text{MEL (mg/day)}}{20 \text{ m}^3/\text{day}} \times \text{PF}.$$

Cleanup Level Determination

Determination of the cleanup level consists of comparing the predicted concentration (C) of toxic material at the biologic receptors with those considered toxicologically safe (AAL). The method considers exposures to individual agents in a single medium, individual agents in multiple media, and multiple agents in multiple media. The following criteria must be met by a cleanup action.

Single Agent/Single Medium

$$\frac{C_i}{AAL_i} \leq 1.$$

Single Agent/Multiple Media

If a substance is present in more than one medium, the combined dose to the biologic receptor is assumed to be additive. Thus, the sum of the ratios of C/AAL in each medium cannot exceed one if the MEL is not to be exceeded. Thus,

$$\sum_{i=1}^{n} \frac{C_i}{AAL_i} \leq 1.$$

Multiple Agents with the Same Toxic Action/Multiple Media

In this scenario, both the total dose from each medium (a sum of media-specific doses) *and* the combined toxic effect on the biologic receptor are assumed to be additive. A cleanup action must proceed until

$$\sum_{j=1} \sum_{i=1} \frac{C_{ij}}{AAL_{ij}} \leq 1,$$

where i is a medium number and j is a substance number.

U.S. ARMY APPROACH

General Concepts

This methodology, which has been used for a number of years by the Army's technical personnel even though it is not officially endorsed by the Army, has been used to assess numerous sites

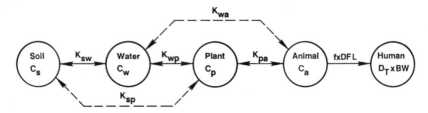

FIGURE 3-2 Pollutant pathway from soil to man through water, plant, and animal compartments.

(Small, 1984). Its primary emphasis is on the environmental fate of chemicals. The methodology views the environment as a set of compartments and a substance as being in equilibrium between these compartments but not between the final compartment and human receptor. This is illustrated in Figure 3-2.

The Army approach uses the following terminology:

- *The acceptable daily dose* (D_T) (mg/kg $\times$ day), is a dose of toxic substance, per kilogram of body weight, that is not expected to produce significant adverse health effects in a population upon chronic exposure.
- *The preliminary pollutant limit value* (PPLV) is a concentration of a chemical in soil that will not produce adverse health effects on chronic exposure either directly to the soil or to one or more secondary environmental compartments, assuming equal partitioning of a chemical among all the environmental compartments, including soil. When the chemical is partitioned only between soil and one other compartment, this soil concentration is referred to as a *single-pathway preliminary pollutant limit value* (SPPPLV).

Derivation of the Acceptable Daily Dose

For the purpose of D_T derivation, substances are divided into threshold and nonthreshold agents. The nonthreshold agents are carcinogens. Although not explicitly stated in the document, the threshold substances can be assumed to include all those that produce toxic effects other than cancer.

TABLE 3-2 Information Sources from Which to Derive Values of Acceptable Daily Doses ($\underline{D}_T$) of Toxic Pollutants for Human Beings (in order of priority)

Input Information	Calculation Required
Existing Standards	
Acceptable daily intake (ADI)	None
Maximum contaminant level (MCL) in drinking water	Adjust for water consumption factor
Threshold limit value (TLV) for occupational exposures	Use factors for breathing rate, exposure time, safety factor of 10^{-2}
FDA guidelines for concentrations in foods	Use factors for consumption of particular foods
Experimental Results in Laboratory Animal Studies	
Lifetime no-effect level (MEL)	Use safety factor of 10^{-2}
90-Day no-effect level (MEL_{90})	Use safety factor of 10^{-3}
Acute toxicity (LD_{50})	Use safety factor of 1.155×10^{-5}

Threshold Agents

The acceptable daily dose applies to chronic toxicity in humans. It is derived either from toxicologic dose-response curves by applying a safety factor to no-effect levels (NELs) or from existing standards or guidelines. The NEL used in this system is conceptually analogous to the better known NOAEL. The term "safety factor" is equivalent to the "uncertainty factor" used in other systems. Table 3-2 lists seven sources of data for D_T derivation and the corresponding safety factors. As shown in Table 3-2, the conversion of standards (threshold limit values, maximum concentration levels, U.S. Food and Drug Administration [FDA] guidelines) to D_Ts requires application of daily intake factors (transfer factors) appropriate to the specific route of exposure.

The conversion factor of 1.155×10^{-5} from animal acute toxicity data lethal dose in 50 percent of animals (LD_{50}) is based on the assumption that a safe limit for the maximum body concentration of a toxic substance is $5 \times 10^{-4} \times LD_{50}$ and on the assumption that the disappearance rate of a toxicant from a body is 2.31 percent per day. Thus,

$$D_T = 2.31 \times 10^{-2} \times 5 \times 10^{-4} \times LD_{50} = 1.155 \times LD_{50} \times 10^{-5}.$$

Carcinogenic Substances

For carcinogenic substances, the acceptable daily dose is that corresponding to an excess lifetime risk of 1 in 100,000 (10^{-5}). The quantitative data on carcinogenic properties is derived chiefly from EPA water quality criteria documents.

Derivation of Single-Pathway Preliminary Pollutant Limit Values

SPPPLVs are calculated from D_Ts using the following formula:

$$SPPPLV \text{ (medium)} = D_T \times \frac{\text{body weight}}{\text{transfer factor} \times K}.$$

K is the partition coefficient or the product of intermedia partition coefficients between the medium from which an agent originated and that through which the actual human exposure occurs (for example, when a substance is deposited in the soil but human exposure occurs through ground water or through fish from contaminated surface water).

Derivation of Preliminary Pollutant Limit Values

In most cases, a toxicant deposited in soil is sufficiently mobile in the environment that the actual human exposure occurs through several media (soil, water, the food chain). In order not to exceed the allowable daily dose through all three pathways, the permissible concentration of the solvent in the original medium, soil, must be adjusted downward from that allowed by any one route. The resulting PPLV is calculated using the following formula:

$$PPLV = [1/(SPPPLV)_1 + 1/(SPPPLV)_2 + 1/(SPPPLV)_3]^{-1}.$$

If a chemical is distributed in only one medium, the formula is reduced to: $PPLV = 1/(SPPPLV)^{-1} = SPPPLV$; that is, the preliminary pollutant limit value equals the single-pathway preliminary pollutant limit value.

This formula does not apply to situations in which several independent sources of a particular pollutant exist.

Cleanup Level

Although not explicitly stated in the document, the implied goal of any cleanup is not to exceed the PPLV value. It is also recommended that, for multiple sources of a particular pollutant, the cleanup level must meet the $D_T \times$ body weight value. The document does not specify whether the cumulative $D_T \times$ body weight value is calculated by addition or multiplication. Because the equilibrium state cannot be assumed for a chemical that partitions itself between soil or water and ambient air, the PPLV calculation excludes air as a route of exposure.

Finally, although the system does not address simultaneous exposure to multiple toxicants, it is assumed that similar toxic effects are additive (Small, 1984; Rosenblatt et al., 1982).

NEW JERSEY CLEANUP LEVELS FOR CONTAMINATED SOILS

General Concepts

This methodology is designed to identify a range of allowable concentrations of organic compounds in soil. For inorganic compounds, acceptable soil concentrations are multiples of background concentrations in New Jersey or U.S. soils (personal communication from R. Dime, New Jersey Department of Environmental Protection, 1986). The methodology is similar to the U.S. Army methodology in that the authors view the environment as a set of compartments and the chemical being in equilibrium between them. Exposure through ambient air is not addressed. Like the EPA manual, the New Jersey methodology focuses on indicator compounds, selected for their toxicity, mobility, and persistence, rather than all chemicals identified at a site.

Acceptable soil contaminant level (ASCL) is the key term used. It is a concentration of a chemical in soil that meets one or more of the following conditions:

- does not present a significant risk to health under average conditions of chronic human exposure to soil;
- is protective of aquatic life in surface water impacted by migration of a chemical from soil; and
- does not present a significant risk to health under average conditions of chronic human exposure to ground water impacted by migration of a chemical from soil.

Derivation of ASCLs to Protect Human Health from Contaminants in Ground Water

ASCLs to protect human health from the effects of drinking the ground water impacted by the leaching of a chemical into an aquifer are derived from either (1) EPA ambient water quality criteria (WQC) for humans or (2) drinking water guidelines, according to the following formula:

$$\text{ASCL} = K_D(\text{standard}) \, (\text{depth factor}) \, (\text{mobility factor}),$$

where K_D is the soil/water partition coefficient; depth and mobility factors are soil parameters; and the standard is the WQC for humans or the EPA drinking water guidelines, whichever is lower.

Derivation of ASCLs to Protect Human Health from Contaminants in Soil

ASCLs for direct human contact are based on the assumption that contaminants enter the human body through the ingestion of contaminated soil. For the purpose of ASCL derivation, substances are classified into one of two groups; carcinogens and noncarcinogens. The ASCL for each group is derived from a health-based acceptable daily intake of a substance by applying an average daily soil intake factor. For carcinogenic substances the health-based acceptable daily intake is that which corresponds to an excess lifetime risk of 10^{-6}. For noncarcinogens, it is equivalent to ADIs published in EPA water quality criteria documents.

The following formulas are used:

Carcinogens

$$ASCL = \frac{(\text{acceptable cancer risk})}{(\text{carcinogenic potency, } kg \times day/mg)}$$

$$\frac{(1,000 \text{ g/kg})}{(\text{lifetime avg. daily soil intake, } g/kg \times day)},$$

where the acceptable cancer risk is 10^{-6}; carcinogenic potency is a slope of dose-response curves in animal bioassay, as calculated by the EPA Carcinogen Assessment Group; and lifetime daily soil intake is 0.0028 g/kg × day.

Noncarcinogens

$$ASCL = \frac{ADI \text{ (mg/day)} \times 1,000 \text{ g/kg} \times 10 \text{ kg}}{\text{daily soil intake by a child} \times 70 \text{ kg}}$$

where ADI is acceptable daily intake; 10/70 is a child/adult body weight conversion factor; and soil intake is for a 10-kg child with pica.

Determination of Cleanup Levels

According to the methodology, site assessment is conducted in two steps. In Step 1, indicator compounds are selected on the basis of the total score, using the following formula:

Score = relative amount score + toxicity score + volatilization score + leachability score + persistence score + bioaccumulation score + aquatic toxicity score

In Step 2, ASCLs for indicator compounds are derived for each environmental pathway (soil, ground water, and surface water). The selection of a cleanup level starts with a listing of ASCLs associated with human exposure through three media and ASCLs associated with aquatic life (two values). The ASCL associated with the most sensitive pathway is selected. (The document does not define "most sensitive pathway.") No consideration is given to multiple route/multiple chemical exposures.

WASHINGTON STATE FINAL CLEANUP POLICY

This is a short in-house manual for the assessment and cleanup of hazardous waste sites. The methodology is based on the assumption that contaminants may migrate from the point of origin to other environmental media although no guidance is given on methods for determining the levels of toxicants in environmental media. The cleanup levels for each medium are derived by one of three methods:

1. specified multiples of existing standards—namely, drinking water standards, ambient air quality standards, occupational standards, and, for chronic air exposure, dangerous waste limit values (not defined in the document);
2. specified multiples (including one) of background levels of the toxicant in the same medium; or
3. biologic tests for water quality (not defined).

These methods are illustrated below.

For *soil*, the method uses 10 times the appropriate drinking water or water quality standard. If no standard exists, then 10 times water quality background is used. If the water quality background is not detectable, then soil background is used.

For *ground water and surface water*, the appropriate drinking water or ambient water quality standard is used; if no standard exists, then background is employed.

For *air*, the method uses U.S. Occupational Safety and Health Administration/Washington Industrial Safety and Health Administration (OSHA/WISHA) limits for air quality over the site prior to backfilling or ambient air quality standards at the site boundaries prior to backfilling. If no standards exist, then background levels are used.

COMPARISON OF THE METHODS

A review of the five methods (EPA, U.S. Army, California, Washington State, and New Jersey) for defining levels of cleanup at hazardous waste sites reveals that their key goal is the protection of public health. Implicitly or explicitly, all assume that chemicals deposited in the primary medium, soil, will migrate into secondary environmental media according to their properties and those of the media. The concentrations of chemicals can be

determined by direct sampling and analysis or by predictive methods. All five approaches recognize that human exposure can occur
through more than one medium. Once a site investigation indicates that human exposure to toxic materials present at the site is
likely, the goal of each cleanup action is to prevent significant adverse health effects in the exposed population. In each of the five
methods the goal of the cleanup is defined through a set of media-
specific numerical permissible concentrations of toxic substances
at the points of human exposure to them. Thus, the methodologies
described here are consistent with the general preference for an
absolute standard-based rather than relative approach to defining
environmental cleanup levels for chemicals.

In addition to conceptual similarities among the five methodologies, there are also some profound differences among them.
These differences are grounded in different applications of the general concepts and include such variables as choice of simplifying
assumptions, degree of reliance on the principles of toxicology,
sources and interpretation of toxicity data, level of detail, terminology, definitions, acceptability of carcinogenic risks, and others.
A number of these variables are discussed in the sections that
follow.

Terminology

It is immediately apparent that each approach uses a unique
set of terms and acronyms that are incomprehensible to all but
those who are very familiar with the documents. Table 3-3 provides
some clarification of terminology.

Environmental Media Addressed

As shown in Table 3-4 the five methods differ in this area. All
methods consider drinking water, but air, soil, and foodstuffs are
not universally included by the five methods.

Environmental Partitioning

The common assumption implicit in the five methodologies
is that the chemicals deposited in the primary medium, soil, will
migrate into secondary media according to their properties and

TABLE 3-3 Terms and Acronyms Used by Different Approaches

Description of Term	EPA	California	U.S. Army	Washington State	New Jersey
Acceptable human daily dose of a substance	Acceptable intake for chronic/subchronic exposure (AIC/AIS), mg/kg x day	Maximum exposure level (MEL), mg/day	Acceptable daily dose ($\underline{D}_T$), mg/kg x day	Not used	Not used
Experimental dose that is considered the threshold of adverse effects	No observed adverse effect level (NOAEL)	No observed adverse effect level (NOAEL)	No-effect level (NEL)	Not used	Not used
Concentration of toxic substance in a medium that does not produce an adverse effect on chronic exposure	Target concentration for chronic exposure	Applied action level (AAL)	Single-pathway preliminary pollutant limit value (SPPPLV) and preliminary pollutant limit value (PPLV)	Not used	Acceptable soil contaminant level (ASCL)
Human dose of a substance expected from contact with contaminant	Subchronic/chronic daily intake (SDI/CDI)	Not used	Not used	Not used	Not used
Average amount of medium consumed daily by an adult	Chronic/subchronic daily intake (CDI/SDI)	Intake factor	Transfer factor	Not used	Intake factor

those of the media. The methodologies differ, however, in their approaches to estimating the media-specific concentrations of chemicals. The Washington State methodology does not address the topic in any detail. In the EPA and California approaches, media-specific concentrations of chemicals in secondary media are determined by direct sampling and by environmental modeling. Thus, the knowledge of current and future concentrations of chemicals in the primary and secondary media is as close to the reality as analysis and modeling permit. The goal of site cleanup under these approaches is to ensure that these concentrations do not exceed previously established chemical-/media-specific numerical criteria.

The U.S. Army and New Jersey methods take a different tack. First, both view the environment as a set of compartments in equilibrium with each other so that the concentrations of chemicals in secondary media can be calculated from soil concentrations by using a set of equilibrium constants. Of course, because in reality equilibrium conditions occur only at compartmental boundaries at best, the calculated concentrations of chemicals are often significantly overestimated. Further, the equilibrium assumption does not apply to assessing the ambient air concentrations of contaminants. Second, by centering around the question "what cleanup level is necessary in the primary medium such that the predicted concentrations in the secondary media do not exceed the health-based acceptable levels?" the two methods attempt to use mathematical formulas that link the last point in the environmental pathway of a chemical to the first one. The EPA and California methods do not do that. Instead, they rely only on comparing concentrations of chemicals in individual media at the points of human exposure with the acceptable health-based levels in these media, with the implicit understanding that cleanup of the primary medium should somehow lead to acceptable levels in the secondary media.

So, whereas the U.S. Army and New Jersey methods may be overly simplistic and stringent, the EPA and California approaches are narrower in scope.

Derivation of Media-Specific Numerical Criteria

As stated earlier, in each of the five methodologies reviewed here, media-specific numerical criteria play an essential function in defining cleanup levels at hazardous waste sites. In short, these

TABLE 3-4 Comparison of the Five Approaches to "How Clean Is Clean?"

Description Of Term	EPA	California	U.S. Army	Washington State	New Jersey
Biologic receptors addressed	Humans	Human biota	Human biota	Humans	Human aquatic life
Media addressed	Air, surface water, soil, ground water, and fish	Air, surface water, soil, and ground water	Air, surface water, soil, ground water, and food chain	Air, surface water, soil, and ground water	Soil, surface water, and ground water
Toxicologic data base	Primary literature	Primary literature	TLV, MCL, FDA standards, ADI, primary literature, and LD_{50}	Not applicable	WQC, drinking water guidelines, and ADI
Duration of exposure considered	Chronic and subchronic	Chronic	Chronic	Chronic (?)	Chronic
Substances considered	Indicator compounds	All detected	All detected	All detected	Indicator compounds

	Ingestion and inhalation	Ingestion and inhalation	Ingestion and inhalation	Ingestion and inhalation	Ingestion
Routes of absorption addressed	Ingestion and inhalation	Ingestion and inhalation	Ingestion and inhalation	Ingestion and inhalation	Ingestion
Derivation of acceptable daily human dose	From no observed adverse effect level (NOAEL)	From maximum exposure level (MEL) and other standards	From no observed adverse effect level and other standards	Standards	From other standards
Treatment of carcinogenic and noncarcinogenic effects	Separate	Separate	Separate	Not addressed	Separate
Carcinogenic risk goals	10^{-4}-10^{-7}	10^{-6}	10^{-5}	Not addressed	10^{-6}
Effects from multiple route exposure	Considered additive	Considered additive	Considered cumulative	Not addressed	Not addressed
Interconversion of media-specific or route-specific standards	Not recommended	Yes, with appropriate adjustment	Yes, with appropriate adjustment	Not addressed	Not applicable
No data	Contact EPA	Not addressed	Not addressed	Cleanup to background	Not addressed

numbers determine "How clean is clean?" Therefore, the method of derivation of these numbers is a cornerstone of each methodology. There are three main conceptual approaches to this task: (1) use media-specific background levels of chemicals or their multiples; (2) use chemical-specific existing standards for air, soil, and water; and (3) develop chemical-/media-specific criteria from toxicity data.

The first approach is simple, but in practice it may be unachievable. Only one of the five methodologies, that of Washington State, uses it.

The second approach is also simple and does not require a knowledge of toxicology, but it suffers from three major limitations. First, environmental standards and guidelines, derived under different laws and based on different sets of requirements and assumptions, are a mixed bag of numbers that are not necessarily protective of the public health of a diverse population. Second, because these numbers are meaningful only when applied to a particular substance in a particular medium, they can not be used to address the multiple media/multiple chemical exposure scenarios that are prevalent at many hazardous waste sites. Third, the number of chemicals for which air and water standards, guidelines, or criteria have been developed is small. Perhaps for these reasons, the use of ambient standards is limited. Only the Washington State methodology makes extensive use of them to define cleanup levels. The EPA approach uses environmental standards to a limited extent; namely, when *all* indicator compounds in all media have them, a very rare event.

The third approach to deriving numerical criteria—from toxicity data—is the most popular (used by EPA, the U.S. Army, California, and New Jersey) and the most difficult. In essence, it consists of the derivation of a chemical-specific ADI (or its conceptual analog), followed by its modification by media-specific intake factors, according to the following formula: criterion (chem, medium) = ADI (chem)/intake factor (medium). Because ADI is a chemical-specific toxicity parameter, it can be modified according to particular exposure conditions, which is the advantage of this approach. Hence, multiple chemical/multiple media exposure conditions can be considered. There are two ways by which the acceptable daily intake is calculated:

1. *Exclusive reliance on toxicity data.* Here, the acceptable

daily intake is calculated by applying an uncertainty factor to a threshold daily dose. In the California and EPA methods the NOAEL (no observed adverse effect level) serves as a threshold dose. In the U.S. Army method the NEL (no-effect level) is used. Only the EPA methodology relies exclusively on this approach. California, the U.S. Army, and New Jersey use it in conjunction with another approach, which is described in the next paragraph.

2. *Conversion of existing guidelines, standards, and criteria into acceptable daily intakes*, according to the formula: Acceptable daily intake (chem) = criterion (medium, chem) × intake factor (medium). For instance, in the California and U.S. Army methods, occupational exposure limits are converted into the MEL and D_T, respectively. Likewise, drinking water standards and food residue limits are converted into D_Ts by the U.S. Army. The conversion methods vary. In the California method, the conversion into maximum exposure levels (MELs, expressed in mg/day) is performed by in-house experts through the application of uncertainty factors, pharmacokinetic factors, intake factors, and professional judgment. The U.S. Army method relies on uncertainty factors and intake factors. The New Jersey method relies only on intake factors to convert numerical criteria into allowable daily doses. (See Tables 3-1 and 3-2 for a list of the uncertainty factors used in the California and U.S. Army approaches.) Clearly, there are differences among the methodologies.

The advantage of approach 1 is its firm reliance on toxicity data and principles of toxicology. Its disadvantage is that it requires extensive data and sophisticated scientific expertise and is resource intensive.

The advantage of approach 2 is its efficiency. Its main disadvantage is that, as stated before, standards and guidelines, derived under different laws and based on different sets of requirements and assumptions, are a mixed bag of numbers that are not necessarily related to toxicity data for a particular chemical. Furthermore, by converting these numbers into acceptable daily doses (MELs, D_Ts), this approach erroneously implies that these are toxicity-based numbers. Despite these clear limitations, approach 2 is used extensively by California, New Jersey, and the Army.

It is apparent that there are significant differences among the four methodologies (excluding Washington State, which uses a totally different approach) in the derivation and use of chemical-/

media-specific numerical criteria. They differ in both their toxicologic data bases and methods of conversion. It is thus unlikely that criteria developed by different methodologies for the same medium/chemical should be the same or even comparable to each other. It is also evident that it is inappropriate to use numbers originating from more than one source to solve a particular problem.

Estimation of Carcinogenic Risks

In all four approaches the lifetime excess cancer risk is a product of carcinogenic potency factor and dose. Where the approaches differ, however, is in the interpretation of carcinogenic potency and the data base used. The New Jersey and EPA methods use the EPA Carcinogen Assessment Group's slope factors (expressed as kg × day/mg). These are 95 percent statistical upper bounds risk estimates that are derived mostly from animal experiments and are not converted to human unit risk values. California relies on its own in-house quantitative risk assessment. The potency factor is based on animal or human data and reflects a 95 percent statistical upper bound of raw data, extrapolated to humans and extrapolated to low doses using the multistage model. The U.S. Army approach uses the unit risk values from EPA water quality criteria documents. These are 95 percent statistical upper bounds estimates, extrapolated to humans and extrapolated to low doses using the one-hit model. Given the above differences one may expect that carcinogenic risks calculated by each method for the same substance/exposure conditions may differ by one or more orders of magnitude.

Acceptability of Carcinogenic Risks

In the four methodologies reviewed here that use chemical-/media-specific criteria to define "How clean is clean?" separate treatment is given to substances with and without carcinogenic properties. For substances with carcinogenic properties the criteria are based on some cancer risk level set as a goal. The three methodologies that address cancer risks for multiple substances/multiple media exposure conditions (California, EPA, and the U.S. Army) assume additivity of cancer risks. The methods vary in what they consider a goal risk level. New Jersey and California use a total risk of 10^{-6}, the U.S. Army uses 10^{-5}, and EPA uses a range of from 10^{-7} to 10^{-4} with 10^{-6} being a preferred goal.

Multiple Chemical/Multiple Route Exposures

The Washington State methodology, which relies mainly on existing media-specific standards, does not address this issue. Neither does the New Jersey approach. Both California and EPA consider cancer risks from multiple routes and/or multiple chemicals to be additive. Also, the adverse effects of multiple chemicals with similar types of toxic response are additive. Finally, the total dose from multiple routes of exposure to a substance is additive. The U.S. Army approach also assumes that multiroute doses of a substance are somehow cumulative but does not specify their exact mathematical relationship (additive, multiplicative, or other). Multiple chemical and multiple carcinogenic risks are not addressed.

SUMMARY AND CONCLUSIONS

Hazard management at waste sites is more complex than at other locations because it involves multiple pathways of exposure. All of the methods reviewed in this paper focus on the protection of public health from the adverse effects of exposure to single toxicants as well as their mixtures, through single or multiple routes of exposure. The most favored approach to defining "How clean is clean?" for hazardous waste sites is that based on chemical-/media-specific numerical ambient acceptable concentrations for specific toxic materials. These criteria are derived separately for substances with and without carcinogenic properties, a practice consistent with many past experiences in regulating air and water contaminants. The rationale used by each method to derive these health-based numbers, however, is unique to each method; thus the results are not comparable.

The similarities and differences among the five approaches were summarized in Table 3-4, which shows that, despite the similarities in defining cleanup levels for hazardous waste sites, the differences in applying the general concepts are vast. The confusion in terminology, although frustrating, is the least of the problem. The most serious differences stem from variations in the basic assumptions about the environmental fate of chemicals, stringency of application of principles of toxicology, data base, use of existing standards/guidelines, use of safety factors, interconversion among routes of human exposure, acceptability of cancer risk, and extent of reliance on expert judgment. Because of this diversity, acceptable ambient concentrations derived by one method are not comparable with those from another. Furthermore, the adoption of numbers derived through one method for use by another is inappropriate.

Finally, it is instructive to look at the results of this analysis in the context of the current emphasis on the separation of risk assessment from risk management. The application of numerical criteria to the "How clean is clean?" question, all related to toxicologic properties of compounds, would imply that this is a risk assessment issue. An examination of the basis of these criteria and the methods for their derivation shows, however, that none of the five methodologies succeeds in the task of separating risk assessment from management. In general, the practice of converting the existing "numbers" into chemical-/media-specific criteria, the need to simplify the complex scenarios, and the need to fill the lack of data with assumptions make it clear that the separation, however desirable, cannot be maintained.

REFERENCES

Department of Health Services, Toxic Substances Control Division, Alternative Technology and Policy Development Section. 1985. The California Site Mitigation Decision Tree. Draft working document.

Dacre, J. C., D. H. Rosenblatt, and D. R. Cogley. 1980. Preliminary pollutant limit values for human health effects. Environmental Science and Technology 14:778–783.

Dime, R., and W. Greim. 1986. Calculation of Cleanup Levels for Contaminated Soils. New Jersey Department of Environmental Protection, Hazardous Sites Mitigation Administration.

Fischhoff, B., S. Lichtenstein, P. Slovic, S. Derby, and R. Kenney. 1981. *Acceptable Risk.* Cambridge: Cambridge University Press.

Kasperson, R. E. 1983. Acceptability of human risk. Environmental Health Perspectives 52:15–20.

Rosenblatt, D. H., J. C. Dacre, and D. R. Cogley. 1982. An Environmental Fate Model Leading to Preliminary Pollutant Limit Values for Human Health Effects. Pp. 474–505 in *Environmental Risk Analysis for Chemicals*, ed. Richard Conway. New York: Van Nostrand Reinhold.

Small, M. 1984. The Preliminary Pollutant Limit Volume Approach: Procedures and Data Base. U.S. Army Medical Bioengineering Research and Development Laboratory, Ft. Detrick, MD 21701. Technical Report 8210.

U.S. EPA, Office of Emergency and Remedial Response. 1985. Superfund Public Health Evaluation Manual. Washington, D.C.

Washington Department of Ecology. 1984. Final Cleanup Policy Technical Guidelines. July.

PROVOCATEUR'S COMMENTS
David Miller

Because the preceding paper is an excellent survey of state approaches to cleanup goals, I would like to spend my time as a provocateur discussing the basic concept of using numerical criteria or setting standards for determining "How clean is clean?" at hazardous waste sites. The thought I would like to get across is that numerical criteria or standards, or whatever you want to call them, are diversions. They are an impediment that removes science from the process of developing rational solutions to soil and ground water contamination problems. As one who has been involved from the start in negotiations on "How clean is clean?" I have watched the numbers and the criteria become more and more stringent. It is not worth arguing over the numbers because almost none of them is achievable.

The natural characteristics of the soil and ground water system at each particular site determine the effectiveness of pumping and treating, capping, or flushing the soil. Aquifers do not give up contaminants either uniformly or completely. Yet most sites can be managed to minimize health and environmental impacts without spending tens of millions of dollars to clean them up to background levels. Contaminated portions of aquifers will never be developed by the waterworks industry as potable water supplies anyway, and further contamination of ground water and surface water sources can be prevented. Our real challenge is not how to set the standard but how to educate the legislator and the public to the reality of the cleanup process.

The money and effort presently being expended to accommodate impossible cleanups should be spent on determining and implementing the best way to protect the rest of the resource.

For example, ground water pumping operations should be located downgradient and not within the boundaries of waste sites where treatment costs are highest and the time required to achieve cleanup standards is greatest. Otherwise, the legacy of the Superfund effort will be the endless operation and maintenance of remedial action systems that originally were justified on the basis of artificial criteria and unscientific risk assessments.

Finally, let me relate some statistics that perhaps can be used later. The average proposed cleanup cost for key Superfund sites has risen from $5 million to about $20 million. This rapid escalation in cost over the past few years is principally driven by a preoccupation with achieving numerical cleanup standards. The potential number of such sites ranks in the thousands.

Investigating Superfund sites has become a million-dollar process, with a million more going into litigation. These expenditures have created a giant data base describing the extent of the problem but very rarely shed much light on the technical and economic feasibility of remedial alternatives. Endless negotiations over "How clean is clean?" have delayed the initiation of remedial actions for more than 3 years at some of the better-known Superfund sites. During these delays, plumes of contamination increase in size as does, proportionately, the ultimate cost of the cleanup.

In conclusion, I am not advocating no action, but I am proposing source control and the treatment of contaminants with the principal objective of protecting what is left and reaching achievable cleanup goals over a reasonable length of time.

4
The California Site Mitigation Decision Tree Process: Solving the "How Clean Should Clean Be?" Dilemma

DAVID J. LEU AND PAUL W. HADLEY

One of the greatest environmental issues facing our nation during this decade is expressed by the cliché "How Clean Should Clean Be?" This cliché refers to the complex problems associated with the mitigation of soils and waters contaminated by chemicals that are produced and used by our modern society. Different federal and state agencies, together with other research and consulting groups, have developed various approaches to this issue. One realistic approach to answering the question "How Clean Should Clean Be?" has been developed by the California Department of Health Services (DHS). This process is contained in a technical guidance document entitled *The California Site Mitigation Decision Tree Manual* (DHS, 1986).

This decision tree manual (also referred to as the decision tree process) was created to fulfill four basic functions. First, it establishes a realistic approach to answering the question of "How Clean Should Clean Be?" Second, it identifies the key

The authors of this paper would like to recognize those individuals who made the development of *The California Site Mitigation Decison Tree Manual* possible. The coauthors of the manual include Michael Kiado; William Quan; Stanford Lau; James Polisini, Ph.D., California Department of Fish and Game; Stephen Reynolds; Richard Sedman, Ph.D.; Judith Tracy; and Caryn Woodhouse. At the same time the authors of this paper especially wish to acknowledge the contribution of Susan Solarz, also a coauthor of the decision tree manual, to the arsenic-contaminated site case study.

decision points needed to set cleanup criteria. Third, it establishes a technical basis for each major decision. Last, it standardizes the decisionmaking process so that it can be applied consistently to all sites.

Fundamental to the decision tree process is a series of distinctive aspects. One such aspect is that the process specifies a multimedia approach to site characterization activities and to establishing cleanup criteria. Specifically, the decision tree process requires one to address analytically the significance of the air, water, soil, and biotic exposure pathways for each site. It also identifies the specific parameters for which such data must be collected. This type of approach promotes a well-focused site characterization effort and minimizes the need for costly revisitations to collect data. Another unique aspect of the decision tree process is that it identifies preferred data gathering, handling, and analytical techniques that should be used to ensure high-quality environmental data.

A critical aspect of the decision tree process is that it quickly sets statewide, health-based criteria called applied action levels (AALs). AALs are specific to substances, media, and biologic receptors. They define exposure levels at which no observed adverse effect would be found.

The decision tree process also allows one to set different cleanup levels for a particular site that reflect the different degrees of effectiveness of various remedial action combinations. Thus, the project manager is in a position to select the final cleanup solution that best suits the conditions of a particular site.

The purpose of this paper is to discuss briefly the basic concepts affiliated with the decision tree process. The paper will conclude with two case studies that illustrate how this process works quickly to reach a cleanup level that has a strong technical and scientific basis. Because this paper is an overview of the decision tree process, the reader is referred to the California site mitigation manual noted earlier (DHS, 1986) for a detailed presentation of the complete approach.

COMPONENTS OF THE DECISION TREE PROCESS

The decision tree process consists of five basic components: (1) preliminary site appraisal, (2) site assessment, (3) risk appraisal (4) environmental fate and risk determination, and (5) development of site mitigation strategies and selection of remedial action.

Each component is made up of several steps, procedures, and decision points. To minimize the time needed to finish a cleanup, the components are designed to be highly interactive and the last four components run concurrently.

Preliminary Site Appraisal

The purpose of this component is to quickly assess a site's potential for environmental and/or public health damage. Sites that are potentially contaminated with hazardous substances are qualitatively assessed using conventional procedures developed for the U.S. Environmental Protection Agency. Based on the characteristics of the wastes that are present and the features of the site itself, the site may be determined to be sufficiently hazardous to be placed on either the National Priority List (for the federal Superfund) and/or dealt with through the state Superfund program. This scoring process, which is referenced in the decision tree, is based on the Mitre model approach developed for EPA and used throughout the nation. The advantage of this approach is that it quickly establishes a priority list of sites based on qualitative data obtained from each site.

Newly enacted statutes within the state of California also assist DHS in establishing its priorities for state-managed cleanups. These statutes create three categories of sites. Each category reflects the degree of willingness and active involvement by the responsible party in addressing the problems that exist. The categories range from proactive participation by the responsible party (thus requiring minimal oversight by the state) to total recalcitrance and strong state participation. (For more details on these priority categories, the reader is referred to the California Health and Safety Code, Division 20, Chapter 6.8, Article 5, Section 25356.)

Site Assessment

After a site has been identified, a detailed quantitative assessment is then conducted by activating the site assessment component. The function of this component is threefold. First, it defines the thought process and procedures used to adequately character-ize a site. Second, it defines the parameters for which data must be collected. Finally, it identifies the preferred data collection, handling, and analytical techniques needed to ensure high-quality environmental information. This is accomplished through the use of a series of decision branches and data checklists. Through the use of these tools, the project manager is able quickly to identify the pathways of concern, the chemical contaminants of concern, and the biologic receptors of concern. The assessment also provides the project manager with site data needed in other components to determine the short-term and long-term health threat of the site.

It should be noted that all of the branches presented in this component need not be used on all sites. In fact, the branching process has been designed to address certain core questions first, a method that allows one to close down a particular branch of analysis before it is pursued very far. For example, if a site only has relatively small amounts of surficial contamination, one may be able to justify not opening up the ground water pathway branch and thus save tremendous time and the costs associated with fully characterizing that medium. Furthermore, this process allows one to document the basis for a particular decision. Thus, if later questioned either through public scrutiny or in the courts, one would have a documented, technical basis for not pursuing that particular branch.

Representations of transport pathways are referred to as mod-ules and are developed from data collected during this component. Each module may consist of observations, deductions, calcula-tions, numerical models, and professional judgments that allow the project manager to make scientifically and technically de-fensible statements and conclusions regarding the behavior and transport of chemical contaminants at the site. The focus of site characterization and the development of environmental modules is ascertaining what the concentrations of toxic chemicals will be at the points of exposure to biologic receptors of concern.

Risk Appraisal

Risk appraisal, the next component, begins while the site as-sessment process is still going on. Here the purpose is to assess quickly whether any immediate corrective action should be consid-ered to mitigate the short-term risk to the public. This assessment

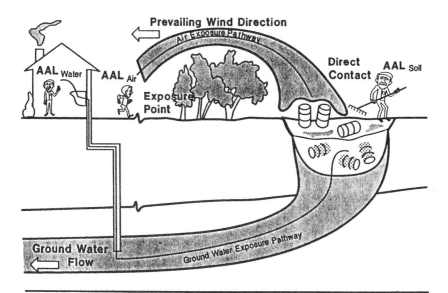

FIGURE 4-1 Illustration of the applied action level (AAL) concept and point of application.

is done using three simple risk appraisal tests. By using these tests the project manager quickly compares the amount of contaminants reaching a biologic receptor to the statewide health-based criterion known as the AAL.

As previously mentioned, the AAL is a substance-medium-biologic receptor-specific value. It defines the maximum exposure value in which no observable adverse effect would be detected. It is viewed as a statewide health-based criterion in that it does not matter where in the state the biologic receptor is located; if he is exposed above this level, he is at risk. AAL values are derived using conventional toxicologic principles and are published by DHS. Figure 4-1 illustrates the AAL concept and how it is applied at the location of the biologic receptor instead of at the site of initial contamination.

The project manager can quickly assess whether or not a biologic receptor is currently at risk through the use of three simple tests contained in the decision tree process. The three tests taken together make up the risk appraisal mechanism.

The first test evaluates whether a biologic receptor receives an excessive exposure to any toxic substance through contact with each contaminated medium (e.g., air, water, soil, biota). The test compares the level of exposure for a substance in the medium (C_{medium}) with a safe exposure level delineated by the AAL criterion. Test 1 is written as follows:

$$\text{if } C_{medium}/AAL_{medium} > 1, \text{ then}$$

a biologic receptor of concern is considered to be at risk to an adverse impact, the test fails, and a risk management process should be initiated.

The second test determines whether a biologic receptor receives an excessive exposure to any toxic substances through contact with all substantially contaminated media. The exposures by various media are assumed to be cumulative.

Excessive exposure is determined by the cumulation of exposure in various media normalized to the AAL standard developed for that medium. Test 2 is written as follows:

$$\text{if } \sum_{medium=1}^{n} C_{medium}/AAL_{medium} > 1, \text{ then}$$

a biologic receptor of concern is considered to be at risk to an adverse impact, the test fails, and a risk management process should be initiated.

The third test in the risk appraisal process determines whether a biologic receptor may receive excess exposure to an aggregate of substances that produces toxic manifestations. This test assumes additivity of such exposures across all media. The test can be modified to account for different types of interactions between toxic substances if shown to exist. Test 3 is written as follows:

$$\text{if } \sum_{sub=1}^{z} \sum_{medium=1}^{n} \frac{C_{medium, \, sub}}{AAL_{medium, \, sub}} > 1, \text{ then}$$

a biologic receptor of concern is considered to be at risk to an adverse impact, the test fails, and a risk management process should be initiated.

It should be noted that additional criteria may be used in lieu of AAL values. For example, if worker exposure and risk appraisal were to be assessed, it might be appropriate to use worker safety standards providing they are health based in their derivation.

Environmental Fate and Risk Determination

As with the previous component, the environmental fate and risk determination component begins soon after the initiation of the site assessment component. Whereas the risk appraisal component evaluates whether a biologic receptor is currently at risk, this subsequent component assesses how the contaminants will behave through time and then evaluates if the receptor will be at risk in the future. The environmental fate and risk determination component establishes methods and procedures to assess the environmental fate of chemicals and their potential to move across media. Conservative projections are then made as to what the concentrations of a substance will be in the future at the exposure point for a biologic receptor.

The process contained in this component allows one to make two critical determinations. First, it allows the project manager to establish the maximum contaminant concentration in each medium that will not pose a health risk (i.e., a health-based cleanup criterion). Second, the process allows one to project the relative efficiencies of different remedial actions and determine whether they will meet the health-based cleanup criterion just established. Because these two actions are the strength of the decision tree process, two case studies are presented later in this chapter to demonstrate each action. The first case illustrates how the decision tree process quickly establishes the cleanup criteria. The second case demonstrates how the decision tree process allows the project manager to evaluate the effectiveness of different remedial actions.

It should be noted that the risk determination process used to establish the cleanup criteria is composed of the three simple tests that make up the risk appraisal mechanism. The difference is that now the concentration values used in each test are those derived through the environmental fate assessment.

A dynamic aspect of the risk determination process is that it allows the transformation of various concentrations of contaminants at a particular location into a single risk value. As shown by Figure 4-2, such a transformation greatly simplifies the evaluation of risk and makes it easier for the project manager to convey this concept to the public. The risk values that are plotted out in Figure 4-2 are defined as risk index scores (RIS). Case study 2 graphically illustrates how risk index scores can be used.

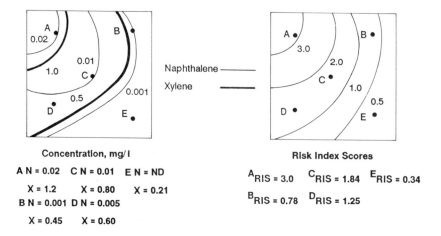

Concentration, mg/l

A N = 0.02   C N = 0.01   E N = ND
    X = 1.2   X = 0.80   X = 0.21
B N = 0.001 D N = 0.005
    X = 0.45   X = 0.60

Risk Index Scores

^{A}RIS = 3.0 ^{C}RIS = 1.84 ^{E}RIS = 0.34

^{B}RIS = 0.78 ^{D}RIS = 1.25

FIGURE 4-2 A comparison between contours of ground water contamination concentrations and risk index scores. The AAL values for naphthalene and xylene are 0.018 mg/l and 0.62 mg/l, respectively.

Development of a Mitigation Strategy and the Selection of Remedial Action

If it is determined, either through the risk appraisal process or the risk determination process, that a biologic receptor of concern is or will be at risk, mitigation of that risk should be investigated. The development, evaluation, and selection of such remedial actions are presented as elements of the last component of the decision tree process. Discussing these activities in the latter portion of this section, however, does not mean that these activities begin late in the decisionmaking process. Rather, they begin during site assessment and run concurrently with the remaining components.

The selection of the remedial action for a project is based on the specific site characteristics (Component 2), the existing toxic concentrations at the location of the biologic receptor (Component 3), and the ability of the contaminants to move across and within media to reach biologic receptors in the future (Component 4). Thus, by initiating the screening process concurrent with site assessment activity, the impractical remedial actions are quickly discarded. Detailed analyses of feasible alternatives can be conducted along with the rest of the investigations to yield a timely solution.

Alternative site mitigation measures are identified and evaluated in the feasibility study component of the development of a remedial action plan. A decision process for the development and evaluation of appropriate alternative remedial actions for a given site is contained in the *EPA Guidance on Feasibility Studies Under CERCLA* (U.S. EPA, 1985). The discussion presented here has been adapted from the discussion presented in that more detailed document. The process for the development and evaluation of appropriate alternative remedial actions for a given site is shown in Figure 4-3.

An example of how this component can be used to define and evaluate the various alternatives is contained in the second case study. The reader is also referred to *The California Site Mitigation Decision Tree Manual* (1986) for a more detailed description of this component.

APPLYING THE DECISION TREE PROCESS: TWO CASE STUDIES

Two case studies are presented below. The first study illustrates how the decision tree process is used to set cleanup criteria quickly. The second study demonstrates how various remedial actions are evaluated so that the best option is selected.

Case Study 1: An Arsenic-Contaminated Site

In this first example, the preliminary site appraisal identified the site as a pesticide-formulating plant that had been in operation for more than 40 years. The facility covered over 10 acres and was located adjacent to a saltwater marsh. Samples showed that extremely high levels of arsenic compounds (up to 10,000 parts per million [ppm] total arsenic) were contained in soils underlying former waste disposal impoundments and storage areas, as well as along former loading and handling areas. Elevated levels of arsenic (up to 100 mg/l) were also observed in samples of the shallow ground water underlying the site. Although the site was located in an industrial zone, a residential neighborhood was less than one-half mile away.

Site assessment activities were undertaken for a better definition of the characteristics of the site and neighboring areas. First, the shallow (6–12 feet) ground water was determined to be

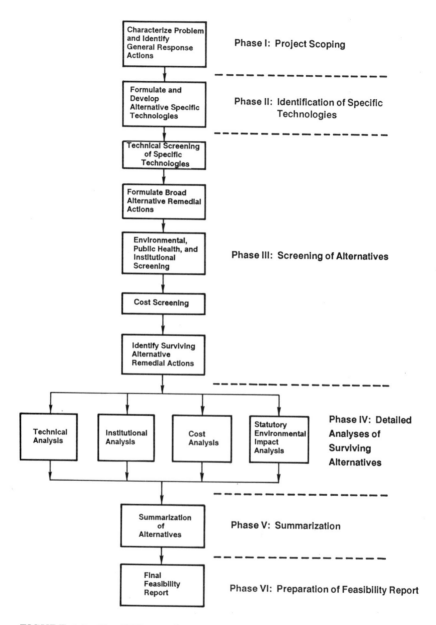

FIGURE 4-3 Feasibility study process.

nearly stagnant and highly saline (about 25,000 ppm total dissolved solids). This aquifer was shown to reside above a drinking water aquifer found at a depth of approximately 200 feet. Domestic wells were so located that they used this deeper aquifer, but they were hydraulically upgradient and located a considerable distance from the site. The drinking water aquifer was separated from the contaminated, shallower aquifer by approximately 100 feet of low-permeability deposits.

The surface and near surface (0–12 feet) soils consisted primarily of silty sands. There were large areas of arsenic contamination as a result of surface transport of the contaminant by seasonal flooding and manufacturing activities. The soil concentration values ranged as high as 10,000 ppm total arsenic for a few "hot spots" but were more typically confined to the 1,000- to 5,000-ppm range.

In addition to soil and water data, meteorological information and marsh flora/fauna data were collected. The California Department of Fish and Game analyzed tissue samples from aquatic species living in the marsh and conducted a vegetation assessment.

While site assessment activities were under way, a risk appraisal was conducted to assess any existing health threats. It was determined that by limiting access to the site the public would be adequately protected. To preclude any surface contamination reaching the marsh and endangering aquatic species, a berm was constructed along the marsh boundary. This barrier eliminated seasonal flooding and surface water runoff into the marsh.

To set a health-based cleanup criterion for the site, the environmental fate and risk determination component was activated. To project what the future concentrations of arsenic compounds would be at the location of the biologic receptors, two conservative scenarios were created. For the first scenario the future site conditions were defined as an undistributed site with all buildings and structures removed; no soil cap or vegetative cover were present, and dry soil conditions existed. The biologic receptor of concern was identified as the general public, and the predominant exposure pathway (medium) was the air. It was assumed that residential development had encroached up to the site boundary. The primary health concern for this first scenario was based on long-term chronic exposure to arsenic compounds.

In the second scenario the site conditions were once again defined as all buildings and structures removed, no soil cap or vegetative cover present, and extant dry soil conditions. In this scenario, however, onsite construction activities using heavy construction vehicles were assumed. Thus, the unsuspecting construction worker was the biologic receptor of concern here, and the predominant exposure pathway was the air. The primary health concern for this second scenario was based on short-term acute exposure to arsenic compounds.

It should be noted that the ground water pathway was excluded from the analyses of both scenarios. It was excluded based on site characterization data, which indicated that the amount of total dissolved solids in the upper aquifer would preclude domestic use.

In order to evoke the risk determination process for the first scenario, the concentration of contaminants that could reach the general public had to be projected. As stated in the decision tree manual (see Section 8.5.5), the estimation of particulate emissions is derived from a modified approach developed by Cowherd et al. (1984). Although the reader is referred to the above-cited reference for a detailed explanation of applicability, the process may be summarized by the following six steps.

Step 1: Determine soil particle size distribution

The determination of the soil particle size may be conducted by sieve analysis. For this site the predominant size fraction was in the 0.05-millimeter (mm) to 0.1-mm range.

Step 2: Estimate threshold friction velocity (U_t)

The threshold friction velocity (U_t) is defined as the wind speed at ground level necessary to initiate soil erosion. The threshold wind velocity depends on such factors as soil particle size distribution, the presence or absence of surface crust, soil moisture content, and the presence of nonerodible elements such as vegetation or stones. U_t was approximately 0.18 meter per second (m/sec) for this site.

Step 3: Determine the roughness height (Z_o), of the site terrain

The roughness height (Z_o) is a measure of the size and spacing of surface irregularities, such as trees or buildings, that obstruct wind flow. This parameter is needed to convert the threshold friction velocity at ground level to wind speed at a typical weather station height of 7 meters. Under this scenario, $Z_o = 1$ centimeter (cm).

Step 4: Determine the threshold wind velocity (U_t)

The threshold wind velocity (U_t) is defined as the wind speed, as measured at a wind sensor station generally 7 meters above the ground, that is necessary to initiate soil erosion. The threshold wind velocity may be determined from the threshold friction velocity, U_f, according to the equation (developed by Cowherd et al., 1984):

$$U_t = U_f(13.1 - 2.5 \ln Z_o),$$

where

U_t = Threshold wind velocity at 7 meters (m/sec),
U_f = Threshold friction velocity (m/sec), and
Z_o = Roughness height (cm).

Step 5: Estimate the respirable particulate emission rate

Cowherd et al. (1984) have developed the following equation to estimate the annual average emission rate of respirable particulate matter from erodible surfaces:

$$E_{10} = 0.036(1 - V)\left(\frac{U}{U_t}\right)^3 [F(X)],$$

where

E_{10} = Emission rate for total respirable particulate
matter (PM10)$^{(gm/m^2 - hr)}$,
V = Fraction of exposed contaminated area that is
vegetated (for bare soil, $V = 0$),
U = Mean annual wind speed (m/sec), and
$[F(X)] = \dfrac{0.18(8x^3 + 12x)}{e^{x^2}}$, where $x = 0.886(U_t/U)$.

Step 6: Project downwind particulate concentrations

Using unscaled concentration values based on a short-term version of the industrial source complex model (Cowherd et al., 1984, Appendix 5) and a mean annual wind speed of 2 m/sec (obtained from two nearby weather stations), a conservative annual estimate of the total dust concentration at the site boundary was calculated to be 0.20 $\mu g/m^3$. Thus, if we assume that the airborne soil particulates are uniformly contaminated across the site at a concentration of 10,000 ppm total arsenic (the maximum concentration found), the annual average airborne arsenic concentration reaching the public at the site boundary would be 2×10^{-3} $\mu g/m^3$.

With this concentration value now in hand, a risk determination can be performed using the three simple tests previously discussed. Because there is only one medium and one substance affiliated with this site, the three tests simplify into the single expression:

$$C_{air}/AAL_{air} = RIS.$$

With C_{air} equal to 0.002 $\mu g/m^3$ and the arsenic AAL_{air} equal to 0.0004 $\mu g/m^3$, this equation derives a risk index score of 5. This score indicates unacceptable risk (i.e., >1), and mitigation measures should be applied.

To establish a health-based cleanup criterion for this scenario, one first recalculates the risk determination equation but this time setting the RIS to equal 1 and solving for C_{air}. Thus,

$$\frac{C_{air}}{0.0004 \ \mu g/m^3} = 1,$$

or

$$C_{air} = 0.0004 \ \mu g/m^3 \text{ at the site boundary.}$$

To transform this air concentration to a soil concentration, one uses the relationship:

$$C_{air} = f(\text{total dust})_{air},$$

where

$$C_{air} = \text{Arsenic concentration in air, and}$$
$$f = \text{Mass fraction of arsenic in soil.}$$

With C_{air} = 0.0004 $\mu g/m^3$ and (total dust)$_{air}$ = 0.2 $\mu g/m^3$, solving for f yields a value of 0.02. To convert f to ppm, one multiplies by 10^6 ppm to obtain 2,000 ppm arsenic in soil.

Thus, for Scenario 1, a soil contamination level of 2,000 ppm total arsenic or less would pose no observable adverse effect to the public if anyone were living adjacent to the site boundary.

Whereas a soil contaminant level of 2,000 ppm total arsenic may satisfy the conditions in the first scenario, the second scenario must be evaluated to assess the potential health impact to workers during intensive earth-moving activities.

In order to compare the occupational exposure of the construction worker, the department reviewed several studies and surveyed various industrial hygienists within the department and Cal-OSHA (California Occupational Safety and Health Administration) regarding particulate monitoring data at actual construction sites. In general, worker particulate exposures will vary depending on soil type, soil moisture conditions, the nature of the equipment used, wind conditions, and the level of worker protection (e.g., as enclosed cabs and soil wetting). From its survey the department concluded that particulate exposures greater than the 10 mg/m^3 occupational standard may be expected for a worker who operates earth-moving equipment without protective measures for the entire 8-hour workday. The range of estimates was 5–100 mg/m^3, with 25 mg/m^3 as a reasonable upper bound estimate for a completely dry, fine-particulate soil.

The 25-mg/m^3 total dust exposure level is also supported by a study of asbestos and total dust exposure to motorcyclists on a dirt road with a high asbestos concentration. This study found that motorcyclists were exposed to an average of 20 mg/m^3 dust from particulates transported from the dirt road to the ambient air (Cooper et al., 1979).

To determine the acceptable soil arsenic concentration, it was assumed that the concentration of arsenic in the ambient air would equal the concentration in air of the total particulates transported to air by wind or mechanical forces such as earth-moving equipment multiplied by the fraction of arsenic in the particulates. Thus:

$$(As)_{air} = f(\text{total dust})_{air}.$$

Thus, if the acceptable arsenic concentration in air is 0.01

mg/m^3 for the short-term exposure level, one can calculate the maximum soil contaminant concentration from:

$$0.01 \text{ mg/m}^3 = f \times 25 \text{ mg/m}^3, \text{or}$$

$$f = 0.01 \text{ mg/m}^3 \div 25 \text{ mg/m}^3 = 0.0004.$$

To convert f to ppm, multiply by 10^6 ppm to obtain 400 ppm.

Therefore, from the analysis of these two conservative scenarios a soil cleanup criterion of 400 ppm total arsenic or less would be required to protect both worker health and residential community health.

Case Study 2: Site with Ground Water Contamination

The following example emphasizes the approach of the decision tree process with respect to the ground water exposure pathway. It is offered as a demonstration of how various remedial actions are evaluated so that the best option can be selected. It should be noted that, for the purpose of illustration, this case study is a fictional example. It was created by drawing from various actual situations, each of which contained certain components (e.g., the location of the municipal well and private well, the river location, the agricultural well). This was done in order to construct a very complex ground water exposure scenario and demonstrate how the decision tree process quickly simplifies the exposure assessment and transforms the situation into a manageable project.

Preliminary Site Appraisal

A plan of the facilities and features of interest in this example problem is shown in Figure 4-4. Through the preliminary site appraisal process, a waste source container leaking chloroform (trichloromethene) was discovered and reported to the appropriate regulatory agencies. Near the site were an agricultural well, a municipal supply well, a private well, and a river.

Site Assessment

Because potential exposures to contaminated ground water

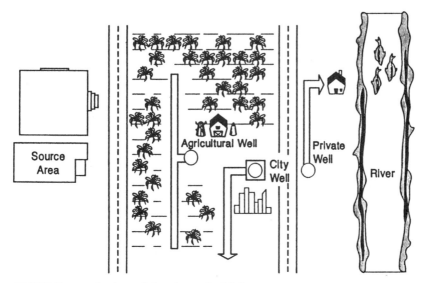

FIGURE 4-4   A view of the site and vicinity.

were of concern, sampling of nearby wells and the river were initiated first. As can be seen in Figure 4-5, samples of ground water collected from the agricultural well were determined to contain chloroform, whereas no contaminant was detected in samples of the city well or of the more distant private well, nor in water samples from the river. This information was immediately used, through the risk appraisal process, to determine whether any biologic receptors of concern were currently at risk. The level of chloroform detected in the sample from the agricultural well exceeded the applied action level (AAL) of 4.3 parts per billion (ppb) for that chemical. As illustrated in Figure 4-5, however, the fate of the water from the agricultural well was application to a field and not consumption by humans or livestock. Therefore, human and other biologic receptors were not at risk from chloroform in the agricultural well, and no immediate action was needed to preclude ingestion exposures to contaminated well water.

Potential downwind exposures to windborne chloroform were evaluated by comparison of the measured concentration of chloroform in air with the AAL value for chloroform in air. No detectable concentrations were found, and it was determined that this pathway posed no health threat.

Concerns over the potential accumulation of chloroform in

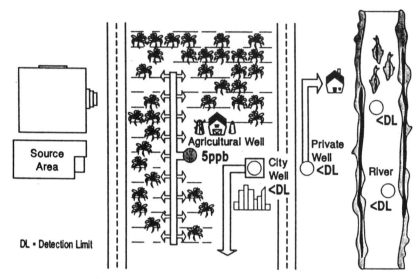

FIGURE 4-5   Risk appraisal for current conditions (AAL = 4.3 ppb for chloroform in water).

the irrigated crop and subsequent food-chain exposures could be evaluated by allocating the maximum exposure level (MEL, given in units of mass/time) for chloroform to the biotic medium of exposure. This procedure would require determining an appropriate rate or amount of ingestion of the crop by the biologic receptor of concern and evaluating the resulting concentration in biota against the AAL developed for biotic exposures. Previous experiences with similar conditions, however, have indicated that volatilization proceeds so rapidly that the uptake of volatiles by plants generally would not be a significant exposure pathway.

As illustrated in Figure 4-5, analysis of surface water samples both upstream and downstream of the leaking tank resulted in no detection of chloroform; thus, the aquatic species identified as biologic receptors of concern currently would not be considered to be at risk.

Through the decision tree process, all other contaminants detected in samples of the ground water from the agricultural well would also be evaluated through test 1 of the risk appraisal mechanism. For toxic chemicals with similar adverse toxicologic manifestations, potential cumulative effects of multichemical and multimedia/multichemical exposures would be evaluated through tests 2 and 3, respectively, of the risk appraisal mechanism. For the sake of brevity in this example, one chemical and one medium of exposure are considered here.

The direction of flow, rate of movement, and flux of the ground water were determined from measurements of the physical and hydraulic characteristics of the ground water system as evaluated at a series of piezometers and wells. To give meaning to the results of the chemical analyses of ground water samples, or of samples of any contaminated medium, the properties of the medium must also be sampled. With respect to ground water, this requires the characterization of the geologic and hydraulic systems controlling the movement of contaminated ground water.

A three-dimensional representation of the ground water system was also developed, illustrating the relationship between the geologic system defined by cross sections and the hydraulic system defined by potentiometric and permeability contrasts and differences. In practice, there are ranges of values of hydraulic properties as well as intrinsic uncertainties associated with geologic interpretations.

Environmental Fate and Risk Determination

Based on site assessment data, a two-dimensional representation of the ground water exposure pathway for the site was constructed (Figure 4-6). The figure shows the extent of contamination, which was defined by data collected from appropriately located, designed, installed, and sampled ground water monitoring installations. The plume of contamination is presented in terms of the risk index score (RIS) associated with the contaminants measured at each point.

In this case, no significant risk was associated with the chloroform-contaminated water pumped from the agricultural well because the water so obtained was not consumed. As shown in Figure 4-7, the flux of contaminants from the site was so small, and the expected pumping rate of the municipal well so great, that simple at-the-wellhead dilution would account for water delivered at the tap containing chloroform at a concentration below the AAL.

Yet, as shown in Figure 4-8, the private well could eventually become contaminated in the future, should the agricultural and city wells not operate. Chloroform is a mobile contaminant and from experience would be expected to migrate very rapidly with

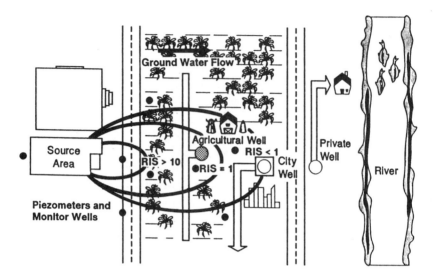

FIGURE 4-6   Site assessment: ground water exposure pathway.

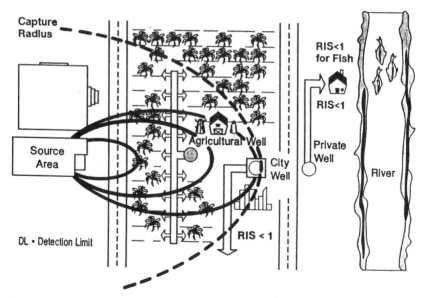

FIGURE 4-7   Environmental fate and risk determination: existing conditions.

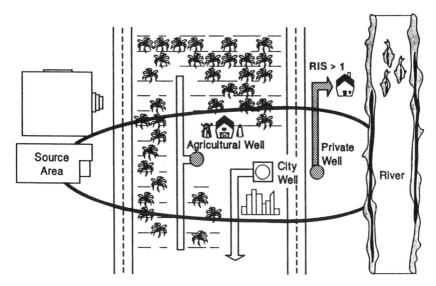

FIGURE 4-8 Environmental fate and risk determination: potential future conditions if the city well is closed.

ground water. The private well is located in the path of the contaminated ground water plume and typically would have such a small capture zone as to preclude at-the-wellhead dilution. The continuing operation of the agricultural and municipal wells to harvest contaminated ground water and thereby work to protect the private well cannot be assumed without formal commitments from the farmer and water purveyor. Therefore, the level of chloroform at the private well would be expected to exceed the AAL in the future; test 1 of the risk appraisal mechanism fails; and a risk management process should be considered to protect those biologic receptors demonstrated to be at risk in the future.

In addition to the existing downgradient biologic receptors, human beings who in the future may wish to use the ground water resource downgradient of the site would be considered at risk. As illustrated in Figure 4-9, this is equivalent to evaluating the site by identifying the biologic receptor of concern as a human being exploiting the ground water just downgradient of the contamination source. Thus, a second biologic receptor has been identified as being at risk, although this second receptor currently does not exploit the ground water and, in reality, may not have been born yet.

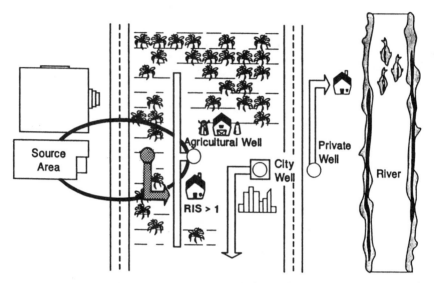

FIGURE 4-9   Environmental fate and risk determination: future beneficial uses of ground water.

As shown also in Figure 4-9, the flux of contaminated ground water that could eventually enter the river in this problem has been determined to be small with respect to the flow of the river. This condition would provide sufficient dilution and result in non-detectable levels of chloroform in the bulk flow of the river. Based on this analysis the aquatic species identified as the biologic receptors of concern would not be considered at significant risk in the future, and a risk management process would not be warranted to protect them.

Development of a Mitigation Strategy and Selection of Remedial Action

At this point in the case study the problems to be solved through remedial action have been identified and defined by investigation and analysis. Specifically, the potential risks of future adverse impacts on biologic receptors of concern have been evaluated and defined through the risk appraisal mechanism. Those risks determined to be significant have been identified as media specific, receptor specific, chemical specific, and site specific. The mitigation strategy to be used must address the defined problems.

In this case, the mitigation strategy must preclude adverse health effects associated with the exposure of humans to chloroform in ground water.

In the fifth component of the decision tree process, the project manager has the opportunity to evaluate various remedial alternatives. The effect of each alternative in reducing the risks associated with remedial actions is evaluated through the decision tree process, again employing the environmental fate modules and the risk appraisal mechanism. Both technical and nontechnical considerations are evaluated by the site manager before proposing plausible remedial alternatives. In this example, four remedial alternatives are evaluated.

Alternative 1—No Action. The no-action remedial alternative would not alleviate or reduce the risk posed to downgradient water users, nor would it protect future human biologic receptors wishing to use the ground water resource as a drinking water supply.

Although humans would be at risk here, the nonhuman biologic receptors of concern, the fish in the nearby river, are not considered to be at significant risk. For this case the no-action alternative would be acceptable with respect to the aquatic species.

Alternative 2—Aquifer Remediation. A second alternative, aquifer remediation, would intend to restore all contaminated ground water to a condition in which the AAL for chloroform is not exceeded anywhere (Figure 4-10). At this particular site, such an alternative protects all biologic receptors of concern but has an associated cost that is extremely high.

Alternative 3—Alternate Water Supply. This third remedial alternative (Figure 4-11) would protect the biologic receptors of concern that have been identified as being at risk, but it would limit the availability of the ground water resource. As shown in Figure 4-11, the alternate source of water would be the existing municipal supply well.

Potential problems in implementing this alternative might arise from a reluctance on the part of the water purveyor either to operate this well in a regime that provides the necessary dilution at the wellhead or to operate such a well at all. At this point it might be appropriate for the risk manager, the water purveyor, and the public to consider the risks associated with other sources

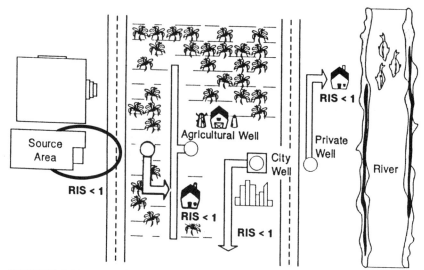

FIGURE 4-10   Remedial alternative: aquifer remediation.

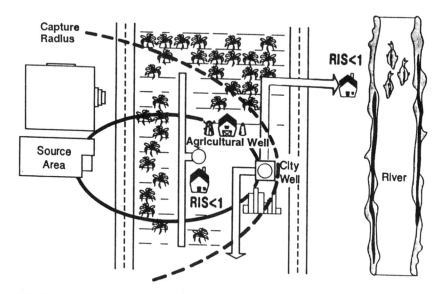

FIGURE 4-11   Remedial alternative: alternate water supply.

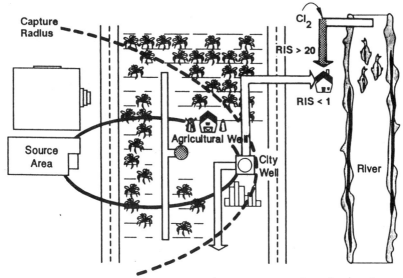

FIGURE 4-12   Risk index scores for surface water supply and ground water supply.

of water, such as chlorinated surface water, and compare the risk index scores associated with both sources of water. Figure 4-12 illustrates the relative risks associated with the water supply alternatives of concern. As can be seen in this figure, exposure to by-products of chlorination, including chloroform, would often be expected to place human biologic receptors at greater risk than they would be from the delivery of untreated ground water.

Alternative 4—Plume Monitoring and Maintenance. A fourth alternative that might be subtitled the "don't go near the water" alternative is shown in Figure 4-13. As the figure illustrates, restricting the use of portions of the ground water system would preclude the exposure of humans to ground water containing chloroform above the AAL. Controlling the pumping of the municipal well would protect downgradient ground water users. This alternative also protects those biologic receptors identified as being at risk and, like other remedial alternatives, has associated costs and problems in implementation.

The four remedial alternatives considered in this example are compared in summary form in Table 4-1. Only one alternative, the no-action alternative, fails to protect the biologic receptors of

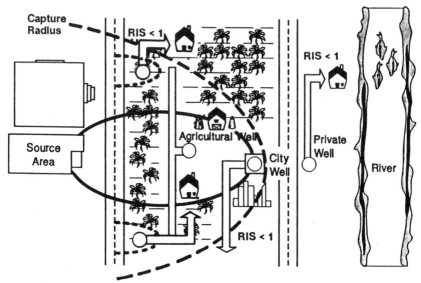

FIGURE 4-13   Remedial alternative: plume monitoring and maintenance.

concern, as discussed above. The aquifer remediation alternative is acceptable under all categories of evaluation but has a cost that is far in excess of the other alternatives. The availability of financial resources to remediate all sites to the standard implied in Alternative 2 is a serious consideration for project managers. Alternatives 3 and 4 rely on administrative and resource management practices rather than the traditional soil removal/ground water treatment program; yet, if rigorously enacted, they would also meet the criterion of protecting the biologic receptors of concern.

It should be noted that the traditional evaluation of "How clean is clean?" for soil contamination is applicable to only one of the four alternatives considered here. It should also be noted that such an evaluation is technically defensible only following a site assessment. As illustrated in Figure 4-14, such an evaluation would rely on the characterization of the soils system as represented by the unsaturated zone module. The construction of such a representation requires the input of several disciplines, as indicated in Figure 4-14. In fact, the multidisciplinary team approach to evaluating hazardous waste sites is an explicit recommendation made throughout the decision tree manual, but it is perhaps most important when evaluating the subsurface behavior of contaminants.

TABLE 4-1 Remedial Alternatives Analysis

Remedial Alternative	Cost	Technical	Public Health	Aquatic Species Concerns	Public Input
No action	None	Unacceptable	Unacceptable	Acceptable	Unacceptable
Aquifer restoration with source control	\$500$\underline{X}$	Acceptable	Acceptable	Acceptable	Acceptable
Alternate water supply	\$50$\underline{X}$	Acceptable	Acceptable	Acceptable	Water agency reluctant
Plume monitoring maintenance	\$20$\underline{X}$	Acceptable	Acceptable	Acceptable	Water agency reluctant

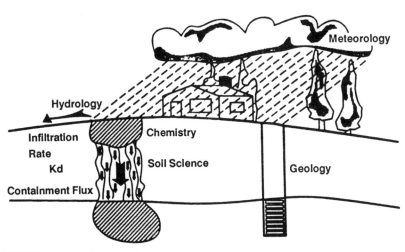

FIGURE 4-14   Unsaturated zone module.

In summary, the project manager who must make the final recommendations regarding this case has been provided with an analysis of the various remedial alternatives considered plausible to implement. The technical basis for each alternative has been constructed through the decision tree process, and the strengths, weaknesses, and costs associated with each alternative have been compared. At this point, it becomes the state decisionmaker's job to select the alternative that is considered the "best" for this particular site. He or she must balance concerns over implementability and public acceptance with the very real-world constraint of cost. The role of the decision tree process is to provide that decisionmaker with the strongest possible technical basis for making such a decision, in part with the goal of making the decision defensible in the event of a challenge in a public or legal forum.

CONCLUSION

The California Site Mitigation Decision Tree Manual has been created as a technical guidance document to assist project managers in making decisions that have a strong analytical basis and technical merit. The process specified in the document was designed to be flexible in application. The decision-branching format allows one to quickly identify the pathways of exposure that must be characterized for each site. Simple sites generally require simple approaches; complex sites require more detailed multipathway analyses.

To facilitate a scientifically based decision process the decision tree incorporates a series of unique aspects. First, it requires a multimedia approach to site characterization and the establishment of cleanup criteria. Second, it identifies the specific parameters for which data must be collected. Third, it identifies the preferred data gathering, handling, and analytical techniques that should be used. Fourth, it establishes statewide, health-based criteria called applied action levels that are specific to particular substances, media, and biologic receptors. They define an exposure level in which no observed adverse effect would be found. Fifth, the decision tree process also allows one to set different cleanup levels for a particular site, a capability that reflects the different degrees of effectiveness of various remedial action combinations. Using the process the project manager is in a position to select the final cleanup solution that best suits the condition of the particular site.

Finally, it should be noted that DHS views the decision tree manual as a dynamic document; as new field techniques and analytical procedures are developed, the document will be updated accordingly. The intent is to have a process that yields decisions with the strongest technical basis.

REFERENCES

California Department of Health Services, Toxic Substances Control Division. 1986. The California Site Mitigation Decision Tree Manual. Sacramento, California.

Cooper, W. C., J. Murchio, and W. Popendorf. 1979. Chryotile asbestos in a California recreation area. Science 206: 685–688.

Cowherd, C. M., G. E. Muleski, P. J. Englehart, and D. A. Gillette. 1984. Rapid Assessment of Exposure to Particulate Emissions From Surface Contamination Sites. Kansas City, Mo.: Midwest Research Institute.

U.S. EPA. 1985. Guidance On Feasibility Studies Under CERCLA. Prepared for Hazard Waste Engineering Research Laboratory, Cincinnati, Ohio, and Office of Emergency and Remedial Response and Office of Waste Programs Enforcement, Washington, D.C.

PROVOCATEUR'S COMMENTS
Joan Berkowitz

The California decision tree process, which is outlined in the report that David was kind enough to send to me, is really a "how-to" manual for conducting a remedial investigation/feasibility study (RI/FS). The document presents a series of flowcharts on what data to obtain and a text on how to obtain them. The material is basically an amplification of the requirements of the national contingency plan. If the directions in the manual were followed, I believe that both the RI and the FS would be of high quality and that they would be linked together. This linkage has not always been achieved with RI/FS studies in the past, as Hirschhorn (1987) points out.

Although the California decision tree manual provides excellent guidance on fact finding, the manual does not provide the last word on how those facts should be used to come to a decision on remedial action. It cannot be emphasized too strongly that facts are fundamental. Without a good factual base, reasonable and defensible conclusions cannot be drawn.

The decisionmaking guidelines in the California model center around AALs (applied action levels). These action levels are set at the point at which contaminants in air, surface water, ground water, and soils impinge on target organisms. The decision itself is based on a comparison between the concentrations (either measured or estimated through a model) at the points of exposure and theoretically derived, health-based AALs. Specifically, the concentration of a chemical in a medium (Cc,m) is compared to an AAL for the same chemical in the same medium. If the ratio, Cc,m/(AAL)c,m, is greater than one, there is a potential risk. Conceptually, this is very nice. However, uncertainties in the measured or modeled concentrations, as well as in the AALs, are both reflected in even greater uncertainties in the ratio. A recent book by Wood et al. (1984), for example, shows that measured concentrations in ground water can vary by an order of magnitude in a given location over relatively short periods. This means that there will be large error bounds on the numerator (environmental concentrations). There will also be large error bounds on the denominator (AAL) because of uncertainty in the data that go into calculating the AAL. The uncertainties are still greater in the sum of the ratios of Cc,m/(AAL)c,m over all chemicals and all media used to reflect overall risks. Therefore, the final answer, taking into account error bounds of the input data, might range from something below one to something above one.

The case example that David gave highlights an additional problem with the AALs. The contaminant selected in the example was chloroform; the AAL was set at 4.3 ppb on the basis of potential carcinogenic effects. Yet the drinking water standard for total trihalomethanes (primarily chloroform) is 100 ppb. Based on conventional dose-response extrapolations, 100 ppb happens to correspond to an increased cancer risk of about 10^{-4}. Admittedly, the drinking water standards are technology based and not health based. In fact, however, the drinking water standards trade off the uncertain risk of cancer as a result of the presence of chloroform against the certain risk of pathogenic diseases if the water were not chlorinated. Chloroform is a byproduct of chlorine disinfection. A dual standard—4.3 ppb for cleanup and 100 ppb for drinking water—may be appropriate. Nonetheless, there is clearly some subjective judgment involved in setting the AALs.

Finally, the California decision tree process and this entire workshop are based on the premise that priority attention must be paid to protecting human health and the environment from hazardous waste sites. After the RI/FS has been completed and a decision has been made to spend, let us say, $20 million on a site, the question is never asked, "If $20 million were made available to this particular community to protect and enhance public health and the environment, what would it be spent on to achieve the maximum overall benefits?" Over the next 5 years, more than $20 *billion* is likely to be spent in the United States for inactive waste site cleanup; the question is never asked, "If that same $20 billion were to be put into a program to improve public welfare in the United States would it all be put into waste sites?" In an even broader context, the question is never asked, "If $20 billion were to be invested in a global public health program, would it be spent on cleaning up hazardous waste sites in the United States?" I am not suggesting that these questions be addressed here; we have a full agenda focused on issues of major national interest. I am suggesting that current national priorities may not be directly proportional to current health and environmental risks in the United States, much less worldwide.

REFERENCES

Hirschhorn, J. S. 1987. Superfund: A Scientifically Sound Strategy Needed. Ground Water Journal, Jan.-Feb.: pp. 3–11.

Wood, E. S., R. A. Ferrara, W. G. Gray, and G. F. Pinder. 1984. Ground Water Contamination from Hazardous Waste. Englewood Cliffs, N.J.: Prentice-Hall.

5

How Clean is Clean? The Need for Action

THOMAS M. HELLMAN AND DEBORAH A. HAWKINS

One of the major impediments to moving remedial cleanup actions under any of the various federal and state laws that apply is the resolution of the "How clean is clean?" issue. The statutory definition of what factors must be considered in determining the acceptable level of cleanup varies from law to law. These definitions, which were developed by legislative processes in Washington, D.C., and various state capitals, often are not clearly translatable to a determination of cleanup levels at remediation sites. Instead, they generate controversy and confusion. The practical result of this situation is that the cost of remediation increases as does the time required to implement solutions. Ultimately, fewer sites will be cleaned up. In this paper, I will discuss the following issues:

- the current legal/regulatory framework relative to cleanup levels;
- the cost and technical implications of various cleanup strategies;
- the balance of today's cleanup costs versus future liabilities; and
- who ultimately pays.

CURRENT LEGAL/REGULATORY FRAMEWORK

EPA has taken the position that a cleanup conducted under the Resource Conservation and Recovery Act's (RCRA) corrective action authority should be no different from a cleanup undertaken under the Superfund program. Both actions target the cleanup of historic contamination, and both have the same health-based cleanup goals. One significant difference is the fact that RCRA sites are generally associated with existing businesses; thus, operating revenues can be used to pay for the cleanup. These costs in turn can be passed on to customers. This is not true for Superfund sites, for which available funds are more limited.

Consistent with this position, EPA has announced its intent to merge RCRA and Superfund cleanup approaches and to implement a single programmatic response to the cleanup of historic contamination. Congress, however, has not cooperated. Notwithstanding EPA's official policy, differences in statutory language and approach make the choice of undertaking a cleanup under the authority of RCRA or Superfund an important one.

The recent enactment of the Superfund Amendments and Reauthorization Act (SARA) has sharpened the differences between RCRA and Superfund. The statutes adopt divergent approaches on a number of critical issues, including cleanup standards, use of alternative concentration limits (ACLs), cost-effectiveness considerations, and public participation. Under RCRA, the requirements can be more stringent as the criterion of cleanup to background is applied with an opportunity to modify cleanup levels using the ACL risk management approach. The Superfund procedure mandates more vigorous public involvement.

In 1987 EPA issued its formal statement of policy on RCRA and Superfund in which it echoed the cleanup goal theme. When identifying those cleanups that should be included on Superfund's National Priority List and those that should be undertaken under RCRA's corrective action program, EPA acknowledged that jurisdiction may lie under both statutes. The agency established a presumption in favor of RCRA-authorized cleanups for RCRA facilities, but it emphasized that similar cleanup approaches would be followed, regardless of whether a cleanup proceeded under RCRA or Superfund. Agency spokesmen explained: "The Agency's goal is to develop RCRA corrective action requirements that remove inconsistencies between remedial actions performed under CERCLA and corrective actions performed under RCRA." In practice, it may be difficult to achieve consistency between the two statutes because cleanup authority under RCRA and Superfund is not similar; in addition, each statute includes important elements that may have significant impact on the cleanup decisions.

As a general rule, RCRA requires that cleanups protect "human health and the environment." Because RCRA is much more of a hazardous waste management statute than a hazardous waste cleanup statute, it provides no additional guidance on cleanup methods. The statute includes no mention, for example, of whether cost-effectiveness can or should play a role in selecting among remedial alternatives, nor does it include any other guidance regarding the type of remedy that should be employed in cleanups. By not mentioning cost-effectiveness, the statute precludes consideration of it. In fact, the legislative history indicates it is not to be considered. The use of ACLs determined by risk assessment is allowed, however.

Even before its recent amendments, Superfund provided much more explicit guidance. Like RCRA, Superfund adopted a health-based standard, but it also specified that cleanups should be evaluated and selected on cost-effectiveness grounds. It also mandated that fund balancing considerations were to be a part of the evaluation whenever Superfund monies are being used for cleanup efforts.

Now, under SARA, the Superfund scheme includes additional guidance and constraints on the selection of remedial actions. Specifically, Section 121 of SARA includes a strong bias in favor of permanent remedies and onsite remedies and requires that applicable or relevant and appropriate state and federal standards be applied. These requirements will ultimately be reconciled in the National Contingency Plan.

Complementing the federal statutes are a number of state laws that drive cleanup activities. Virtually every state has its own form of the Superfund law, which requires the cleanup of sites not addressed by the federal Superfund. Several states are taking innovative approaches toward remediation of contaminated sites. New Jersey has, under its Environmental Cleanup Responsibility Act (ECRA), established a process by which the transfer of industrial or commercial properties on which hazardous materials have been handled must be reviewed and approved by the New Jersey Department of Environmental Protection to ensure that any contamination has been cleaned up. This approach is being considered in a number of other state legislatures. Massachusetts approaches property cleanups using another method called Superlien. Under Superlien laws, the state has the first lien on properties on which the state has expended money to clean up contamination. The banking community in Massachusetts has become very concerned about the potential consequences of making loans secured by contaminated property and has required environmental reviews of properties before making loans. Each of these laws ultimately drives a decision on whether a property is deemed to be contaminated and, if so, what cleanup levels are appropriate. The "How clean is clean?" issue is usually resolved on a site-by-site basis using a combination of risk assessment techniques and applicable standards.

The three criteria most often used by states to address the level-of-cleanup issue are:

- cleanup to background (the level at which no industrial activity had taken place, allowing only for natural contamination, pH, radioactivity, and so on);
- cleanup to background, holding other responsible parties accountable for the contamination they caused on the property; and
- human health and environmental protection standard of care.

COST VERSUS CLEANUP LEVELS

The two parameters most significantly affected by cleanup levels are the costs of the cleanup and the time required to accomplish the remediation. The overall impact of SARA on the Superfund process has caused EPA staff to project a 9-month increase in the time it takes to handle a Superfund cleanup—that is, from 58 months to 67 months. The remedial investigation/feasibility study (RI/FS) work plan is supposed to be developed within 6 months of the commencement of discussions with cooperative potentially responsible parties (PRPs). The RI/FS itself will take another 18 months. The health assessment should be available toward the end of the second year. Public and state comment will occur in the third year, after which the record of decision (ROD) is prepared. The remedial design will be available around the end of the third year, and consent decrees may be entered at any time there is a settlement. Thereafter, review and contracting will occupy most of the fourth year. Remedial action, which takes an average of 2.5 years, will bring EPA's estimate of total elapsed time to over 6.5 years—that is, the remedy is even further away.

This schedule illustrates that SARA has created a cleanup process with great potential for inflating costs. New cleanup standards, health assessments, state and public participation, and

TABLE 5-1 Summary of Record of Decision Results

Cleanup Options	Average Cost Increase Multipliers	Revised Program Cost
EPA remedy	1.00	$16 billion*
Containment remedy	2.61	$39 billion
Least-cost permanent solution	5.49	$81 billion

*These estimates were derived from the EPA average cleanup cost estimate provided in the Superfund Section 301(a)(1)(c) study of future funding needs. In that study the average site cleanup cost was estimated at $8.84 million, and 1,800 sites were assumed to be listed on the National Priority List. This volume results in a total program cleanup cost of approximately $16 billion. The revised program costs are estimated by applying the cost multiplier to design, construction, and operation and maintenance costs but not to remedial investigation/feasibility study costs, which should stay the same.

other new requirements of the statute all contribute to this potential. EPA has estimated that the cleanup requirements in SARA would drive the cost of a Superfund cleanup from its present average of about $8 million–$9 million per site to between $25 million and $30 million per site. States are responsible for paying 10 percent of the cleanup costs at fund-financed sites, and many state officials have expressed concern about the increased cost potential.

In a study carried out in 1986, Putnam, Hayes, and Bartlett, Inc., examined all the RODs issued after January 1, 1985, to determine the costs associated with various cleanup options. Thirty-five of these RODs were useful for the purpose of this study (Table 5-1).

The practical result of the increased cost per site would mean that either the Superfund tax would need to be adjusted to reflect the added cost of the more stringent cleanup requirements or fewer sites would be cleaned up.

The following case studies address the cost issue on a smaller scale.

Case Study 1

A relatively small electric equipment repair shop located in the southeastern United States had a polychlorobiphenyl (PCB)

TABLE 5-2 Costs of Different Cleanup Levels

Remediation Level (ppm PCB)	Volume (cu. yd)	Cost ($000s)
50	2,260	1,000
10	3,750	1,750
1	8,290	3,500

contamination problem. The solution was deemed to be offsite disposal at an approved hazardous waste land disposal facility. The costs were a direct function of the amount of soil to be removed (Table 5-2).

In addition to cost considerations, a judgment must be made on the wisdom of using limited hazardous waste disposal facilities to dispose of a relatively low-risk waste—that is, PCB-contaminated soil.

Case Study 2

A trichloroethylene (TCE) ground water contamination problem was discovered at a plant in the western part of the United States. Cleanup of the ground water contaminated with 20 ppm TCE was initiated by airstripping at a rate of 85 ppm. After 900 days of continuous pumping the TCE concentration in the aquifer had dropped to 1.3 ppm. After an additional 700 days the concentration was 1 ppm. Thus, additional pumping had arrived at a point of decreasing benefit because with time the concentration was asymptotically approaching a nonzero value. The estimated costs to reach various cleanup levels are given in Table 5-3.

The case study demonstrates the costs and the length of time that would be required if low parts-per-billion cleanup levels are required. It raises the practical question of who will be responsible for these kinds of abatement systems 20 to 50 years from now when the companies deemed responsible may no longer exist.

TABLE 5-3   Estimated Costs for Several Cleanup Levels

Total Cost ($000s)	Cleanup Level (ppb)	Time (years)
222	1,300	2.5
312	1,000	4.5
~1,100	100	20.0
~10,000	10	100.0

TECHNOLOGY CONSIDERATIONS

Basically, the universe of cleanup problems we face can be analyzed in terms of three major technology challenges: (1) concentrated residues—sludges and drums containing hazardous materials are examples; (2) contaminated ground water—typically having relatively low levels of organic and inorganic contaminants; and (3) contaminated soil—with a wide variety of contaminants.

At least two of these problems are currently capable of solution. Adequate technology exists for concentrated residues because they are essentially the same hazardous wastes managed under the RCRA program. Ground water cleanup is in some respects merely a different form of water pollution control. Obviously, these characterizations are an oversimplification, and yet, clearly much of the technology for destroying residues and cleaning ground water exists. The challenge is how to get that technology to the site needing remediation. The cleanup of contaminated soil remains a problem to be solved. For example, incinerating soil is extremely expensive, and the "burnt soil" product may be as hazardous as the original contaminated soil. Table 5-4 shows various cleanup options for PCB-contaminated soil and their costs.

BALANCING CLEANUP COSTS VERSUS
FUTURE LIABILITIES

In today's litigious society, more people are suing companies over environmental contamination-related issues (e.g., drinking water, property devaluation, illness, etc.). For most large companies, the annual transactional costs alone are measured in the millions of dollars.

TABLE 5-4 Cleanup Options and Costs for PCB-Contaminated
Soil (100 ppm PCB)

Treatment	Estimated Cost/cu. yd
Landfill--no pretreatment	$200-$400
Fly ash/cement stabilization	$60-$80
Fixation onsite with inorganic polymer/cement mixture	$180
Chemical destruction onsite	$100
In situ vitrification (glassifying the soil) maxtrix with complete destruction of PCBs	$200-$250
Incineration of soil onsite (PCB destruction)	$200-$300

The quandary we face is that the lower the cleanup standards—that is, the more stringent they are—the higher the cost per site and the longer each cleanup will take, with the result that fewer sites will be cleaned. On the other hand, lower cleanup standards may also result in lower future liabilities for responsible parties with respect to the site being remediated. Clearly, when responsible parties are evaluating what constitutes an adequate cleanup level, consideration should be given to the impact of the cleanup on future liabilities.

WHO PAYS?

The final important question is, who pays? The answer is, we all do. An examination of the magnitude of the monies being expended today on cleanups may be instructive. Over the last few years, based on the original Superfund, EPA's spending rate has been about $20 million per month. It is now about $30 million per month, about one-half of which is spent at waste sites. About 50 percent of waste site money goes for RI/FS; the remainder goes for cleanup. Thus, $5 million to $10 million per month is being spent by EPA on cleanup efforts. SARA will ultimately boost that spending rate to $100 million per month. EPA has indicated that some 13 cleanups have been completed and about 300 are beyond the RI/FS stage. Companies with significant involvement in national priority site listing, which essentially includes most of industrial America, are spending $15 million to $30 million per year for cleanups. In addition, a number of states have passed mini-Superfund legislation to generate the necessary matching funds and to undertake the cleanup of sites that are not on the National Priority List. New Jersey and New York have significant funds available for cleanup. As with the federal Superfund, these state programs are generally funded by industry, and their costs are ultimately passed on to customers in the form of higher prices for American goods and services. Yet American industry pays an additional price by being further disadvantaged in relation to foreign competition in a world economy. The point is that we should all feel responsibility for making sure that the limited resources available to address environmental contamination problems are spent in the most effective manner. Some form of overall risk assessment should be used to determine what action represents the greatest risk reduction potential per dollar spent. EPA could then evaluate its performance against a meaningful yardstick.

CONCLUDING REMARKS AND RECOMMENDATIONS

In the arena of hazardous waste site cleanup, the price we pay for inaction is elevated risk to the impacted population. The decisionmaking process is often prolonged by the desires of certain interested parties to achieve the ultimate solution, despite the necessity of working from an imperfect data base and using complex yet unverified modeling systems. The attempt to distinguish between risk rates of 10^{-5} to 10^{-7} is somewhat analogous to trying to distinguish between the third and fourth decimal place using a slide rule—it is in the error bracket. Clearly, a balancing of issues, including public health, environmental protection, and economy, must take place with a premium on cleanup action.

We often lose sight of the tremendous disjunction between the "How clean is clean?" issue and the real world. Through increased political and agency pressure, we are tightening cleanup requirements to degrees of stringency that push the cost of cleanup beyond what is possible, thus inducing further delays. We spend too much time on site-specific data development and modeling—especially considering the complex "chemical soup" that exists at most sites, which is too complicated for our current techniques to model accurately. These issues may be some of the underlying causes of the lack of achievement in the Superfund program to date.

We need more objective future-use considerations in our remediation planning. We need to take site-specific actions consistent with good engineering practices and the circumstances of the site. We must also develop a decisionmaking system that can be applied on a mass production basis. The premium must be on getting cleanup activities under way with incentives built in for those who are willing to go forward. The solutions may not always be perfect, but let us opt for some imperfection versus paralysis.

REFERENCE

Putnam, Hayes, and Bartlett, Inc. 1986. Cost Implications of Changes in Superfund Cleanup Standards. Study conducted for U.S. Environmental Protection Agency, Washington, D.C.

PROVOCATEUR'S COMMENTS
Toby Page

I thought that Tom Hellman's paper was thoughtful and interesting. He said in the paper that we have a confusing set of criteria that counteract each other and lead to inefficiencies. He also said there are diminishing returns that waste cleanup. Nonetheless, he pointed out that we have to do some sort of balancing because we have mixtures of goals and mixtures of costs. As a practical result we end up having a few big sites treated to a large extent, and we lose efficiency in the course of that. We might do better with less treatment and more sites and quicker treatment. This is a theme that makes sense to me.

To move from this summary to something a little more provocative, I will say that what we really need to do is think about what is driving the present system and what we will need to change in order to drive it in the direction we would like to see. One of the things that is driving the system is liability. The liability issue is certainly affecting the way industry is doing things. It is also affecting the way regulators are doing things, and this is not as well known. But I think it is important. Liability from a regulator's point of view has to do with how much trouble he can get into from making a decision. When you think of liability in that sense, it explains some of the delay that we are seeing. If you put off a decision and have another study, wait a few years, get a contractor's report, all of this puts distance between you and the liability you might feel for your decisions. I think this is part of the problem. Another part of the problem is that if you ever sign off on something, saying, "This is clean enough, let's stop work," you might get into trouble. If you drag on the process and insist on more and more, then you put off the day of reckoning and you put off the liability. Therefore, liability affects not only what industry does but also the way regulators work, and the combination of the two can lead to some of the things Tom has observed—especially the phenomenon of a small number of large-scale cleanup sites.

A second thing driving the system and leading to inefficiencies is the old-fashioned way of looking at uncertainty and making decisions on the basis of it. In contrast to our management of toxic wastes, there has been a shift in economics, and the decision sciences quite generally, toward the ideas of de Finetti, Ramsey, Savage, and others. These decision theorists are more explicitly judgmental and subjectivist than traditional scientists and statisticians. The modern decision theorists do not believe in probabilities being "really out there." They do not think of probabilities being in the dice or in the toxic chemical; they believe that probabilities are "really in here," in the judgment, in the mind of the assessor. This newer perspective changes the way one looks at decisionmaking. It means that one makes probabilistic evaluations of scientific uncertainty, including both systematic error and measurement error. Probabilistic assessment of systematic error is often lacking in current risk assessments. We often substitute analyses of measurement error for analyses of the assessment of systematic error. Instead of saying a model is useful in the sense that it yields information for a decision in a particular way, we say it is either valid or not valid in a very brittle kind of way. This either/or approach has gotten us into trouble when we deal with decisionmaking under uncertainty.

A third thing driving the system is our difficulty in dealing with criteria other than efficiency. To an economist the criterion of economic efficiency is precise. It can be translated under varying kinds of assumptions into criteria having to do with cost-benefit analysis, risk-benefit analysis, cost-effectiveness, the minimization of costs not just for the particular project but in the design of the institutional device to make it work, and the minimization of costs over an entire decision process. All of this is a well-trodden field. I do not think it has been applied very well in the case of the Superfund program, but actually the consideration of efficiency is the easy part. The hard part is that other criteria are also important, criteria that have to do with distributional considerations such as the protection of victims and restitution for those who are harmed. Another criterion has to do with corrective justice, the holding to account of a perpetrator of bad actions. In the case of Superfund, this is usually translated into money that the polluter should pay. Distributional criteria are important and help explain why we have had so much trouble implementing straightforward cost-benefit analysis, which tends to neglect them. A concern for distributional criteria also helps to explain another anomaly: we seem to be spending enormous amounts of money on the remediation of hazardous waste-sites, whereas we seem to be much more accepting of hazardous materials in other media, such as air or surface water. If you think of what it takes to identify a source, it may be easier in the arena of ground water protection than it is in the air, and that may help explain why there is greater political salience for one rather than the other.

These three things—our current approaches to liability, uncertainty, and distributional criteria—can be added to the obvious fourth factor, the traditional conflicts between the potential gainers and losers from any collective decision. The four factors help explain not only what is driving the system but also why it is so hard to get to a satisfactory destination.

6

How Clean is Clean?
An Environmentalist Perspective

LINDA E. GREER

The selection of cleanup levels for hazardous waste dump sites has been a priority issue within the environmental community since the original passage of the Superfund legislation. After lobbying the issue during the debate over the 1980 bill, the Environmental Defense Fund (EDF) oversaw the implementation of the statutory language and participated in the rule making that generated the National Contingency Plan (NCP), the set of regulations governing cleanups nationwide. EDF subsequently filed suit against EPA in 1982 over the agency's failure to resolve the cleanup standards issue in the NCP, arguing both that the agency's approach was not what was contemplated by Congress when it passed the law and that the approach was not adequate to protect human health and the environment from the toxic hazards posed by dump sites.

Since 1982, the "How clean is clean?" question has expanded to include not only the question of the level of cleanup appropriate at dump sites but also the technology to be selected in undertaking a cleanup and the point of compliance at which the cleanup goals will be attained. These three issues have been addressed by environmental and citizens groups at particular sites as well as in lobbying efforts on the 1986 reauthorized Superfund bill.

CLEANUP LEVELS

EPA currently sets cleanup levels using the largely unmodified methodology originally proposed in its 1982 NCP. This approach allows cleanups to vary from site to site depending on a number of factors. Dubbed the "maximum flexibility/minimum accountability" approach by community groups living around the dump sites, this approach allows EPA to take into account numerous variables, most notably cost, in addition to the need to protect human health and the environment when cleaning up sites. The current EPA approach results in the establishment of different acceptable levels of contamination in the ground water, surface water, and air from site to site across the country after cleanup. Thus, for example, some of our Superfund sites have been cleaned "down" to 50 ppm PCB in the soil, whereas others have been cleaned to 10 ppm and even 1 ppm. The major objection that environmental and community groups have about the current EPA approach is that it does not guarantee a minimum level of protection to citizens across the country; rather, a number of factors, many of which are never quantified or explicitly discussed, appear to determine the amount of contamination that will remain at the site after cleanup.

EPA justifies its case-by-case approach to cleanup by citing the many technological complexities inherent in cleaning up dump sites as well as the scientific uncertainties involved in determining safe levels of exposure to various toxic chemicals in the environment. Although the environmental community does not dispute the premise that these decisions are inherently difficult, we strongly disagree with the idea that the solution is to make cleanup decisions case by case. Rather, it would be more equitable and efficient for the agency to establish a baseline of protection at toxic dump sites that would be guaranteed to all citizens. This baseline would comprise acceptable levels of contaminants in the ground water, surface water, soil, and air that would be achieved at the end of each and every cleanup (barring physical impossibility or truly exorbitant costs). Such a baseline would minimize the role that politics and short-term economics play in the selection of cleanup goals.

It is important to note here that there are many in the industrial community who agree with environmentalists that a case-by-case approach to establishing cleanup levels at dump sites is not desirable public policy. They agree because uncertainty in the appropriate cleanup levels for a site substantially complicates both negotiations between private parties and the agency concerning voluntary cleanups and settlements with responsible parties at Superfund sites. The fact that no site serves as a precedent for other sites, even those contaminated with identical chemicals, precludes easy decisions on the part of corporate management to end cleanup negotiations as well as to initiate voluntary cleanup of sites not yet in the public eye. It was the agreement between industry and environmentalists concerning the desirability for predictable outcomes at Superfund cleanups that inspired detailed and successful consensus discussions on this topic at the Keystone Center in 1985 and 1986.

The EDF has suggested since its lawsuits with EPA in 1982 that the baseline of protection for Superfund cleanups should comprise drinking water standards, ambient water quality criteria, hazardous air pollutant standards, and other relevant and appropriate numbers that have been developed in various EPA programs over the years. Such numbers exist for many relatively common industrial pollutants, and they are numbers whose origin lies in the desire to protect human health and the environment. They thus provide objective, quantitative cleanup goals and can be used without undue delay in the Superfund program.

It is important, however, to distinguish between the need to establish a baseline of protection and the selection of appropriate numbers to constitute such a baseline. That is, it is possible to agree with environmentalists on the need for an objective baseline for cleanup but disagree on the appropriate numbers to be used to construct it. In this vein, some grass roots citizens groups have taken the position that EPA standards and criteria should not form the baseline for protection at Superfund sites. Rather, these groups prefer that ambient background levels be used to establish acceptable levels of contaminants in the environment. They are interested simply in returning the site to the condition of the surrounding area as it existed before the dump was sited and in fact do not trust the EPA health-based numbers to protect them.

As a result of successful work by the environmental lobby the 1986 reauthorized Superfund requires the use of all relevant and appropriate standards and criteria in establishing nationwide levels of cleanup. The law explicitly directs EPA to use requirements established by all federal environmental legislation including the Toxic Substances Control Act; the Safe Drinking Water Act; the Clean Air Act; the Clean Water Act; the Marine Protection, Research, and Sanctuaries Act; and the Solid Waste Disposal Act. The laws to be applied also include any state environmental requirement that is more stringent than a comparable federal requirement, including state requirements where there is no comparable federal requirement.

As a result of this new statutory language the environmental community expects that consistent levels of cleanup will be selected across the country, levels that are adequately protective of human health and the environment. Yet there are several ambiguous areas of the law on cleanup levels that remain for EPA to clarify, the successful implementation of which are critical to the success of the Superfund program.

First, the standards and other guidance available to EPA and the states have been developed largely for water and to a small extent for air. There are no standards for contaminated soil, which presents a hazard through both direct contact, as when children play at the dump site, and through the soil's ability to contaminate other media (by leaching its hazardous constituents into ground water and by volatilization and/or contaminated dust entrainment in the air). EPA must therefore develop a decision methodology for contaminated soil in order to provide a comprehensive baseline for cleanup at Superfund sites.

Second, the legislation is vague as to the level of risk that is allowed to remain at dump sites after cleanup. This silence is unfortunate because nearly all of EPA's guidance numbers for carcinogenic chemicals provide a range of risk figures, and the selection of the acceptable level of risk could thus be left to the decisionmaker on a case-by-case basis. Much has been made of the inability to attain a zero-risk situation at a hazardous waste dump site no matter what level of cleanup is selected, given the one-hit model for the mode of action of carcinogens.

The zero-risk issue has been hotly debated for many years, both inside and outside the Superfund program, and it is a good example of decisionmakers allowing the perfect to become the enemy of the good. Because it is impossible to attain a zero level of risk, the agency has moved slowly to regulate carcinogens at all. Such issues as the role of the ever-decreasing analytical detection limit and the distinction between individual and population risk have rendered the EPA essentially incapable of responding to carcinogenic hazards, be they in dump sites, industrial discharges, or ambient air. An expeditious solution to the complexities of regulating carcinogens is, at a minimum, to regulate them to levels below current detection limits. In this way, society is doing the best it is capable of doing to minimize the hazards of exposure to carcinogens. Over the years, as our abilities to detect chemicals improve, the debate can continue over the appropriate levels for regulation. For now, however, a large number of carcinogens, regulated at their current detection level, would pose no less than a 1×10^{-6} risk. Some carcinogens, such as dioxin, in fact pose risks much higher than 10^{-6} at their detection level.

POINT OF COMPLIANCE

In contrast to the detail the 1986 Superfund statute provides on the issue of the level of cleanup to be obtained at dump sites, the statute is thin on the issue of point of compliance. That is, the statute speaks to "How clean is clean?" but is silent as to "where." On this issue the agency has three major points at which to achieve protective levels: (1) at the dump itself (at the edge of the waste or at the center of the dump), (2) at the property boundary, or (3) at the point of actual exposure (e.g., the wellhead). Although it is theoretically possible to achieve equal levels of protection for human health and the environment under each of these alternatives, the choices differ substantially in the extent to which they require sophisticated hydrogeologic transport and fate models and institutional controls on future development, as well as the extent to which they require remedial technologies that are not yet within our grasp. It is only in considering our capabilities to implement each of these alternative strategies that the distinguish themselves.

Achieving protective levels of contaminants beyond the property boundary has two major drawbacks from an environmental perspective. First, it requires extensive sampling and sophisticated mathematical modeling. Competent professionals who are skilled in these tasks are still quite rare in our society, and of the handful of persons capable of doing these jobs, few if any are employed by federal or state governments. Because the strategy of allowing contaminants to attenuate out to the property boundary requires technical expertise that is difficult to obtain, it will often be carried out incompetently. Thus, it is undesirable as a public policy option. Furthermore, some well-qualified scientists believe that many Superfund dump sites are too complex, both geologically and chemically, for accurate modeling or sampling to occur. Therefore, prudent policy suggests that an alternative means of essuring protection at dump sites be considered even in situations in which experts can be retained for cleanup work.

A second drawback to the selection of the property boundary as the point of compliance is that it encourages polluters to buy up property rather than clean up ground water. In fact, we have seen this occur in the RCRA program. Clearly, this policy can lead to undesirable results if we are not careful to prohibit the purchase of property under these circumstances.

Third, the use of the property boundary requires extensive control of future land uses surrounding the dump. As our experience at Love Canal and countless other dumps has shown, we do not have the ability to predict accurately or control where future populations will live. Consequently, it is shortsighted to allow contamination to occur in currently undeveloped areas.

Selecting the wellhead as the point of compliance has developed support in several circles that advocate this alternative on the grounds that it is the most cost-effective. This option would address contamination only at the point at which it begins to contaminate a water supply well. Yet the alternative is flawed on several counts. It overlooks the technical uncertainties associated with the accurate prediction of ground water movement into the well drawdown zone and the cost of contaminating future water supplies. Furthermore, it is an option that is only applicable to sites with contaminated community well fields; individual homes could not be expected to install treatment units. As a general rule, it would not be cost-effective to treat contamination at the wellhead because the contamination would be most dilute in this location. Wellhead cleanups may have low annual costs, but they have to be operated for many more years than a cleanup that addresses the concentrated source in an expeditious manner.

The remaining option is to attain the required cleanup level at the edge of the waste. This alternative is clearly the most stringent and the one least subject to problems with scientific uncertainty or institutional control of land use. For this reason, under most circumstances, it is the preferred option of environmentalists. Yet EDF and many other national environmental groups agree that there are some circumstances in which cleanup at the edge of the waste would not be necessary to provide adequate assurances of protection for the public. For example, in those cases in which the hydrogeology around a site is simple (and ground water models therefore can be applied more accurately) and effective methods are available to preclude exposure to soil or air at dangerous levels at the site itself, it would be reasonable to use some of the property around the waste to attenuate the contaminants. We suggest that in these cases we use reasonable worst-case assumptions about such phenomena as adsorption, biological degradation, and ground water velocity to ensure a conservative result to the modeling exercises. In situations in which the geology is complex, however, or it is difficult to control access to the soil or air directly onsite, the only acceptable alternative is cleanup at the source itself.

CLEANUP TECHNOLOGY

Since the inception of Superfund in 1980, EPA has demonstrated a distinct preference in the technologies it selects to clean up dump sites. For the most part the agency has chosen to remove some of the most highly contaminated materials at a given site, opting for redisposal at an operating hazardous waste landfill followed by containment (with clay caps and slurry walls) of the remaining materials. Often, ground water pumping is also used to isolate the waste and complete the "containment" strategy.

For good reason the 1986 Congress severely criticized EPA for its nearly exclusive choice of containment. This criticism was founded on evidence that the containment structures were extremely short-term solutions. It was found that caps eroded within months of installation, and slurry walls often failed almost as soon as construction was completed. Furthermore, an investigation of the operating landfills used for disposal of highly contaminated wastes from Superfund sites revealed that the large majority of these sites were already leaking their toxic contents into the ground water. Thus, we had the ironic situation of the government paying large sums of money to private industry to move and dispose of toxic waste from existing Superfund sites for disposal in licensed dumps that were themselves well on the way to becoming future targets of Superfund action.

Much of the justification EPA gave for selecting these removal and containment strategies was its peculiar definition of cost-effectiveness; EPA was considering only the up-front cost of constructing containment facilities and did not factor in long-term operation and maintenance costs or the cost of technological uncertainty in the performance of these structures. As a result, the agency's policy was extremely shortsighted.

The environmental community lobbied hard in Congress to insert a presumption for permanent treatment technologies at dump sites, and it was successful in obtaining strong and specific permanent treatment language in the 1986 bill, which requires that EPA use such treatment at Superfund sites to the maximum extent practicable. Permanent treatment is defined as treatment that permanently and significantly reduces the volume, toxicity, or mobility of the hazardous substances, pollutants, or contaminants at the site. The statutory bias toward the implementation of permanent technologies is designed to encourage such methods as biological degradation, incineration, and other destruction technologies as well as chemical fixation and stabilization processes for metals. It is hoped that, in the long term, these types of treatments will be more effective in addressing the contaminant sources at the dump sites.

Furthermore, the environmental lobby obtained new statutory language on the role of cost in making both cleanup and technology decisions. As of the end of 1986, an analysis of cost-effectiveness can begin only after a remedial action has been selected in compliance with health and environmental protection requirements as well as permanent treatment requirements. Thus, cost will not play a role in the selection of the correct course of cleanup action; rather, it will come into play only after the cleanup strategy has been selected. It is hoped that this secondary role for cost considerations will allow the agency to select permanent technologies with high up-front costs but low long-term operation and maintenance costs.

CONCLUSION

There has been considerable dissatisfaction on the part of community and environmental groups concerning the "How clean is clean?" decisions made to date by EPA. The decisions made so far in the program have been inconsistent, and they have not always been adequate to protect human health and the environment. In light of this problem the national environmental groups expended a great deal of time and money to improve the language of the Superfund legislation and redirect EPA. We were largely successful in our attempts to improve the law and are looking over the next 5 years for these legislative improvements to show up in regulations, in guidance documents, and, most importantly, at the Superfund sites themselves.

PROVOCATEUR'S COMMENTS
Leo M. Eisel

In both her written and spoken remarks, Linda Greer followed very closely these major areas: How clean is clean?; what are the cleanup levels?; what are the standards?; where is the point of compliance: is it out at the edge of the dump, or is it someplace off property?; and what kind of technology should be used? In all these areas I think she comes across very strongly for no-nonsense standards, little flexibility, and the use of minimum engineering, essentially using the same techniques and the same standards at all sites. She suggests the use of existing standards such as the Safe Drinking Water and ambient stream standards, and calls for no off-property containment and, again, the minimizing of dependence on ground water models, engineering calculations, and so on. She appears to have little trust of major corporations, EPA, and the consulting industry in general.

I have been on both sides of this. I have a lot of sympathy for the simple, straightforward, no-nonsense approach. I was director of the state of Illinois' EPA at one time. Outside of my office was a big couch, and this is where major industry heads in the state would sit with their state representative before entering my office and saying, "Oh, please be reasonable, please allow some flexibility, please let me pollute just a little bit more." So, I can understand the problem with a lot of flexibility. However, I wonder if this apparent distrust and emphasis on very straightforward and simple solutions is really politically and economically feasible.

I heard Tom Hellman talk about balancing and about going out and putting the spade in. By this I took him to mean, let's get some data, let us proceed on the basis of the data, and let us tailor our solutions to the individual conditions. I just wonder whether Tom Hellman and his consulting engineer—and I presume that Tom has a good consulting engineer—are really going to allow Linda to push this concept of a uniform solution and inflexible standards at every site. I also wonder whether they will continue to put up the money for what can be a quite costly and expensive uniform solution at every site, or whether they are only going to do this after a very long litigation process.

From experience at a few sites where I have put on my little plastic suit and respirator and actually gone out and walked around, there is enormous variability, ranging from mining sites in western Colorado to the Rocky Mountain arsenal. There is enormous variability, and I just cannot help but wonder whether we have to allow some flexibility in the conditions, the standards, and the solutions that we apply to each of these sites and whether the type of program that Linda has proposed is economically and politically viable. Her suggestion essentially to use Safe Drinking Water standards, ambient water quality standards, and other existing standards as the appropriate guidelines or cleanup criteria tends to ignore that even within these standards a great deal of variability exists. For example, the ambient water quality standards within the state of Colorado for a trout stream are far stricter than those for the drinking water that we can consume. Where do we come down in that? How much flexibility do we allow? In conclusion, I would just ask Linda to take into account longer-term political and economic viability. If we go with limited flexibility, where are we going to be in 10 years? Are things going to be cleaner? Are they going to be stalled because of continued litigation by Tom Hellman and his very skilled attorneys and engineers who are going to say we must have some flexibility? Or are we going to have to have a cleaner site and solve some of the neighborhood problems that Linda Greer brought out?

7

Ground Water Contamination Issues in Santa Clara County, California: A Perspective

RONALD R. ESAU AND D. J. CHESTERMAN

In the last few years, Santa Clara County has been the focus of state and federal attention in the area of hazardous materials regulation. The discovery of major ground water contamination in 1981 set in motion a local regulatory response that has been the pattern for similar action throughout the state of California. Responsible agencies have also forged new ground with regard to remedial actions associated with existing incidents of contamination. Millions of dollars have been spent by private industry on cleanup activities while a cooperative relationship has been maintained between industry and government to the extent that expensive and time-consuming litigation has been avoided in almost all cases. Now that cleanups are in progress at over 125 sites in the county, difficult decisions with regard to the level of cleanup required must be faced. In addition, it is becoming more evident that funding for cleanups will be a major hurdle in the very near future. Efficient mechanisms must be in place to permit a rapid response to high-priority cases of contamination.

BACKGROUND

The Santa Clara Valley Water District is a public agency established by special act of the California legislature to provide overall flood protection and supply water to Santa Clara County residents. The county comprises 15 cities, the largest being the city of San Jose. The district's flood protection responsibilities include the planning and construction of facilities to prevent floodwater damage to the county's expanding urbanized areas; its water supply functions include the planning, construction, and operation of facilities to provide an adequate supply of water for the growing municipal and industrial demand. The district is also responsible for contracting with appropriate state and federal agencies to import additional water to supplement the available local supply.

Funding for flood control is generated from property taxes, benefit assessments, and some federal assistance. Funding sources for water supply responsibilities include revenue from taxes, water sales, and ground water extraction charges. In terms of direct sales the district is essentially a wholesaler, providing treated water to several private and municipal entities distributing within Santa Clara County. Figure 7-1 shows the boundaries of the various water retailers located in the county.

The total quantity of water needed to supply the approximately 1.4 million county residents is currently 400,000 acre-feet per year. This requirement is satisfied by a combination of treated surface water and ground water, with ground water accounting for about 60 percent of the total consumption countywide. The ground water basin underlying the county is relied on heavily, not only for its natural yield but also to treat, store, and distribute a major portion of the imported water the county uses, along with water conserved in local reservoirs.

It was recently recognized that authorities were literally overlooking a serious threat to the water quality of that basin arising from activities associated with a major industry in a part of the county popularly referred to as "Silicon Valley." In 1981 a large electronics firm reported to the San Francisco Bay Regional Water Quality Control Board (Bay Regional Board) the loss of about 60,000 gallons of waste solvents and water from an underground storage tank farm. A week later, on December 7, 1981, a nearby well of a water utility company was shut down after detecting contamination with trichloroethane (TCA) at a concentration of 5,800 ppb.

During the next year, the Bay Regional Board conducted extensive surveys of all industry that might have underground solvent storage tanks on their property. Fuel products were omitted from the initial survey. Solvents were considered a higher priority because of their extreme toxicity, their higher solubility in water, their specific gravity, and their persistence, or resistance to

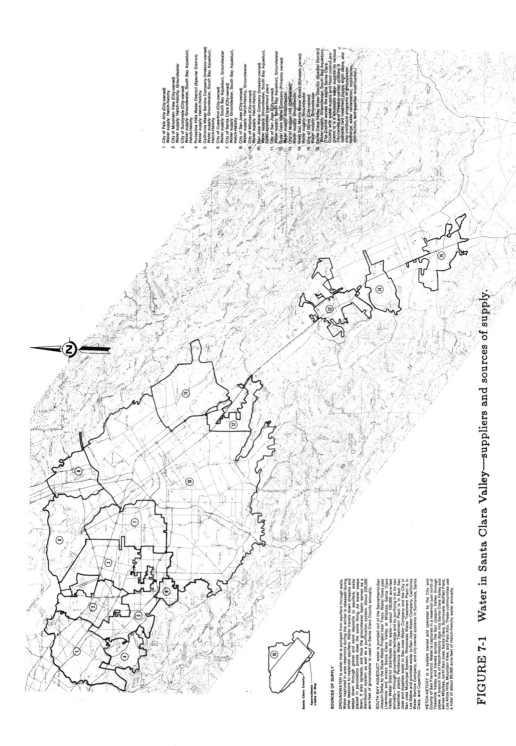

1. City of Palo Alto (City-owned)
   Water supply: Hetch-Hetchy
2. City of Mountain View (City-owned)
   Water supply: Hetch-Hetchy, Groundwater
3. City of Sunnyvale (City-owned)
   Water supply: Groundwater, South Bay Aqueduct, Hetch-Hetchy
4. Purisima Hills Water District (Special District)
   Water supply: Hetch-Hetchy
5. California Water Service Company (Investor-owned)
   Water supply: Groundwater, South Bay Aqueduct, Hetch-Hetchy
6. City of Cupertino (City-owned)
   Water supply: South Bay Aqueduct, Groundwater
7. City of Santa Clara (City-owned)
   Water supply: Groundwater, South Bay Aqueduct, Hetch-Hetchy
8. City of San Jose (City-owned)
   Water supply: Hetch-Hetchy, Groundwater
9. City of Milpitas (City-owned)
   Water supply: South Bay Aqueduct, Hetch-Hetchy
   SJWC-operated treatment plant
10. San Jose Water Company (Investor-owned)
    Water supply: South Bay Aqueduct, Groundwater
11. City of San Jose (City-owned)
    Water supply: South Bay Aqueduct, Groundwater
12. Great Oaks Water Company (Privately owned)
    Water supply: Groundwater
13. City of Morgan Hill (City-owned)
    Water supply: Groundwater
14. West San Martin Water Works (Privately owned)
    Water supply: Groundwater
15. City of Gilroy (City-owned)
    Water supply: Groundwater
16. Santa Clara Valley Water District (Special District)
    Water supply: Groundwater, South Bay Aqueduct
    (The District serves the entire Santa Clara
    County with water supply and flood control pro-
    grams. It is a wholesale water supplier to various
    retailers and treatment plants, eight dams, and
    also conducts programs on groundwater
    recharge, water reclamation, importation,
    distribution, and weather modification.)

SOURCES OF SUPPLY

GROUNDWATER is water that is pumped from aquifers through wells. Water captured in area reservoirs during the winter is released during other seasons to replenish aquifers. Water travels down streams and seeps down through gravel and sand deposits to aquifers, water placed in percolation ponds does the same thing. As water seeps down, it also spreads, and then the groundwater basin serves as a distribution system as well as a purification system. About 235,000 acre-feet of groundwater is used in Santa Clara County annually.

SOUTH BAY AQUEDUCT water is pumped out of the Sacramento-San Joaquin Delta by the State Water Project near Tracy. Water flows past Livermore and enters Santa Clara Valley at Milpitas. Santa Clara Valley Water District distributes this water—about 100,000 acre-feet annually—through its two treatment plants (Penitencia Water Treatment Plant is in the northeast part of San Jose and the City of San Jose Municipal System, Rinconada Water Treatment Plant is in Los Gatos and provides water to San Jose Water Company, California Water Service Company, and city-owned systems in Sunnyvale, Santa Clara, and Cupertino.

HETCH-HETCHY is a system owned and operated by the City and County of San Francisco. Water is captured in a reservoir just north of Yosemite Valley and travels across the San Joaquin Valley through pipes. A branch line of Hetch-Hetchy digs off into Santa Clara Valley and serves Milpitas, north San Jose, Santa Clara, Sunnyvale, Mountain View, and Palo Alto. These communities use a total of about 65,000 acre-feet of Hetch-Hetchy water annually.

FIGURE 7-1   Water in Santa Clara Valley—suppliers and sources of supply.

biochemical degradation, as compared to petroleum products. In the survey, it was found that a significant number of the companies had leaks or spills on their property that warranted further investigation.

This discovery concurrently set in motion a response from local regulatory agencies that resulted in the adoption of the nation's first hazardous materials storage ordinance (HMSO), which went on to become the model after which the California state regulations were patterned. The HMSO had two primary purposes: (1) to ensure the safe storage and onsite handling of hazardous materials and (2) to protect the quality of the underlying ground water. The ordinance requires soil sampling around all tanks to detect past leaks as well as periodic monitoring to detect future leaks at an early stage before major soil and/or ground water contamination can occur. Through the implementation of the HMSO, a number of new cases of solvent contamination have been discovered, along with numerous instances of petroleum product contamination.

Today, the Bay Regional Board is overseeing the investigation of over 125 ground water contamination cases. In addition, there are over 350 cases of petroleum product contamination uncovered so far that are receiving essentially no response at all because of a severe lack of staffing. As the remedial actions at the solvent contamination sites proceed the Bay Regional Board is rapidly approaching a most difficult set of decisions—that is, to what levels should contamination in the soil and ground water be reduced. These decisions are not only technically complex but are further complicated by economic, political, and value considerations introduced by a concerned public rightfully involved in the process. It is the purpose of this paper to consider these issues and how they are currently addressed in the existing regulatory framework. Portions of case studies are provided for examples, as appropriate.

REGULATORY AGENCY ROLES AND RESPONSIBILITIES

Because the roles and responsibilities of regulatory agencies may vary from state to state, a brief outline of the regulatory framework governing remedial actions for ground water contamination in Santa Clara County follows. This is by no means an exhaustive review but rather an attempt to describe succinctly those responsibilities that directly relate to the cleanup operations.

Regional Water Quality Control Board

There are nine regional boards in California with surface and ground water quality responsibilities covering the state's various surface drainage basins. Portions of Santa Clara County lie within the jurisdiction of boards in two different regions: the San Francisco Bay Region and the Central Coast Region. The regional boards have responsibility for the oversight of remedial actions, which includes issuing cleanup and abatement orders after the initial definition of the extent of the contamination, as well as issuing permits for the discharge of polluted or contaminated water to streams. The boards derive their authority from the state's 1969 Porter-Cologne Water Quality Control Act, which provides "that the statewide program for water quality can be most effectively administered regionally, within a framework of statewide coordination and policy." The State Water Resources Control Board, under whose policy guidance the regional boards operate, is the mechanism to provide the framework of "statewide coordination and policy."

California State Department of Health Services

The California State Department of Health Services (DHS) has some responsibilities that overlap those of the regional boards in the area of soil contamination. DHS is primarily concerned with the levels of contamination permissible in case of human contact with the soil. The regional boards' concern, on the other hand, is with the leaching of contaminants from the soil down to ground water.

DHS also has oversight responsibilities for the transportation of hazardous materials. Therefore, all removal of soil or other contaminated materials from a site is done under DHS-issued permits.

Finally, DHS administers a state Superfund program similar to the federal Superfund. One function of the state Superfund is to provide 10 percent matching funds to federal Superfund sites. In addition, it provides emergency cleanup for surface spills requiring immediate action, as well as funds for relatively small ground water contamination investigations.

Environmental Protection Agency

EPA administers the federal Superfund provided for in the Comprehensive Environmental Response, Compensation, and Liability Act (CERCLA). This fund provides for the ranking of sites on the National Priority List. Funds are subsequently encumbered for the cleanup of contamination at sites with no identifiable responsible party (so-called orphan sites) or at sites at which the responsible party fails to cooperate with the regional board in a timely manner. Such recalcitrant parties are usually prodded into action by the threat of EPA's expending funds for remedial actions that it will later recover from the responsible party through litigation.

The EPA has had another role in the ground water contamination in Santa Clara County through a special study called the Integrated Environmental Management Plan (IEMP). The purpose of the plan has been to evaluate public health risks from ground water contamination, along with risks from contamination in other media, to compare the relative risks and make recommendations on how best to minimize them in a cost-effective manner through better management practices. In the study, EPA addresses many of the same issues to be discussed in this paper.

REMEDIAL ACTION STRATEGIES

The primary goal of any remedial action is to enable the continued safe use of the ground water basin, both as an important source of water as well as an efficient mechanism for treatment, storage, and distribution of local and imported water recharged into the basin. With this in mind, two general approaches toward remedying ground water contamination can be presented: the active versus the passive approach.

Active Approach

The active approach, as used herein, refers to specific steps taken, first of all, to define the extent of a particular plume of contamination and then to proceed to effectively reduce levels of contamination while maintaining hydraulic control of the plume. Reducing the level of contamination can either be accomplished by some sort of in situ treatment technology or by removing the contaminated soil and/or water for treatment or disposal.

In situ treatment of soil can mean aeration of contaminated soil by injecting air into the ground to volatilize the contaminants. In situ treatment of ground water refers to the encouragement of biochemical degradation by creating a more favorable environment for the natural degradation processes to occur. Because these treatment technologies are in a more experimental state of development, the method of choice is, almost exclusively, the latter method noted in the previous paragraph: removal and treatment or disposal.

Generally, the grossly contaminated soil will be removed and disposed of in a Class I landfill. Contaminated ground waters are removed by extraction wells located in the center of the plume. The extracted water is then treated to acceptable levels and discharged to nearby streams. By hydraulically controlling the contamination, the extraction wells also prevent the plume from spreading further and threatening nearby drinking water wells. Another method of controlling the plume is to introduce a physical barrier at the contamination source—usually a bentonite slurry cutoff wall in the ground. This procedure is economically feasible only when extremely high concentrations are present in a relatively small area. The method will almost always be used in combination with extraction wells.

Passive Approach

The passive approach involves essentially allowing the plume of contamination to spread and dealing with it at the water extraction wells that are affected. The water from these wells is then treated to some technically feasible levels that are acceptable to the public, the ultimate consumers. Wellhead treatment includes either air stripping or activated carbon adsorption of contaminants—essentially the same procedure used in the active approach at wells within the plume.

Discussion

In considering these two approaches to ground water contamination, it is important to recognize first that, because of technical considerations, the solution will necessarily be some combination of both alternatives. That is, it is widely accepted that concentrations of contaminants in ground water cannot be reduced to zero or to nondetectable levels within any practicable amount of time. This is due to the reasonably well-documented physical processes that govern the movement of contamination in ground water. Therefore, with active cleanup measures, when an acceptable contaminant level is attained and the extraction wells cease pumping, the remaining "plume" can eventually migrate to nearby drinking water wells and result in some measure of low-level contamination.

As discussed earlier, however, this scenario is quite different from the passive approach in the extreme case, in which potentially high levels of contamination would be migrating to any nearby drinking water wells. There are many unknowns inherent in this approach that make it very difficult to evaluate, both technically and economically. Technical unknowns include the rate of movement of the plume, the number of wells that might ultimately be affected, and the concentration of contaminant that might be involved. Solute transport models have been used to attempt to predict these unknowns, but they are very often combined with a limited knowledge of important parameters. The resultant predictions, therefore, are subject to criticism or very often found to be of little value.

Economically, the cost of reducing relatively low levels of contamination to "acceptable" levels must be evaluated. It is well documented in the literature that techniques for the removal of volatile organic chemicals from water are less effective at lower concentrations. Therefore, the cost-effectiveness of treating much higher quantities of water at low levels of contamination suggests that the passive approach could potentially cost much more over the period of time that surrounding wells require treatment. More research is in progress in this area, specifically through the EPA IEMP study mentioned previously.

In addition to the such technical and economic considerations, there are other issues that must be weighed when considering the passive approach. First of all, some mechanism—a local "Superfund," if you will—would be necessary to reimburse the drinking water well owner who has been damaged, in a legal sense, by one or more incidents of contamination. Also, in our litigious society, it would seem naïve to think that this situation would not provoke a barrage of civil actions, not only from aggrieved well owners but from adjacent property owners as well, citing alleged effects on property values. Lawsuits of this nature could require costly hydrogeologic investigations to determine liability or relative liability in cases with more than one responsible party involved. Therefore, hidden costs could increase the total cleanup "cost to the nation" significantly.

Finally, there are social factors to consider; that is, what is the social value of being able to extract uncontaminated water from a generally pristine ground water basin, as presently exists in Santa Clara County? Will a public with keen awareness of the risks associated with the consumption of these toxic chemicals tolerate a policy allowing the degradation of what is considered to be an important local resource?

In contrast, the active approach when strictly applied prevents the migration of contaminants to nearby wells and helps ensure that the "owner" of the plume will continue to assume liability for the cleanup. It also results in a more efficient operation because it treats water with the highest concentrations of contaminants. Critics might argue that this approach results in a significant waste of water. Yet during periods of average to above average rainfall a major ground water basin can perhaps afford to "waste" the relatively small quantities of water required to effect the hydraulic control of a plume. Responsible parties are currently investigating the feasibility of treating and recharging extracted waters to reduce or eliminate such discharges to local streams and, ultimately, to San Francisco Bay.

This discussion has noted only the extremes of each approach and ignored various qualifying hydrogeologic factors. It has also disregarded the issue of what constitutes, in either case, an "acceptable" level of contamination. Whereas the "acceptable" level in the passive case might be the applicable drinking water standard, appropriate objectives for ground water cleanup are not as simple to define.

Case Studies

As mentioned earlier, there are over 125 cases of ground water contamination currently being investigated under Bay Regional Board oversight. Two of the cases that have been subject to intensive cleanup efforts are briefly described as examples of the active cleanup technology. A third case—one without an identifiable responsible party—is discussed as an example of a case in which a combination passive/active approach is appropriate, at least until the source of contamination can be identified.

IBM, San Jose

The IBM case, first reported in October 1980, is one of the earliest cases of contamination in Santa Clara County. It is located near the middle of the county in a part of the basin that is particularly sensitive because of the relatively coarse-grained geologic materials underlying the site. For this reason the general area is used extensively for artificial and natural recharge of the ground water basin. The primary contaminants include TCA, trichloroethylene (TCE), and freon 113, all of which have various associated adverse health effects.

IBM responded to the urgency of the situation in an exemplary fashion and to date has expended in the vicinity of $40 million on remedial actions at the site. The boundaries of the contamination plume have been defined to a point about 3 miles downgradient at which concentrations decrease to less than 10 ppb at a narrow geologic constriction. A few wells downgradient of that point have shown trace levels of 2 ppb but are essentially considered beyond the plume area, which measures about 3 miles long and a maximum of 400 feet in width.

The cleanup method being used—an active approach—is to create a situation of hydraulic ground water control by extracting contaminated water from wells located near the center of the flow-path to create a cone of depression toward which tainted water will flow. The plume is gradually decreasing in size and concentration as contaminated water is extracted.

The extracted water is treated either by passing it through activated carbon or by air stripping; it is then discharged to the nearby storm sewer. The Bay Regional Board was at first allowing the discharge of water with a contamination of 100 ppb, but recent evidence that the recharge of that water is causing contamination in a distant well has caused it to revise those requirements. Discharged water in areas of potential recharge now must be treated to a concentration of 1 ppb.

IBM is currently extracting water at the rate of about 10,000 acre-feet per year–about 7 percent of total ground water extraction countywide. The company has recently submitted, by request, a draft comprehensive plan, which addresses final cleanup objectives for the site. Because of concerns regarding the amount of water "wasted" to complete the cleanup, IBM has proposed treating to 1 ppb and delivering the treated water to district-operated recharge facilities.

Fairchild Camera & Instrument Corporation, San Jose

In 1981 Fairchild reported the loss of about 60,000 gallons of TCA and water, which resulted in the shutting down of a nearby water supply well contaminated at a level of 5,000 ppb TCA. The Fairchild site is located less than 2 miles southeast of the IBM site in the same sensitive area of the basin. Fairchild has displayed an equivalent level of effort in defining the boundaries of the plume of contamination and proceeding with interim cleanup efforts. The plume extends about 1 mile offsite with high-level contamination remaining in the soil and ground water directly underlying the property.

The cleanup approach has been similar to that of the IBM case in that hydraulic control has been maintained by means of strategically located extraction wells. Problems were encountered, however, when shallow aquifer materials became dewatered because of the rate of extraction from deeper aquifers. In order to flush the contaminated shallow aquifer soils, Fairchild reinjected treated water into wells perforated in the shallow zone.

This procedure eventually proved to be too time consuming, however, and the company subsequently proposed and implemented an additional measure to enhance the cleanup operation. A bentonite clay slurry wall has been installed around the perimeter of the property to encapsulate the onsite heavy contamination down to a natural clay layer at a depth of about 100 feet. Although the construction cost about $4 million, the company decided that the potential benefits justified the cost. The physical barrier allows Fairchild to extract water at a much lower rate within the containment to maintain an inward gradient at the walls of the containment. The offsite operation is also enhanced by ensuring that additional contamination will not migrate from the heavily contaminated area to continue "feeding" the plume. Fairchild will soon be submitting a comprehensive plan to propose final cleanup objectives for the site.

California Water Service Company Well, Los Altos

In 1982 it was discovered that a 400-foot-deep standby well owned by California Water Service Company (Cal Water), an area water purveyor, was tainted with carbon tetrachloride at a concentration of about 10 ppb. The source of the contamination to date is unknown. After consultation with the responsible regulatory agencies and public meetings with neighborhood residents, it was determined that the well water should be treated by air stripping at the wellhead. By spraying the water into a holding tank, concentrations have been effectively reduced to about 1–2 ppb.

Although the circumstances—the unknown contamination source—obviously create the need for a passive approach, there remains a concern about finding the source of contamination and defining the plume to protect other wells in the area that are more critical to the water supply. Based on existing and historical land use in the general vicinity, certain landowners are being asked to conduct relatively inexpensive soil gas surveys of their property to identify possible sources of contamination. In addition, DHS will be using the state Superfunds to investigate the area around the subject well by installing monitoring wells to begin defining the extent of the plume. As the investigation proceeds, the approach may be changed to one of active cleanup.

CLEANUP OBJECTIVES—HOW CLEAN?

When considering to what extent concentrations should be reduced in cases of ground water contamination, the regulatory agency has the unenviable task of balancing the cost of remedial actions against the public health risk associated with consumption of tainted drinking water. Even for those chemicals for which drinking water standards or action levels exist, the decision is not an easy one. There are many uncertainties associated with the standards that must be considered when applying drinking water criteria to ground water restoration activities.

Current Cleanup Policies

As noted previously, there are three agencies—the Regional Water Quality Control Board, DHS, and EPA—that have responsibility for the oversight of remedial action activities. Although each has a different methodology for addressing cleanup objectives, there are basically two schools of thought: (1) cleanup to predetermined standards or (2) cleanup to criteria based on an evaluation of site-specific circumstances. The predetermined standards approach simply requires the cleanup to proceed until concentrations in ground water are reduced to applicable drinking water standards or state "action levels."

In the case-by-case approach, which has been applied by the Bay Regional Board, cleanup to standards is considered a minimum level of effort. Beyond that the discharger is asked to prepare a report estimating the cost of three higher levels of effort: cleanup to action levels, cleanup to nondetectable levels, and cleanup to a third level at some intermediate point. The board then considers each case in a public forum to allow comments to be heard from all interested parties. The cost of each cleanup alternative is used as a guideline in deciding on overall cleanup objectives. Other factors, such as the underlying hydrogeology, the areal extent of contamination, and the proximity of drinking water wells, are used to evaluate the risk of contamination spreading to nearby wells or affecting significant portions of the underlying aquifer.

Discussion

When standards exist for the chemical contaminants in a particular case, the simplest approach, administratively, is to require cleanup to those standards. In sensitive regions of the basin, however, this approach may be inadequate to satisfy not only legislative mandate but also the concerns of the public who are ultimately affected.

The Bay Regional Board, in its strategy for establishing cleanup objectives, is attempting to incorporate all relevant information into its decisionmaking. In the hearing process, the state's nondegradation policy is used as a starting point for subsequent discussion. That policy requires the maintenance of preexisting water quality unless the board finds that, because of economic and technical considerations, some level of water quality degradation is "consistent with maximum benefit to the people of the state" and "will not unreasonably affect" beneficial uses. This policy is necessarily quite broad and leaves much interpretation to the board members. There are many important factors for their consideration in reviewing a case.

The location of the contamination is of primary importance. In Santa Clara County, there are widely varying hydrogeologic conditions that affect the way contamination can move once it is released into the ground water basin. The Bay muds, existing along the edge of San Francisco Bay, provide an example of a nearly complete natural containment; contamination at the surface would, for all practical purposes, never reach deeper aquifer materials used for water supply. Therefore, in that region of the basin, removing only the heavily contaminated soil may be acceptable. In the forebay zone of the basin, however—the area that recharges the deeper confined aquifers—much greater efforts are required. In that area, there are direct hydrogeologic connections between the surface soils and deeper aquifer materials, and the contamination of nearby wells is almost certain unless extensive extraction of contamination is mandated.

In addition to the relevant technical aspects of a case the public hearing process permits input from all concerned parties—the retail water agencies, the water district, and, most importantly, the public. The public in Santa Clara County and throughout California is very aware of and concerned with water quality issues. Statewide public opinion was strongly voiced by the overwhelming passage of a recent ballot proposition imposing, among other things, stringent notification requirements on any designated public official with knowledge of any potentially hazardous discharge to waters of the state. Clearly, the public is demanding accountability on the part of public officials and therefore should certainly be included in any decisions involving health considerations.

Retail water agencies are equally concerned in that local liability, with respect to serving unsafe water, must be taken seriously. In the wake of a recent multimillion-dollar lawsuit, at least one local water retailer has refused to pump ground water with *any* detectable level of organic chemicals.

Finally, the district, with management responsibility for the ground water basin, takes a very conservative view on cleanup requirements. One concern is that many of the chemical standards are based on a relatively short time span of data collection and research. As more is learned about the proven or potential effects of these chemicals, a gradual lowering of the standards can be expected. In that case, wellhead treatment may be required for what was once considered safe contaminant levels in ground water. Ultimately, the question of equity arises as to whether the resultant liability and costs are those of the public or of the responsible party. It would seem inequitable to require the public to bear the cost of such treatment when a responsible party was once assuming liability for the contamination.

CLEANUP COSTS—WHO IS RESPONSIBLE?

As experience in Santa Clara County has shown, the costs associated with remedial actions to remove ground water contamination can be staggering. In general, responsibility for most of the cases of organic solvent contamination in Santa Clara County is being assumed by the company involved in the illegal discharge. The ideal situation is one in which (1) a responsible party can be identified and (2) the identified responsible party has the resolve and financial means to undertake the necessary remedial actions. It has been fortunate that some of the largest incidents in the most sensitive areas of the ground water basin have been caused by large, responsive corporations. In general, they have cooperated with the regional board and proceeded with remedial actions in a timely manner. This is not an assured situation, however.

In an increasingly competitive business world, there are obviously strong economic disincentives for companies that have caused contamination to proceed in a timely manner or even to proceed at all with remedial actions. Furthermore, there are a growing number of cases being discovered in Santa Clara County for which the owner simply does not have the necessary financial means to remove the contamination. Most of these latter types of cases are small businesses storing motor fuels in underground tanks that have been found to be leaking. Other such contamination is caused by small businesses who illegally or negligently handle or dispose of toxic solvents. The threat to the public health from incidents such as these can be as serious as from those caused by larger companies with greater resources. Therefore, because cleanup of these incidents must proceed expeditiously, alternative funding sources must be available.

SUMMARY

The Santa Clara Valley Water District, as a wholesaler of water and the management agency of the ground water basin, has a responsibility to ensure that the basin remains usable as an important element of the water supply in Santa Clara County. As discussed earlier, recent contamination, primarily from leaking underground tanks, has threatened that vital resource. In response, regulatory activity in recent years has greatly reduced the possibility that future leaks might cause serious problems. The various regulatory agencies involved in cleaning up past contamination have sorted out their respective roles, and an effective working relationship has evolved.

Two approaches to remedial action have been discussed: the active versus the passive approach. Although only the extremes of these cases were discussed, various permutations are possible. The consensus of the affected parties—the public, the retailers, and this agency—has been that the passive approach is definitely not acceptable. Only when a situation arises in which the source of contamination is unknown has wellhead treatment been considered a feasible solution.

In their oversight responsibilities the regulatory agencies are faced with difficult decisions with respect to ultimate cleanup objectives. The Bay Regional Board, as a lead agency in cleanup oversight activities, has forged an effective policy for determining cleanup objectives. Its approach considers economic, technical, and public health risk factors in a process aimed at achieving a cost-effective cleanup that is safe and acceptable to the public.

Funding for the increasing number of contamination cases being discovered is a growing problem in Santa Clara County. Hundreds of fuel leaks have received little or no oversight due to understaffing in regulatory agencies. As a result, these cases are receiving an unknown level of cleanup effort from facility owners who may or may not have the technical and financial means to address these problems adequately.

CONCLUSIONS

This paper has attempted to outline the current situation and describe issues that have been faced and continue to be faced in Santa Clara County. Perhaps the primary conclusion reached by responsible agencies in this area is that an informed public input must continue to be an integral part of decisions affecting the public health and environment. Public education and involvement mechanisms must be incorporated into the process—not only to allow public input on decisions affecting human health but also to enlighten the public with regard to the difficult trade-offs surrounding environmental decisions. This kind of process will enable mutually acceptable solutions to be reached with much greater ease.

A final conclusion that becomes more evident as the technical realities of ground water contamination become more widely understood—not only by the regulatory community but also by the public at large—is that there is necessarily some degree of risk that simply must be accepted. Various preventative programs are now in place to drastically reduce the possibility of future incidents causing serious ground water contamination. Yet existing contamination caused by past handling and storage practices will be present for many years. The reality is that even if sufficient funds were available, it would prove technically impossible to remove all of the contaminants from the ground. The obvious result is that some trace level of contamination in the water supply in some areas may, unfortunately, be inevitable. Admittedly, the health risk associated with consuming tainted water may be minimal in comparison to other environmental risks with which we live. It continues to be important, however, to strive for ways to reduce those risks as much as is technically and economically feasible.

BIBLIOGRAPHY

California Department of Water Resources. 1975. Evaluation of Groundwater Resources: South San Francisco Bay, vol. 3. Sacramento. December.

California Regional Water Quality Control Board, San Francisco Bay Region. 1986. South Bay Site Management System Reports. Oakland, Calif. May.

Ford, J. 1978. The Story of the Santa Clara Valley Water District, San Jose, Calif.: Santa Clara Valley Water District.

Himmon, K., D. Schwartz, and E. Soffer. 1986. Santa Clara Valley Integrated Environmental Management Project, Revised State I Report. San Francisco, Calif.: Environmental Protection Agency. May.

Suffet, I. H., and M. J. McGuire. 1980. Activated Carbon Adsorption of Organics from the Aqueous Phase, vols. 1 and 2. Ann Arbor, Mich.: Ann Arbor Science Publishers, Inc.

TRS Consultants, Inc. 1984. South Bay Groundwater Contamination Task Force, Agency Coordination Project. San Francisco, Calif. December.

U.S. EPA. 1984. Groundwater and Drinking Water in Santa Clara Valley: A White Paper. San Francisco, Calif.

Provocateur's Comments
Norbert Dee

I would like to make some general comments about the paper and about other related issues. First, the paper is very good in discussing risk management and the hazardous waste management issues facing a water district. What we have learned over the last 5 years of RCRA and Superfund implementation is that not all ground water is equal. In addition, we have learned that we can make very costly and technical mistakes by going in with a shovel just to do something.

In the Superfund discussion earlier, the point was made that not all ground water is equal and that therefore, in making cleanup decisions, consideration must be given to the use, value, and vulnerability of ground water. This is a differential protection policy, which is not accepted by everyone. At present, EPA has a classification system based on differential protection that has been sent out for public review and comment. In the example discussed in the paper, $40 million was spent cleaning up a site. Should we do the same level of cleanup if the site had no effect on a public water supply? The Safe Drinking Water Amendments of 1986 also protect drinking water from contaminants that could affect human health by protecting the wellhead area. This is a form of differential protection.

Earlier, some arguments were made against the macro approach of classification and data collection and in favor of a micro approach. My response to that brings to mind an incident from *Alice in Wonderland*. Alice was walking down a path when she reached a fork. She asked the Cheshire Cat which way she ought to go. The cat responded by asking where she wanted to go, and when Alice said she didn't know the cat said, "Then it doesn't matter which way you go." We need to do better than Alice, and a macro policy can direct us. This, to some degree, has been the problem we have had over the last 5 years. If we focus our attention on priority areas based on classification, then we know which path we are taking and the issue of specific data will be answered by the implementation of the policy.

I would like to make a few more comments on the paper. Because I do not know the specifics of the Fairchild or the IBM sites, the question I pose may be unanswerable. The question is this: Would or should California have proceeded differently if the areas were not vulnerable, if they did not have an irreplaceable water supply, or if a public water supply had not been threatened? In other words, if the site had been in another location in California, would we have made or should we make the same decision? This is a risk management question.

Another point about the cleanup at the Fairchild site also concerns risk management. If the cleanup of the site requires air stripping and we are in a nonattainment area on volatiles, is this good management? In addition, the pump-and-treat method used in these site cleanups did not look at the depletion of the ground water resource by discharging the treated ground water to the San Francisco Bay. Again, are we looking at the full picture, managing our risk properly? This is the same question David Miller asked earlier. What are we trying to do?

The last point I would like to address is that the approach followed in the paper is differential protection and risk management. Yet the state has a nondegradation policy. How are these two compatible?

8
Using Models to Solve
Ground Water Quality Problems

JAMES M. DAVIDSON AND P. S. C. RAO

A comprehensive national survey to assess ground water contamination has not been undertaken to date; yet the contamination of portions of various aquifers in different states is well documented (Holden, 1986; Pye et al., 1983). The reason for this contamination, as well as the potential for further contamination, is rooted in the fact that nearly all facets of modern life (urban, industrial, agricultural, etc.) use and/or discard chemicals on a daily basis. Because of the ubiquity of man-made chemicals in our society, the potential for ground water contamination is real, and the problem is one of national, regional, state, and local interest. Not only are regulatory and policymaking agencies faced with monitoring the presence of ground water contaminants, but they are also responsible for developing policies that will prevent further contamination of this valuable and limited natural resource.

The use of mathematical models to simulate the behavior and movement of water and toxic chemicals in water-unsaturated and saturated porous media for ground water management is a controversial issue within the scientific community as well as among users of these models. Yet many of those responsible for ground water quality protection consider models to be the most pragmatic approach to a complex problem. To complicate the issue further, there is urgency in the problem facing regulatory and policy agencies and their need to respond in a manner that is environmentally and fiscally objective. Some of those developing models, as well as those who promote the use of models for ground water management, speak positively about their ability to accomplish this task.

This manuscript briefly discusses the general types of models that are available, their potential role in managing and protecting ground water, the concerns of those who use models for policy issues, and risk assessment. These topics are raised in hopes of helping the reader focus on and understand specific issues and alternatives and the need for a response to the problem of ground water protection.

MODELS FOR PREDICTING MOVEMENT AND FATE AND/OR RANKING RISK OF CHEMICALS IN GROUND WATER

There is no model that will adequately describe *all* ground water quality problems because the assumptions and simplifications generally associated with models do not adequately mimic all the processes that influence the movement and behavior of the water and/or the chemicals of interest. This is especially true for the chemical and biological processes that influence the movement and fate of chemicals in porous media. Although major advances have been made in recent years in our understanding of the behavior of chemicals in water-unsaturated and saturated porous media, research in this area is still in its infancy. This is especially true for those cases in which water-miscible organic solvents may enhance the mobility of selected organic chemicals, in which immiscible solvents exist, and in which chemical movement occurs in fractured rock and well-structured soils.

At least two distinct modeling approaches can be identified. In the first, models are needed to provide site-specific predictions of the behavior of a particular chemical. This approach requires the use of sophisticated mathematical models that explicitly accommodate site-specific characteristics (e.g., hydrogeology, soils, chemical loading) in sufficient detail so as to provide predictions about the spatial distribution of a chemical's concentration or flux, or both, in porous media. Thus, there are numerous input coefficients required for this type of model to function. An example of a situation in which such a model might be used is the prescription of remediation actions for a hazardous waste disposal site covered under the Comprehensive Environmental Response, Compensation, and Liability Act (CERCLA). Because of the large financial and technical resources generally available for remediation of a Superfund site and the fact that the problem is narrowly focused, one may be justified in using a large, complex model. Also, this application makes feasible the possibility of continued refinement and calibration of the model using site monitoring data.

In contrast, the second modeling approach seeks to establish regulatory policies that will prevent or minimize ground water contamination on a regional, state, or national level. For this case the use of a complex model is unrealistic, primarily because of the large quantity of input data that must be provided and the spatial variability of the area under consideration. Also, for these cases, one is generally more interested in evaluating the potential of a particular aquifer to become contaminated whether certain chemicals pose a greater threat than others to a ground water supply. For such applications (e.g., development of regulations and permitting policies), the simulation of a chemical's distribution over time in porous media may not be essential. Rather, it is the relative behavior of the chemical that is of interest. For such applications, simplifications of the more complex models may be adequate.

When considering which of the above modeling approaches are better suited to addressing a potential ground water contamination problem, three questions should be asked:

1. How likely is it that a particular aquifer (or a portion of an aquifer) may be contaminated? To answer this question, it is necessary to assess the *site vulnerability* of an aquifer to become contaminated.

2. Given the use patterns of chemicals and their physical, chemical, and biological properties, which chemicals are most likely to intrude ground water? This answer will require determining the *contamination potential* of a group of chemicals.

3. If a specific chemical or group of chemicals have already contaminated an aquifer, are the concentrations of sufficient magnitude to pose an adverse health risk? This question is answered after evaluating the *toxicological potency* of the chemical.

Aquifer vulnerability may be assessed on the basis of the physiographic setting and the hydrogeologic characteristics of a site. The contamination potential may be estimated from the chemodynamic properties of the chemicals of interest. Finally, toxicological potency may be determined by comparing the action level set by the Office of Safe Drinking Water with that measured or predicted through the use of a model. Various schemes for dealing with these three factors are reviewed in the paragraphs that follow.

Empirical approaches rather than simulation models are frequently used to rank a site's vulnerability or contamination potential. Aller et al. (1985) have proposed a numerical rating technique called DRASTIC for evaluating the likelihood of ground water contamination at a specific site, given the site's geohydrologic setting. The acronym for this rating technique is derived from the seven factors considered in the rating scheme: (1) *d*epth to ground water, (2) *r*echarge rate, (3) *a*quifer media, (4) *s*oil media, (5) *t*opography, (6) *i*mpact of vadose zone, and (7) *c*onductivity of the aquifer. A combination of weights and rating is assigned to each of these factors, and a numerical rating called the DRASTIC index is calculated for a site or area of interest. The DRASTIC scheme currently is being used to design and guide EPA's national survey for ground water contamination (Alexander et al., 1986).

The Arizona Department of Health Services (1982) and the Florida Department of Agriculture and Consumer Services (1986) have developed numerical rating schemes to establish lists of "priority pesticides" that pose a threat to ground water. The procedures are based on assigning numerical values to pesticide properties (solubility and persistence), the quantities of pesticides used in the state or local region, and the human health effects. Other approaches based on the numerical ratings of several factors have been proposed for evaluating the suitability of sites for land disposal of hazardous wastes and/or the application of contaminants to a site (Seller and Canter, 1980; Gibb et al., 1983; LeGrand, 1983; Michigan Department of Natural Resources, 1983; U.S. EPA, 1983). These ranking schemes, in the strictest sense, are not descriptive models.

Comprehensive mathematical models that include procedures for describing each process influencing the movement, sorption, degradation, and transformation of a specific chemical are more complex than ranking schemes. A primary question of concern in the use of complex simulation models is how chemical processes that occur at the interstitial level of porous media are represented on a field scale. Cherry et al. (1984) reviewed this subject for both organic and inorganic chemicals in ground water systems. Currently, there are insufficient field data available on the behavior of chemicals to test the available simulation models properly. Most information regarding processes has been collected under controlled laboratory conditions and, in general, under equilibrium or steady-state conditions. Thus, any attempted simulation encounters the problem of the reliability of extending laboratory-scale behavior to field conditions.

Of all the processes responsible for organic chemical attenuation within the unsaturated and saturated zones, only biologically mediated transformations may lead to complete degradation of organic chemicals. Although the capacity for microbial degradation in surface soils has been studied extensively, the characterization of microbial activity in the vadose zone and in aquifers has received considerable attention only recently. Given the oligotrophic conditions of the vadose zone and deep aquifers, these areas were believed not to support or sustain significant microbial populations. As evidence gradually accumulates to suggest that diverse and active microbial populations can survive and function in aquifers, it has been proposed that aquifers might have a certain "assimilatory capacity," that is, the ability to degrade chemicals to some acceptable concentration. Thus, the feasibility of biodegradation as an in situ aquifer restoration technique is currently being explored. Comprehensive process-level models are being formulated, but their validation and integration into larger ground water models are far from complete. We must also note that even through biodegradation the zero concentration of a contaminant is approached asymptotically. Thus, this technique may only be acceptable for noncarcinogenic chemicals and then only for those with a large maximum contaminant level (MCL) or maximum contaminant level goal (MCLG). As long as the legislative history of the Safe Drinking Water Act justifies zero concentrations for carcinogens in ground water, biodegradation as an in situ remediation technique may not be a viable alternative.

The foregoing discussion of simulation models raises some significant questions about their reliability for predicting and/or ranking site vulnerability or contamination potential. Given the seriousness of the problem and the risk to human health that is involved, Wagenet (1986) concluded the following:

> Our current understanding of the basic principles that determine pesticide fate in the field is incomplete, yet we must make decisions now considering pesticide regulation and management. Current pesticide models used by regulators and academics represent the best tools we have to estimate pesticide fate as a function of soil, climate and management factors. Yet, we have every indication

that their predictions are not universally reliable, and almost no proof of their credibility in the field. The question is whether we can feel comfortable about the predictions produced by these models, or whether we should abstain from their use as predictive tools until their credibility is better established. A healthy and continuing intellectual argument is in progress on this issue, and will probably persist for some time. During this debate, the use of existing models for regulatory and management purposes will continue, and will result in some good decisions, and probably some mistakes. Several points are clear. First, no pesticide model exists that has been proven to estimate consistently and accurately the spatial and temporal distribution of pesticide concentrations in the unsaturated zone. This is true regardless of the resolution used to represent basic principles in the model, and whether the model falls into the research or management category. Second, it follows that current models should be used only to compare the relative, not absolute, behavior of pesticides in field soils. Third, the first two points indicate that our approach to modeling pesticide fate in unsaturated field soils must change if we are to develop a new generation of pesticide models that do not suffer from the limitations of the current models. (pp. 339–340)

Although this statement pertains to mathematical models that describe the fate and transport of pesticides, it eloquently summarizes the issues pertinent to the application of simulation models for most organic pollutants.

Quality Control/Quality Assurance for Models

Before any model is used to describe or simulate the behavior of a chemical in porous media, its validity should be independently established by some individual or institution other than its developer. Code testing is generally considered to encompass verification and validation of the model (Adrion et al., 1982). To evaluate ground water models in a systematic and consistent manner, some institutions have developed model review, verification, and validation procedures (Morgan and Mezga, 1982; van der Heijde et al., 1985). Generally, the review process is qualitative in nature, whereas code testing results are evaluated by quantitative performance standards.

In April 1984, EPA Order 5360.1, "Policy and Program Requirements to Implement the Mandatory Quality Assurance Program," was issued and for the first time provided a regulatory basis for the agency's quality assurance program. Quality assurance is the procedural and operating structure required in model development to ensure technical execution of all aspects of the model. The primary goal of the EPA ground water modeling quality assurance program is to ensure that all modeling efforts supported by EPA are of a known and scientifically acceptable quality in terms of computer code, documentation, and operation.

Concerns of Those Using Water Quality Models

In a recent report by van der Heijde and Park (1986), the following concerns and needs were identified by national and regional EPA staff using water quality models:

- a limited knowledge of what types of water quality models are available;
- the need for assistance in selecting and using available models for specific sites;
- guidance in model reliability and interpretation of simulations;
- the need for additional models for multiphase flow and contaminant behavior in the vadose zone;
- improved interaction and communication with technical staff located in other regional offices, headquarters, and EPA laboratories;
- training in basic processes (e.g., geology, hydrology, fate and transport, geochemistry) for the project officers as well as modeling training for technical experts in the region; and
- the hiring and retention of technical staff who have received special training in modeling.

Role of Ground Water Quality Models
in Regulatory or Policy Issues

A policy for resource protection based on monitoring is by nature reactive, not preventive. Policies and regulations based on models, however, can be both preventive and reactive. A discussion of some of the principal areas in which mathematical models can and are being used to assist in managing EPA state and/or local government ground water protection programs follows.

Development of Regulations and Policy

Evaluation of the impacts (economic, health risk, etc.) of regulations on policy scenarios requires process-oriented generic models. Some specific uses of such models in the evaluation of existing or proposed policies and regulations include: (1) developing standards for well setbacks with respect to pesticide applications and waste disposal sites, (2) evaluating the potential impact of various types of "failures" of injection wells, (3) providing technical justification for restricting land disposal of hazardous wastes at specific sites, and (4) evaluating the need and effectiveness of ground water monitoring programs for hazardous waste injection wells.

Permitting

Ground water models are being used on a site-specific basis by owners/operators of hazardous waste facilities to show compliance with permit requirements; they are being used by regulatory agencies to validate information provided for permitting purposes. Models are also being used to evaluate hazardous waste site characteristics to determine the optimal locations for monitoring wells, to estimate the transport and fate of contaminants below a waste disposal site, and to assess corrective action should a failure occur.

EPA's Office of Waste Programs Enforcement (OWPE) is currently using models to evaluate the following source types: sanitary landfills; municipal, industrial, and mining surface impoundments; underground storage tanks; septic tanks; agricultural feedlots; road de-icing chemicals; hazardous waste landfills; and hazardous waste surface impoundments. OWPE is also investigating the use of ground water modeling for fund-financed CERCLA actions, with an emphasis on using simple, desktop fate and transport calculations to predict leaching to ground water from residual soils at Superfund sites.

EPA's Office of Pesticide Programs (OPP) is using models to assess the leaching potential of registered pesticides as well as to evaluate new pesticides prior to registration. Past and present modeling efforts have focused on predicting whether various pesticides are likely to leach to ground water under normal usage. This focus results from the fact that pesticides are considered a nonpoint loading problem by OPP as opposed to a point source (usually the case for other EPA program offices).

Remedial Action

Ground water models are being used increasingly in the CERCLA response process for remediation of the potential release of hazardous substances. A typical model application for a Superfund-financed or enforcement-related remedial response action includes both site investigation to assist in problem definition and system conceptualization to identify the contamination source and to predict future contamination and health risk. Models are also being used to develop and evaluate remedial alternatives during the remedial investigation/feasibility study stages and to analyze design specifications for remedial action alternatives. In addition, models are frequently being used to assess required cleanup levels, set the level of required source removal, and project performance characteristics for remedial action design as well as formulate postoperation and closure requirements.

Risk Assessment

Risk to human health and the environment owing to the presence of trace concentrations of toxic chemicals in ground water used for domestic purposes is a matter of major concern to modern society. However, the detection of a hazardous chemical in ground water is not necessarily a cause for immediate alarm. Modern chemical detection techniques are so sensitive that it is possible to detect concentrations at levels below federal or state action levels (MCLs or MCLGs). In fact, chemical detection techniques are constantly improving, causing detection levels to be pushed lower and lower. For chemicals that pose acute toxicity problems, the no observable adverse effect level (NOAEL) may be established; for chemicals that induce chronic effects, however, NOAEL values are less well defined and generally contain a safety factor of two to three orders of magnitude. Thus, concentrations like these that induce chronic effects may be quite low, and at times they may fall below current analytical detection levels. For those chemicals that have been shown to be carcinogenic, there is no acceptable concentration level; however, an exposure risk may be calculated using various exposure models.

SUMMARY AND CONCLUSIONS

Mathematical models for describing the fate and transport of chemicals in porous media and numerical ranking schemes for assessing site vulnerability and contamination potential, although not satisfactorily validated to date, appear to have a guarded role in policymaking, the development of environmental regulations, and the establishment of remedial actions for regulatory agencies responsible for ground water. The models should not, however, be used without some monitoring effort for the purpose of validation and/or calibration. The extent to which such efforts are conducted will depend on the purpose of the model as well as the areal extent to which the model is expected to be representative. The alternative to modeling is one of reaction through an extensive soil and ground water monitoring program, a position that is not realistic if pristine ground water conditions are the anticipated goal. The release of a chemical to the soil surface will eventually result in some portion of it reaching the ground water, be it a large concentration or a very low concentration. Such attenuation results from degradation, sorption, and volatilization. Complete chemical containment or stabilization is the only waste disposal procedure currently available that provides ground water protection; yet even these procedures are subject to engineering failures.

REFERENCES

Adrion, W. R., M. A. Branstad, and J. C. Cherniasky. 1982. Validation, verification and testing of computer software. ACM Computing Surveys 14:159–192.

Alexander, W. J., S. K. Liddle, R. E. Mason, and W. B. Yeager. 1986. Groundwater Vulnerability Assessment in Support of the First Stage of the National Pesticide Survey. Washington, D.C.: EPA.

Aller, L., T. Bennett, J. Lehr, and R. Petty. 1985. DRASTIC: A Standardized System for Evaluating Groundwater Pollution Potential Using Hydrogeologic Settings. Washington, D.C.: EPA Office of Research and Development.

Arizona Department of Health Services. 1982. Pesticides with groundwater pollution potential in Arizona. Prepared by Rich and Associates, Phoenix, Arizona.

Cherry, J. A., R. W. Gillham, and J. F. Barker. 1984. Contaminants in Groundwater: Chemical Processes. Pp. 46–64 in Groundwater Contamination, J. D. Bredehoeft, panel chairman. Washington, D.C.: National Academy Press.

Florida Department of Agriculture and Consumer Services. 1986. Pesticide assessment procedure: An assessment procedure based on pesticide and hydrogeologic factors developed for selective pesticide monitoring of groundwater in Florida. Prepared by the Pesticide Review Council. November.

Gibb, J. P., M. J. Barcelona, S. C. Schock, and M. W. Hampton. 1983. Hazardous Waste in Ogle and Winnebago Counties: Potential Risk Via Ground Water Due to Past and Present Activities. Document No. 83/26. Illinois Department of Energy and Natural Resources.

Holden, P. W. 1986. Pesticides and Groundwater Quality: Issues and Problems in Four States. Washington, D.C.: National Academy Press.

LeGrand, H. E. 1983. A standardized system for evaluating waste-disposal sites. National Water Well Association, Worthington, Ohio.

Michigan Department of Natural Resources. 1983. Site assessment (SAS) for the Michigan priority ranking system under the Michigan Environmental Response Act. Ann Arbor.

Morgan, M. S., and L. J. Mezga. 1982. Evaluation factors for verification and validation of low-level waste disposal site models. DOC/OR/21400-T119. Oak Ridge, Tenn.: Oak Ridge National Laboratory.

Pye, V. I., R. Patrick, and J. Quarels. 1983. Groundwater Contamination in the United States. Philadelphia: University of Pennsylvania Press.

Seller, L. E., and L. W. Canter. 1980. Summary of selected groundwater quality impact assessment models. Report No. NCGWR 80-3. National Center for Ground Water Quality Research, Norman, Oklahoma.

U.S. EPA. 1983. Surface Impoundment Assessment National Report. EPA-570/9-84-002. Washington, D.C.

Van der Heijde, P. K. M., P. S. Huyakorn, and J. W. Mercer. 1985. Testing and validation of groundwater models. In: Practical Applications of Groundwater Modeling. Proceedings of the NWWA/IGWMC Conference, Columbus, Ohio, August 19–20.

Van der Heijde, P. K. M., and R. A. Park. 1986. U.S.E.P.A. ground-water modeling policy study group: Report of findings and discussion of selected ground-water modeling issues. International Ground Water Modeling Center, Holcomb Research Institute, Butler University, Indianapolis, Indiana.

Wagenet, R. J. 1986. Principles of modeling pesticide movement in the unsaturated zone. Pp. 330–341 in Evaluation of Pesticides in Groundwater, ed. W. Y. Garner et al. Symposium Series 315. Washington, D.C.: American Chemical Society.

PROVOCATEUR'S COMMENTS
Ishwar P. Murarka

I have known Jim for a while. Some of my comments are motivated by that. The rest are motivated by the paper itself. Let me make several comments to raise underlying questions for models, modelers, and model users. I really think the problem is that of predicting or assessing ground water quality and not quantity. So can ground water quality problems be addressed by models? To answer this question, we need to address the following: (1) Who are the users of these models? (2) Who expects what from models' and those uses? (3) How good should the models' performance be?

Let me interject here that ground water quality problems are not going to be solved by models. Liabilities are not going to be assigned by models. What models will do is provide some skills and analyses and some answers to "what if" questions that can be used for discussion regarding the nature and extent of ground water quality problems. If a model is incomplete, the corresponding uncertainties will be reflected in its predictions, and the discussions will have to recognize that. If the models are complete but the users do not know how to use them, then the ground water quality problems are neither defined nor solved.

The next issue raised by the paper is that of discarding materials that contain chemicals. Is the question one of discarding or not discarding, or is the real question one of proper or improper management of the discarded materials? These distinctions have different implications for ground water quality problems and the use of models. Models used to simulate ground water contamination for improperly disposed wastes will give a very different answer than when the same models are used to simulate ground water quality changes that result from a well-managed disposal facility.

The issue is not one of using models or not using models but rather the accuracy, precision, and reliability of models. Contributing to the problem is a lack of objective performance requirements for models and model users. Is the problem the accuracy/completeness of the models, or is the issue that of availability of data to use models? I will be brave here and state that I can predict with and without models. But why should you or I believe any one of my predictions and for what use? This is the area in which the importance of models, modelers, and model users cannot be overemphasized. If we want proper answers to our questions, we must ask those questions clearly and make known a priori the degree of confidence we require in those answers.

Let me conclude my comments by stating that models are also used for summarizing and organizing data. Indeed, models are nothing more than mathematical descriptions used by those who know how to use them. These same models, however, are also available for use by those who do not quite know how to use them. As a result, we develop perceptions or labels such as toxic substances or hazardous materials. Scientifically though, I have to leave you with this question: Are we all of a sudden concerned about a "toxic or hazardous" chemical or is the concern really that of "quantities" of a chemical that causes adverse and unacceptable biological effects?

9
Estimating Health Risks at Hazardous Waste Sites: Decisions and Choices Despite Uncertainty

ROBERT G. TARDIFF AND MICHAEL GOUGH

The purpose of this paper is to discuss the approaches currently being used to estimate the risks posed by hazardous waste sites. We present some of the complex characteristics of waste sites, a synopsis of risk assessment methodology, and a summary of several examples of comprehensive quantitative risk estimations. Finally, we discuss some of the inherent uncertainties in risk assessments—and somes means of dealing with them—to reach conclusions usable in risk management.

BACKGROUND

By definition, hazardous waste sites contain a myriad of substances, the composition of which is known to varying extents at each site. Because most sites offer incomplete containment, the substances escape at differing rates into surface and ground water and into air. (This situation is particularly true for those facilities constructed without the benefit of state-of-the-art containment technology, as is the case for virtually all sites identified by EPA for remediation under the Comprehensive Environmental Response, Compensation, and Liability Act.) Such dynamic processes can expose humans in a number of ways. For example, at a single site, workers might for several months of their lives inhale highly volatile compounds and experience skin contact with substances bound to dust; by contrast, nearby residents might ingest for many decades contaminants that had migrated from the site to the water in their wells.

Waste substances are absorbed into the body at different efficiencies through the skin, gastrointestinal tract, and respiratory system. They vary greatly in their toxic properties—for example, some can cause cancer, others birth defects, injury to neural functions, and a panoply of damage throughout the body. Their toxic potencies also vary considerably under differing and identical conditions of exposure. Often other characteristics, such as flammability and explosivity, also contribute to the complexity of the chemical makeup and the evaluation of risks to humans.

ASSESSMENT OF RISKS TO HUMAN HEALTH

Regardless of the details of the situation at any site, the four steps of risk assessment (as described originally by a committee of the National Research Council, 1983) provide an orderly means for analyzing scientific information, identifying critical data, elucidating uncertainties, and comparing estimates of risk and safety (i.e., acceptable risk). Briefly, the four steps are hazard identification, dose-response assessment, exposure assessment, and risk characterization, the definitions of which are provided in the National Research Council report and further elaborated in a publication by the ENVIRON corporation (1986).

In practice, risk assessments are usefully divided into those done for substances that cause cancer and mutations and those done for all other toxic effects. The underlying premise for such a distinction is that the essential molecular step in mutation and at least some forms of cancer is an irreversible change in the DNA that is passed on to subsequent generations of cells. A single interaction, therefore, is sufficient to cause a mutation or to initiate cancer. For other forms of toxicity a critical concentration or "threshold" of a toxicant is needed, occasionally for a substantial period, before functional damage occurs, and such damage is generally repaired on cessation of exposure.

A consequence of this distinction is that any exposure, no matter how small, to carcinogens (at least, to "initiators") and mutagens is associated with a probability of injury. By contrast, for other toxicants, there are definable levels of exposure above which injury (whether mild or severe will depend on the magnitude of the dose) can occur and below which no harm is expected; these are called reference doses (RfD) or acceptable daily intakes (ADI).

Historically, risk assessments have been applied largely to single substances, but the need for comprehensive evaluations of complex exposure from operations such as manufacturing facilities and waste sites has spurred the development of methods for assessing risks from mixtures. The assessment of mixtures is usually complicated by data on constituents that vary enormously in quality and magnitude.

In practice, assessing the risks of exposures to mixtures has been approached in one of three ways: (1) relative potency, (2) toxicity/carcinogenicity equivalency, and (3) comparative toxicity. For carcinogens, unit cancer risk (UCR) values are derived by considering the data generated from standard tests and applying standardized extrapolation techniques (U.S. EPA, 1985). The results permit consistent comparisons (i.e., relative potency) between individual carcinogens to help in deciding on the allocation of resources for controls. They are particularly useful in providing convincing evidence for setting priorities to maximize public health benefits through intervention. To deal with mixtures of carcinogens, EPA (1986) proposed guidelines by which to amalgamate cancer risks. Primarily, the guidelines call for the use of an additivity model, and they make provisions for dealing with synergism should data indicate its existence among groups of carcinogens at waste sites.

Gold et al. (1984) reviewed the world literature on animal testing of carcinogens and for each of 770 chemicals calculated the dose necessary to cause cancer in half of a group of exposed animals. The potency of those carcinogens varied by approximately eight orders of magnitude. Figure 9-1 scales the animal carcinogens from the most potent (2,3,7,8-tetrachlorodibenzo-p-dioxin, or TCDD) to the least potent (FD&C Green No. 1).

Because of the enormity of the expense in obtaining cancer bioassay data, only a small fraction of the compounds in commerce has been subjected to such experimental scrutiny. Consequently, the toxicologic data base for numerous substances at waste sites is grossly deficient for risk estimation purposes. To remedy that deficiency, toxicity/carcinogenicity equivalence schemes have been devised for substances that cause (or are presumed to cause) the same type of toxic injury (e.g., cancer, liver damage, central nervous system disability). The schemes are based largely on the

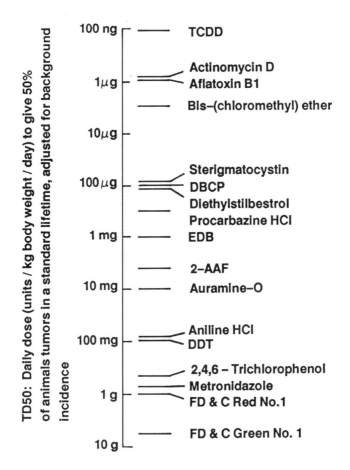

FIGURE 9-1   Range of carcinogenic potency in male rats.

proposition that chemicals of like structure cause similar types of injury but have different potencies. Such analytic judgments are more commonly referred to as structure-activity relationships. An example is an EPA scheme to compute the carcinogenic potency (i.e., the toxicity equivalence factors) of 75 chlorinated dioxins and 135 chlorinated furans in the absence of cancer test data for most of the congeners (Bellin and Barnes, 1986). A similar scheme is currently under development for the class of polynuclear aromatic hydrocarbons (PAHs or PNAs). Such schemes afford the opportunity to achieve a collective estimate of cancer risks without ignoring biologic reality about differences in potency.

TABLE 9-1 Chronic Toxicity Scoring

Unit Cancer Risk (mg/kg/day)$^{-1}$	ADIs for Non-carcinogens (mg/kg/day)$^{-1}$	Chronic Score
$> 10^2$	$< 10^{-7}$	9
$< 10^2$-10	$> 10^{-7}$-10^{-6}	8
< 10-1	$> 10^{-6}$-10^{-5}	7
< 1-10^{-1}	$> 10^{-5}$-10^{-4}	6
$< 10^{-1}$-10^{-2}	$> 10^{-4}$-10^{-3}	5
$< 10^{-2}$-10^{-3}	$> 10^{-3}$-10^{-2}	4
$< 10^{-3}$-10^{-4}	$> 10^{-2}$-10^{-1}	3
$< 10^{-4}$-10^{-5}	$> 10^{-1}$-1	2
$< 10^{-5}$	> 1	1

[a]Exposure at the acceptable daily intake (ADI) level is assumed to be associated with a 10^{-5} risk of a toxic effect; ADIs for carcinogens are doses associated with a 10^{-5} risk of cancer.

For noncancer toxicity the potencies of substances damaging the same target organ are combined for the same degree of injury, and a determination of the appropriate margin of safety is then made for the group. The final step is to amalgamate the conclusions about the risks from noncarcinogens with those for carcinogens. A procedure to convert ADIs and UCRs to a comparable scale has been developed for this purpose. ADIs are calculated to cause no risk, and UCRs assume that there is some risk at all doses. To make a common scale, ADIs are assigned a finite risk (10^{-5} is suggested). As shown in Table 9-1, the ADI and UCR of a substance can be compared to select a single chronic toxicity score.

EXPOSURE CONSIDERATIONS

Hazardous substances can escape from waste sites as vapors or fumes, dissolved in water, or attached to dust particles and carried by wind and water. Vapors, fumes, and particulates can be inhaled; some chemicals carried by dirt can be absorbed through the skin; particulates can be ingested; and contaminants can elute into drinking water.

An additional route of exposure results from chemicals entering the food chain. Examples of this exposure route include incorporation into plants eaten directly by humans and those consumed by food-producing animals such as fish. Fish are a particularly serious concern because they bioconcentrate highly lipid-soluble substances present in their aqueous environment.

Water in the vicinity of waste sites is another grave concern. The United States has many ground water reservoirs that are ideally situated to receive liquid wastes deposited in unlined cavities. In the worst of situations, such wastes are actually buried beneath the water table, where solubilization and distribution are greatly enhanced. Once distributed in ground water, pollutants often biodegrade extremely slowly, if at all, because of anaerobic conditions; and they may remain in the aquifer for geologic time because of the extreme difficulty of their removal. Such wastes are also known to migrate to surface waters where they are subject to the same natural forces as other industrial substances present in streams.

Human exposure to water-borne wastes can occur by ingestion (direct and during food preparation), inhalation (e.g., while showering), and dermal contact (e.g., while bathing). For water that is extracted directly for human use without benefit of treatment, exposure is to the wastes themselves or their degradation products (e.g., vinyl chloride is at times a product of trichloroethylene metabolism by soil microorganisms). Where water is drawn by a community utility for treatment and distribution, exposure is more difficult to determine or estimate because of competing influences. First, the filtration system is likely to remove, to varying degrees of effectiveness, substances absorbed to particulate matter, thereby reducing exposure to waste substances. Second, the oxidizing processes (e.g., chlorination for disinfection) will probably change the chemical character of the pollutants, in some cases to more toxic halogenated products.

The assessment of human exposure to the diverse substances likely to emanate from a hazardous waste site is a highly complex and sometimes speculative enterprise. All too often the characterization of risks is more dependent on exposure assessment than on knowledge of the type and quality of the hazard data.

ILLUSTRATIONS OF RISK ASSESSMENTS
AT HAZARDOUS WASTE SITES

ENVIRON has been involved in assessing risks and providing information from those assessments to decisionmakers concerned with many different types of waste sites. Five of those sites, depicting widely differing circumstances, are described briefly in the paragraphs that follow. These illustrations indicate site complexity as well as the diversity of bases for public health concern. At some sites, for example, inhalation and dermal contact are the most important routes of exposure; at others, fish and water are much more significant.

Manufactured Gas Sites

Before the widespread availability of natural gas after World War II, public utilities manufactured "town gas" from coal or oil by a process known as gasification. During their decades of operations, gasification sites produced many PAHs, phenols, and aliphatic compounds as by-products; several inorganic chemicals from the coal or oil were also deposited in the soil around the plants.

For its risk analysis, ENVIRON sifted through lists of all the chemicals found at gasifier sites on the bases of toxicity, likelihood of exposure, and regulatory status. Substances such as cyanide, which is lethal at low concentrations, and carcinogens were ranked high on the basis of toxicity. Substances that are present in high concentrations and that are likely to migrate from the site were scored high on the basis of likelihood of exposure. The third factor reflected governmental concerns about hazardous substances and the need for risk assessors to devote some attention to those chemicals singled out for public concern. The sifting produced a list of 30 chemicals. Thirty is a manageable number; the complete list of chemicals was too large.

Along with the identification of the 30 substances, we made a detailed examination of nine former gasifier sites. Information was collected about the presence of ground and surface water, about whether the site was paved or bare soil, and about nearby activities. (A nearby school or residential area is of more concern than a sparsely populated industrial area.) In addition, the types of wastes were characterized as liquid (tar), buried wastes, and surface wastes.

Models of air, water, and dust transport of the wastes were used to make estimates of exposure. In general, inhalation and skin absorption appeared to be the most important exposure routes at the sites. Combined with information about toxicity, those exposure estimates were used to calculate various health risks (Table 9-2).

As benchmarks, the levels of exposure to the 16 PAHs and 14 other chemicals from the sites will be compared to "background" levels of exposure to the same chemicals from all other sources. Because the 30 chemicals are ubiquitous, these comparisons will provide information about how much additional risk may be associated with the former gasifier plants. The intensity of remediation efforts will probably depend, in part, on whether exposure from the gasifier sites constitutes a large or small fraction of background exposures.

The Hyde Park Landfill

Love Canal is probably the most notorious waste site in the world. It is, in fact, only one of four large sites formerly used for the disposal of industrial chemical wastes in the Niagara Falls, New York, area. Another of the four, the Hyde Park landfill, contains between 0.5 and 1.5 tons of TCDD, more than at any other site in the world. In addition, the Hyde Park landfill contains tons of chlorinated organic compounds, pesticides, and pesticide by-products.

The levels of possible exposures of nearby residents were estimated under two different circumstances: (1) improving containment and collecting and destroying leachate from the site and (2) excavation and removal of the contents of the landfill. Our analysis showed that risks from vapors and dusts during an excavation would far outweigh risks from improved containment. EPA and New York State accepted the analysis and its conclusions and selected containment as the better management choice.

Another significant route of exposure is through the migration of leachate to surrounding waters and the bioconcentration of chemicals in fish. In the case of the landfill, this route is made more important because fish consumption around Niagara Falls is higher than the national average and because the concentration of TCDD in fish is 5,000-fold the concentration of the chemical in water. Yet little is known directly about the chemical's concentration near

TABLE 9-2 Cancer Potencies and Acceptable Daily Intakes
(ADIs) for Gasifier Wastes

Chemical	Cancer Potency $(mg/kg/day)^{-1}$		ADI $(mg/kg/day)^{-1}$
	Inhalation	Ingestion	
Noncarcinogenic PAHs			
Acenaphthene			0.10
Acenaphthylene			0.02
Anthracene			0.0006
Fluoranthene			0.02
Fluorene			NA[a]
Naphthalene			0.005
Phenanthrene			0.007
Pyrene			0.06
Carcinogenic PAHs			
Benzo(a)anthracene			
Benzo(a)pyrene	6.10	11.5	
Benzo(b)fluoranthene			
Benzo(k)fluoranthene			
Benzo(ghi)perylene			
Chrysene			
Dibenzo(a,h)anthracene			
Indeno(1,2,3-cd)pyrene			
Volatile Inorganics			
Benzene	0.026	0.0445	
1,2-Cresol			0.11
1,4-Cresol			0.11
Ethylbenzene			0.10
n-Hexane			0.29
Phenol			0.01
Toluene			0.42
Xylenes			1.00
Inorganics			
Arsenic	50.0	15.0	
Cadmium	7.8		
Chromium	41.0		0.003[b]
Cyanide			0.15[c]
Lead			0.02

[a] No suitable data available.
[b] ADI for total inorganic Cr, adjusted to account for other routes of
exposure.
[c] Adjusted to account for other routes of exposure.

NOTE: PAH = polynuclear aromatic hydrocarbon.

the landfill. These uncertainties have led the company responsible for the landfill, along with EPA and New York State, to fund a study about the amount of dioxin in local fish. Table 9-3 presents illustrative risk estimates for several routes of exposure, including fish consumption.

In summary, at this site, TCDD was present in large amounts, and consideration of its toxicity and the potential exposures to it drove the risk assessment. Yet risks from other compounds are also being considered, despite the predominance of concern about dioxin; a monitoring program will analyze air and water from the Hyde Park landfill to detect possible contamination from other chemicals. This detection effort should be easier, given that the other contaminants are more mobile and are present in larger amounts.

Widespread Ground Water Contamination

This example involves a chemical company that manufactures several hundred different products: dyes, epoxy resins, specialty chemicals, plastics, and others. At various times in the past, wastes were disposed onsite in a sludge disposal area, an unlined landfill, in various lagoons and basins, and in the process areas of the plant. A plume of volatile organic chemicals and base/neutral extractable compounds that is about 380 acres in area is now present in the ground water near the plant.

The flow of the plume was analyzed, and it was found that it endangers no currently used drinking water wells. The plant owner offered to seal irrigation wells that contained chemicals in excess of drinking water standards; now only a single well, which is used for lawn irrigation, is active. Those findings and actions eliminated most of the concerns about ingestion but not all of them: some ground water seeps into recreational marshlands and into a recreational river. In both those cases the expected chemical contamination was analyzed, and it was determined that, although contamination was widespread, it was at low levels. No chemical on EPA's list of priority pollutants was present above the detection limit. ENVIRON analyzed possible exposures through ingestion of and skin contact with contaminated water and soil, as well as through inhalation of volatile organic chemicals. The estimated upper bound to risks for cancer following lifetime exposure in the

TABLE 9-3 Examples of Risk Estimates Derived for Select Exposure Scenarios
Related to the Hyde Park Landfill

Compound	Fish Ingestion Carcinogen (mg/kg)	Fish Ingestion Noncarcinogen (mg/kg)	Inhalation (High) Carcinogen (mg/m³)
	RISK*	MDD/ADI	RISK*
1. Acenaphthene	NA	NA	NA
2. Acenaphthylene	NA	NA	NA
3. Aldrin	NA	NA	NA
4. Anisole (methyl phenyl ether)	NA	3.17E-07	NA
5. Anthracene	NA	NA	NA
6. benzo(a)-Anthracene	NA	NA	NA
7. dibenzo(a,h)-Anthracene	NA	NA	NA
8. Arsenic	NA	NA	1.17E-18
9. Benzene	7.34E-13	NA	9.81E-10
10. Benzidine	9.36E-11	NA	1.55E-06
11. Benzochlorodifluoride	NA	NA	NA
12. 2,3-Benzofuran	NA	NA	NA
13. Benzoic acid	NA	1.12E-07	NA
14. Bromobenzene	NA	NA	NA
15. Bromodichloromethane	NA	NA	NA
16. p-Bromofluorobenzene	NA	NA	NA
17. Bromoform	NA	NA	NA
18. Bromomethane	NA	NA	NA
19. 4-Bromophenyl phenyl ether	NA	NA	NA
20. n-Butylbenzene	NA	NA	NA
21. sec-Butylbenzene	NA	NA	NA
22. tert-Butylbenzene	NA	NA	NA
23. Butyl benzoate	NA	1.34E-07	NA
24. Butyl benzyl phthalate	NA	NA	NA
25. di-n-butyl phthalate	NA	7.59E-09	NA
26. Carbon tetrachloride	5.46E-14	NA	4.21E-11
27. Chlorendic acid	3.44E-09	3.19E-04	2.72E-17
28. Chlorobenzene	NA	1.06E-06	NA
29. m-Chlorobenzoic acid	NA	3.42E-07	NA
30. o-Chlorobenzoic acid	NA	NA	NA
31. p-Chlorobenzoic acid	NA	NA	NA
32. m-Chlorobenzotrifluoride	NA	NA	NA
33. o-Chlorobenzotrifluoride	NA	NA	NA
34. p-Chlorobenzotrifluoride	NA	2.07E-07	NA
35. 1-Chlorocyclohexene	NA	NA	NA
36. Chloroethane	NA	1.17E-11	NA
37. bis(2-Chloroethoxy) methane	NA	NA	NA
38. bis(2-Chloroethyl) ether	NA	NA	NA
39. 2-Chloroethylvinyl ether	NA	NA	NA
40. Chloroform	1.13E-12	NA	3.25E-09
41. Chloromethane	NA	1.16E-11	NA
42. 4-Chloro-3-methyl phenol	NA	NA	NA
43. 2-Chloronaphthalene	NA	NA	NA
44. 2-Chlorophenol	NA	2.91E-08	NA
45. m-Chlorotoluene	NA	2.90E-10	NA
46. o-Chlorotoluene	NA	7.71E-08	NA
47. p-Chlorotoluene	NA	3.97E-08	NA
48. o/p-Chlorotoluene	NA	NA	NA
49. Chrysene	NA	NA	NA
50. Cumene	NA	NA	NA
51. Cyclopropylbenzene	NA	NA	NA
52. p-Cymene	NA	NA	NA
53. p,p-DDD	NA	NA	NA
54. p,p-DDE	NA	NA	NA
55. p,p-DDT	NA	NA	NA
56. Dibromochloromethane	NA	NA	NA
57. m-Dichlorobenzene	NA	1.66E-08	NA

	Inhalation (High) Noncarcinogen (mg/m^3)	Inhalation (Lower) Carcinogen (mg/m^3)	Inhalation (Lower) Noncarcinogen (mg/m^3)	Dermal (Water) Carcinogen (mg/kg)	Dermal (Water) Noncarcinogen (mg/kg)
	MDD/ADI	RISK*	MDD/ADI	RISK*	MDD/ADI
1.	NA	NA	NA	NA	NA
2.	NA	NA	NA	NA	NA
3.	NA	NA	NA	1.93E-12	NA
4.	7.51E-05	NA	2.96E-06	NA	8.39E-07
5.	NA	NA	NA	NA	NA
6.	NA	NA	NA	NA	NA
7.	NA	NA	NA	NA	NA
8.	NA	1.32E-20	NA	1.14E-12	NA
9.	NA	1.11E-11	NA	5.25E-13	NA
10.	NA	1.76E-08	NA	7.91E-10	NA
11.	NA	NA	NA	NA	NA
12.	NA	NA	NA	NA	NA
13.	1.72E-06	NA	6.80E-08	NA	5.37E-07
14.	NA	NA	NA	NA	NA
15.	NA	NA	NA	NA	NA
16.	NA	NA	NA	NA	NA
17.	NA	NA	NA	NA	NA
18.	NA	NA	NA	NA	NA
19.	NA	NA	NA	NA	NA
20.	NA	NA	NA	NA	NA
21.	NA	NA	NA	NA	NA
22.	NA	NA	NA	NA	NA
23.	4.79E-07	NA	1.90E-08	NA	5.37E-09
24.	NA	NA	NA	NA	NA
25.	8.16E-12	NA	3.21E-13	NA	8.16E-12
26.	NA	4.78E-13	NA	2.31E-14	NA
27.	2.24E-13	3.08E-19	8.80E-15	5.43E-11	9.31E-06
28.	7.07E-06	NA	2.78E-07	NA	7.90E-08
29.	8.69E-08	NA	3.42E-09	NA	2.56E-07
30.	NA	NA	NA	NA	NA
31.	NA	NA	NA	NA	NA
32.	NA	NA	NA	NA	NA
33.	NA	NA	NA	NA	NA
34.	NA	NA	NA	NA	1.28E-08
35.	NA	NA	NA	NA	NA
36.	1.76E-09	NA	6.96E-11	NA	2.01E-10
37.	NA	NA	NA	NA	NA
38.	NA	NA	NA	1.54E-13	NA
39.	NA	NA	NA	NA	NA
40.	NA	3.70E-11	NA	1.75E-12	NA
41.	1.74E-09	NA	6.87E-11	NA	1.99E-10
42.	NA	NA	NA	NA	NA
43.	NA	NA	NA	NA	NA
44.	1.51E-07	NA	5.93E-09	NA	2.34E-09
45.	5.05E-09	NA	1.99E-10	NA	5.49E-11
46.	9.49E-07	NA	3.74E-08	NA	1.06E-08
47.	6.38E-07	NA	2.51E-08	NA	7.12E-09
48.	NA	NA	NA	NA	NA
49.	NA	NA	NA	NA	NA
50.	NA	NA	NA	NA	NA
51.	NA	NA	NA	NA	NA
52.	NA	NA	NA	NA	NA
53.	NA	NA	NA	NA	NA
54.	NA	NA	NA	NA	NA
55.	NA	NA	NA	5.75E-14	NA
56.	NA	NA	NA	NA	NA
57.	8.00E-08	NA	3.14E-09	NA	8.94E-10

TABLE 9-3 Continued

Compound	Fish Ingestion Carcinogen (mg/kg)	Fish Ingestion Noncarcinogen (mg/kg)	Inhalation (High) Carcinogen (mg/m^3)
	RISK*	MDD/ADI	RISK*
58. o-Dichlorobenzene	NA	3.48E-09	NA
59. p-Dichlorobenzene	NA	6.74E-09	NA
60. Dichlorobenzotrifluorides	NA	8.06E-08	NA
61. Dichlorodifluoromethane	NA	NA	NA
62. 1,1-Dichloroethane	NA	1.62E-11	NA
63. 1,2-Dichloroethane	1.06E-14	NA	9.21E-11
64. 1,1-Dichloroethylene	7.31E-14	NA	3.76E-10
65. trans-1,2-Dichloroethylene	NA	2.85E-10	NA
66. 2,4-Dichlorophenol	NA	1.58E-10	NA
67. 1,2-Dichloropropane	3.89E-15	NA	1.32E-11
68. cis-1,3-Dichloropropylene	2.04E-13	NA	1.33E-10
69. trans-1,3-Dichloropropylene	NA	NA	NA
70. Dichlorotoluenes	NA	1.69E-07	NA
71. Dieldrin	NA	NA	NA
72. Diethylphthalate	NA	NA	NA
73. 2,4-Dimethylphenol	NA	NA	NA
74. Dimethylphthalate	NA	NA	NA
75. 2,4-Dinitrophenol	NA	NA	NA
76. 2,4-Dinitrotoluene	NA	NA	4.65E-12
77. 2,6-Dinitrotoluene	NA	NA	NA
78. Dioctylphthalate	NA	NA	NA
79. 1,2-Diphenylhydrazine	NA	NA	NA
80. Endosulfan I	NA	NA	NA
81. Endosulfan II	NA	NA	NA
82. Endosulfan sulfate	NA	NA	NA
83. Endrin	NA	NA	NA
84. Endrin aldehyde	NA	NA	NA
85. Ethyl benzene	NA	1.26E-08	NA
86. bis-(2-Ethylhexyl)phthalate	1.76E-13	NA	3.48E-13
87. Fluoranthene	NA	NA	NA
88. benzo(b)-Fluoranthene	NA	NA	NA
89. benzo(k)-Fluoranthene	NA	NA	NA
90. Fluorene	NA	NA	NA
91. Heptachlor	NA	NA	NA
92. Heptachlor epoxide	NA	NA	NA
93. Hexachlorobenzene	3.28E-11	NA	6.51E-11
94. Hexachlorobutadiene (C-46)	7.75E-12	NA	1.27E-11
95. α-Hexachlorocyclohexane	NA	NA	1.38E-09
96. β-Hexachlorocyclohexane	NA	NA	4.77E-12
97. δ-Hexachlorocyclohexane	NA	NA	NA
98. γ-Hexachlorocyclohexane	9.48E-11	NA	9.92E-10
99. Hexachlorocyclopentadiene (C-56)	NA	9.48E-06	NA
100. Hexachloroethane	3.59E-14	NA	4.39E-12
101. Isophorone	NA	NA	NA
102. Mercury	NA	NA	NA
103. Methyl benzoate	NA	3.42E-10	NA
104. Methyl chlorobenzoate	NA	NA	NA
105. 2-Methyl-4,6-dinitrophenol	NA	NA	NA
106. Methylene chloride	1.11E-15	NA	1.93E-11
107. Mirex	2.76E-11	4.18E-06	1.13E-12
108. Napthalene	NA	NA	NA
109. Nitrobenzene	NA	NA	NA
110. 2-Nitrophenol	NA	NA	NA
111. 4-Nitrophenol	NA	NA	NA
112. n-Nitrosodiphenylamine	NA	NA	NA
113. n-Nitrosodi-n-propylamine	NA	NA	NA

Inhalation (High) Noncarcinogen (mg/m^3)	Inhalation (Lower) Carcinogen (mg/m^3)	Inhalation (Lower) Noncarcinogen (mg/m^3)	Dermal (Water) Carcinogen (mg/kg)	Dermal (Water) Noncarcinogen (mg/kg)
MDD/ADI	RISK*	MDD/ADI	RISK*	MDD/ADI
58. 2.15E-08	NA	8.50E-10	NA	2.40E-10
59. 3.81E-08	NA	1.50E-09	NA	4.25E-10
60. 8.30E-08	NA	3.27E-09	NA	9.26E-10
61. NA	NA	NA	NA	NA
62. 8.15E-09	NA	3.21E-10	NA	9.31E-11
63. NA	1.05E-12	NA	4.92E-14	NA
64. NA	4.27E-12	NA	2.06E-13	NA
65. 4.39E-07	NA	1.72E-08	NA	4.91E-09
66. 2.13E-09	NA	8.38E-11	NA	8.23E-11
67. NA	1.50E-13	NA	7.24E-15	NA
68. NA	1.51E-12	NA	7.28E-14	NA
69. NA	NA	NA	NA	NA
70. 3.40E-07	NA	1.33E-08	NA	3.78E-09
71. NA	NA	NA	5.14E-12	NA
72. NA	NA	NA	NA	NA
73. NA	NA	NA	NA	NA
74. NA	NA	NA	NA	NA
75. NA	NA	NA	NA	NA
76. NA	5.27E-14	NA	5.24E-14	NA
77. 4.38E-07	NA	1.72E-08	NA	1.03E-07
78. NA	NA	NA	NA	NA
79. NA	NA	NA	1.30E-13	NA
80. NA	NA	NA	NA	NA
81. NA	NA	NA	NA	NA
82. NA	NA	NA	NA	NA
83. NA	NA	NA	NA	NA
84. NA	NA	NA	NA	NA
85. 2.86E-07	NA	1.12E-08	NA	3.19E-09
86. NA	3.95E-15	NA	4.32E-15	NA
87. NA	NA	NA	NA	NA
88. NA	NA	NA	NA	NA
89. NA	NA	NA	NA	NA
90. NA	NA	NA	NA	NA
91. NA	NA	NA	5.70E-13	NA
92. NA	NA	NA	NA	NA
93. NA	7.40E-13	NA	1.41E-12	NA
94. NA	1.44E-13	NA	6.55E-15	NA
95. NA	1.57E-11	NA	3.34E-10	NA
96. NA	5.41E-14	NA	4.51E-11	NA
97. NA	NA	NA	NA	NA
98. NA	1.12E-11	NA	1.10E-10	NA
99. 3.07E-06	NA	1.20E-07	NA	1.70E-06
100. NA	5.08E-14	NA	2.40E-15	NA
101. NA	NA	NA	NA	NA
102. 3.23E-08	NA	1.27E-09	NA	NA
103. 8.78E-08	NA	3.46E-09	NA	9.80E-10
104. NA	NA	NA	NA	NA
105. NA	NA	NA	NA	NA
106. NA	2.19E-13	NA	1.03E-14	NA
107. 1.52E-08	1.28E-14	5.97E-10	7.04E-13	1.98E-07
108. NA	NA	NA	NA	NA
109. NA	NA	NA	NA	NA
110. NA	NA	NA	NA	NA
111. NA	NA	NA	NA	NA
112. NA	NA	NA	8.32E-16	NA
113. NA	NA	NA	NA	NA

TABLE 9-3 Continued

Compound	Fish Ingestion Carcinogen (mg/kg)	Fish Ingestion Noncarcinogen (mg/kg)	Inhalation (High) Carcinogen (mg/m^3)
	RISK*	MDD/ADI	RISK*
114. Octachlorocyclopentene	NA	NA	NA
115. PCB, 1016/1242	NA	NA	NA
116. PCB, 1221	NA	NA	NA
117. PCB (Aroclor 1248)	6.34E-09	1.60E-04	1.52E-09
118. PCB, 1254	NA	NA	NA
119. PCB, 1260	NA	NA	NA
120. Pentachlorobenzene	NA	4.51E-08	NA
121. Pentachloroethane	3.28E-15	NA	8.50E-13
122. Pentachlorophenol	NA	NA	NA
123. benzo(ghi)-Perylene	NA	NA	NA
124. Phenathrene	NA	NA	NA
125. Phenol	NA	2.62E-07	NA
126. Phenyl benzoate	NA	6.37E-09	NA
127. n-Propylbenzene	NA	NA	NA
128. Pyrene	NA	NA	NA
129. benzo(a)-Pyrene	NA	NA	NA
130. ideno(1,2,3-cd)-Pyrene	NA	NA	NA
131. Styrene	NA	NA	NA
132. 2,3,7,8-TCDD	3.42E-08	7.20E-03	1.91E-09
133. 1,2,3,4-Tetrachlorobenzene	NA	7.71E-07	NA
134. 1,2,4,5-Tetrachlorobenzene	NA	6.09E-06	NA
135. 1,1,2,2-Tetrachloroethane	3.05E-14	NA	6.48E-11
136. Tetrachloroethylene	2.64E-12	NA	1.04E-09
137. Tetrachlorotoluenes	NA	NA	NA
138. Toluene	NA	9.50E-09	NA
139. 1,2,3-Trichlorobenzene	NA	4.26E-08	NA
140. 1,2,4-Trichlorobenzene	NA	1.90E-06	NA
141. 1,3,5-Trichlorobenzene	NA	2.36E-09	NA
142. 1,1,1-Trichloroethane	NA	1.97E-10	NA
143. 1,1,2-Trichloroethane	6.13E-15	NA	1.86E-11
144. Trichloroethylene	6.64E-13	NA	6.76E-10
145. Trichlorofluoromethane	NA	2.93E-11	NA
146. 2,4,5-Trichlorophenol	NA	3.46E-07	NA
147. 2,4,6-Trichlorophenol	5.79E-14	NA	2.06E-12
148. Trichlorotoluenes	NA	2.99E-08	NA
149. 1,2,4-Trimethylbenzene	NA	NA	NA
150. 1,3,5-Trimethylbenzene	NA	NA	NA
151. Vinyl chloride	NA	NA	NA
152. m-Xylene	NA	2.97E-07	NA
153. o-Xylene	NA	1.43E-06	NA
154. p-Xylene	NA	9.62E-07	NA

*Upper bound lifetime cancer risk.

NOTE: ADI = acceptable daily intake, MDD = maximum daily dose, and NA = not applicable.

	Inhalation (High) Noncarcinogen (mg/m^3)	Inhalation (Lower) Carcinogen (mg/m^3)	Inhalation (Lower) Noncarcinogen (mg/m^3)	Dermal (Water) Carcinogen (mg/kg)	Dermal (Water) Noncarcinogen (mg/kg)
	MDD/ADI	RISK*	MDD/ADI	RISK*	MDD/ADI
114.	NA	NA	NA	NA	NA
115.	NA	NA	NA	NA	NA
116.	NA	NA	NA	NA	NA
117.	3.41E-06	1.73E-11	1.34E-07	4.04E-11	1.89E-06
118.	NA	NA	NA	NA	NA
119.	NA	NA	NA	NA	NA
120.	8.35E-09	NA	3.29E-10	NA	9.35E-11
121.	NA	9.64E-15	NA	4.56E-16	NA
122.	NA	NA	NA	NA	NA
123.	NA	NA	NA	NA	NA
124.	NA	NA	NA	NA	NA
125.	1.47E-05	NA	5.78E-07	NA	4.51E-06
126.	1.19E-07	NA	4.71E-10	NA	1.34E-09
127.	NA	NA	NA	NA	NA
128.	NA	NA	NA	NA	NA
129.	NA	NA	NA	NA	NA
130.	NA	NA	NA	NA	NA
131.	NA	NA	NA	NA	NA
132.	3.58E-05	2.17E-11	1.41E-06	2.37E-10	9.26E-05
133.	1.42E-07	NA	5.58E-09	NA	1.54E-09
134.	1.42E-06	NA	5.58E-08	NA	1.54E-08
135.	NA	7.35E-13	NA	3.55E-14	NA
136.	NA	1.18E-11	NA	5.58E-13	NA
137.	NA	NA	NA	NA	NA
138.	9.15E-07	NA	3.61E-08	NA	1.02E-08
139.	3.56E-08	NA	1.40E-09	NA	3.86E-10
140.	1.83E-06	NA	7.23E-08	NA	2.05E-08
141.	1.21E-09	NA	4.76E-11	NA	1.35E-11
142.	3.31E-08	NA	1.30E-09	NA	3.78E-10
143.	NA	2.11E-13	NA	1.02E-14	NA
144.	NA	7.69E-12	NA	3.63E-13	NA
145.	2.76E-09	NA	1.09E-10	NA	3.15E-11
146.	1.84E-07	NA	7.23E-09	NA	3.13E-09
147.	NA	2.34E-14	NA	3.36E-15	NA
148.	1.50E-08	NA	5.89E-10	NA	1.29E-10
149.	NA	NA	NA	NA	NA
150.	NA	NA	NA	NA	NA
151.	NA	NA	NA	3.11E-15	NA
152.	1.91E-05	NA	7.54E-07	NA	2.13E-07
153.	3.51E-05	NA	1.38E-06	NA	3.91E-07
154.	2.18E-05	NA	8.60E-07	NA	2.44E-07

marsh or river ranges from 10^{-7} to 10^{-12}, which is less than that generally found to be significant by public health officials.

Single-Compound Disposal

For more than 15 years, a facility manufacturing metal components depended on one solvent, trichloroethylene (TCE), to carry out its fabrication process. A few other chemicals were used but in much smaller quantities. Whereas the disposal of all chemicals presumably was carefully controlled, the company was unable to account for all of the TCE (in contrast to near complete accountability for other substances); however, the missing TCE was explained as resulting from the chemical's high volatility and its consequent loss to the atmosphere.

Although large losses to the atmosphere certainly had occurred, it became clear that the underground holding tank for the solvent had also ruptured and leaked considerable quantities of TCE into the ground. Furthermore, records indicated that on several occasions drums of the solvent had been ruptured accidentally by the improper use of forklifts, also discharging large volumes of the solvent to the ground. By this time, a plume of the solvent had begun to migrate offsite in the direction of a city's potable water well field, more than 2 miles away.

A risk assessment was performed to determine the nature and magnitude of the possible health threat to the local community. In the meantime, the use of all privately operated wells for human consumption was halted, and replacement water was provided from another source known not to contain TCE. The risk assessment concluded that if the plume were allowed to migrate unchanged, the unwanted substance would contaminate the water supply of the entire community of some 80,000 residents in 2 to 5 years. The anticipated risk was conservatively estimated to be on the order of 1 per 100,000, a value in excess of EPA's guideline for concern of 1 per 1,000,000. On this basis, corporate management decided to excavate the contaminated soil that was feeding the plume and to construct monitoring wells to determine if the contamination was being abated. In addition, a community information program, in which the state health agency was a participant, was instituted to ensure the dissemination of all relevant information to potentially affected residents.

Future Risk to a Major Aquifer

In the southeast United States, local officials learned accidentally of an illicit ("midnight") waste dumping activity immediately adjacent to a well field that supplied more than half of the potable water to a population in excess of 600,000. Indirect evidence suggested that some of the wastes were in liquid form, that the volume was probably quite large (hundreds, perhaps thousands, of tons), and that the wastes were buried over several acres. Limited sampling of the site revealed the presence of large numbers of metal drums and a handful of toxic compounds, all present below the water table. Most important, a hydrogeologic investigation revealed that the ground was porous (no clay lens was present to act as a barrier against migration); that the materials had been deposited in a sinkhole that acted as a funnel into the underground aquifer; that the rock formation underlying one part of the area was greatly fractured, providing direct pathways to the well field; and that the direction of the flow of ground water was from the waste site to the well field.

On the strength of such evidence the authorities obtained judicial authorization to excavate the site before the well water, whose quality up to that time had been exceptionally high, became irreparably damaged. During the excavation, additional, albeit limited, sampling indicated that the volume of wastes was indeed large and that the number of compounds necessarily of commercial origin was greater than 100.

After the excavation the water authority sued the owners of the waste site to recover remedial costs. The court required the authority to demonstrate, postremediation, that there had been sufficient danger to the well field and to the health of those served by it to warrant reimbursement for its remedial initiative.

A risk assessment was undertaken to estimate the danger the waste site had posed and might have posed in the future, had the source of chemicals not been removed. In addition to data about the landfill contents the results of water analyses from monitoring wells demonstrated that the more mobile pollutants were intruding into the well field.

The risk assessment focused on 100 compounds (Table 9-4); examined their chronic toxicity (including the ability to cause cancer) particularly in relation to the older members of a population (because the community was composed largely of senior citizens);

TABLE 9-4   Future Risk to a Major Aquifer

Chemical	UCR $(\mathrm{mg/kg/day})^{-1}$	ADI $(\mathrm{mg/kg/day})$
Acenaphthene	1.1×10^{1}	5.7×10^{-3}
Acenaphthylene		
Acetone		2.9
Anthracene		
Arsenic	1.5×10^{1}	
Benzene	2.9×10^{-2}	7.0×10^{-4}
Benzidine	2.3×10^{2}	1.3×10^{-3}
Benzo($\underline{a}$)anthracene	1.1×10^{1}	
Benzo($\underline{k}$)fluoranthene	1.1×10^{1}	
Benzo($\underline{ghi}$)perylene		
Beryllium		5.0×10^{-4}
Bromodichloromethane		6.0×10^{-3}
Bromophenyl phenyl ether, 4-		
Butyl benzyl phthalate		
Cadmium	6.1×10^{1}	2.4×10^{-3}
Carbon tetrachloride		7.0×10^{-4}
Chlordane	1.6	5.0×10^{-5}
Chlorobenzene		3.0×10^{-2}
Chloroethane		5.4×10^{-1}
Bis(2-chloroethoxy)methane		
Bis(2-chloroethyl)ether	1.1	
Chloroform	8.1×10^{-2}	1.0×10^{-2}
Bis(2-chloroisopropyl)ether		1.0×10^{-3}
Chloro-3-methyl phenol, 4-		6.3×10^{-3}
Chlorophenol, 2-		4.4×10^{-3}
Chloro-$\underline{m}$-cresol, $\underline{p}$-		6.3×10^{-3}
Chromium		1.0
Cyanide		2.0×10^{-2}
DDD		
DDE		
DDT	3.4×10^{-1}	5.0×10^{-4}
Diazinon		2.0×10^{-3}
Dibromochloromethane		
Dichlorobenzene, 1,2-		9.0×10^{-2}
Dichlorobenzene, 1,3-		6.9×10^{-2}
Dichlorobenzene, 1,4-		1.1×10^{-1}
Dichlorobenzidine, 3,3-	1.7	
Dichloroethane, 1,1-		1.2×10^{-1}
Dichloroethane, 1,2-	9.1×10^{-2}	
Dichloroethylene, 1,1-	1.2	1.0×10^{-2}
Dichloroethylene, $\underline{cis}$-1,2-		1.1×10^{-2}
Dichloroethylene, $\underline{trans}$-1,2-		1.1×10^{-2}
Dichloromethane	1.4×10^{-2}	6.0×10^{-2}
Dichlorophenol, 2,4-		3.0×10^{-3}
Dichloropropane, 1,2-	6.1×10^{-2}	
Dichloropropylene, $\underline{cis}$ and trans-1,3-		
Diethyl phthalate		1.0×10^{1}
Dimethyl phthalate		1.0×10^{1}
Dimethylphenol, 2,4-		1.1×10^{-2}
Dinitrophenol, 2,4-		2.0×10^{-3}

TABLE 9-4 Continued

Chemical	UCR $(mg/kg/day)^{-1}$	ADI $(mg/kg/day)$
Dinitrotoluene, 2,4-	3.1×10^{-1}	1.3
Di-n-butyl phthalate		1.0
Di-n-octyl phthalate		1.3×10^{1}
Ethyl benzene		1.0×10^{-1}
Bis(2-ethylhexyl)phthalate	8.5×10^{-3}	2.0×10^{-2}
Fluoranthene		
Fluorene		
Heptachlor epoxide		3.0×10^{-5}
Hexachlorobenzene	1.7	
Hexachlorobutadiene	7.8×10^{-2}	2.0×10^{-3}
Hexachlorocyclohexane	1.3	
Hexachlorocyclohexane, β-		
Hexachlorocyclohexane, γ-	1.3	3.0×10^{-4}
Hexachloroethane	1.4×10^{-2}	3.3×10^{-2}
Hydrogen sulfide		2.0×10^{-3}
Isophorone		2.0×10^{-1}
Kelthane (Dicofol)		
Lead		
Malathion		2.0×10^{-2}
Mercury		2.0×10^{-3}
Methyl chloride		1.0
Methyl-4,5-Dinitrophenol, 2-		
Methyl-4,6-Dinitrophenol, 2-		
Methyl ethyl ketone		5.0×10^{-2}
Methyl isobutyl ketone		1.0×10^{-1}
Naphthalene		1.3×10^{-1}
Nickel	1.2	1.5×10^{1}
Nitrobenzene		5.0×10^{-4}
Nitrophenol, 2-		
Nitrophenol, 4-		
Nitrosodimethylamine, N-	2.6×10^{1}	
Nitrosodi-n-propylamine, N-		
Parathion		5.0×10^{-4}
Pentachlorophenol		3.0×10^{-2}
Phenanthrene		1.0×10^{-4}
Phenol		1.0×10^{-1}
Pyrene		
Selenium		1.0×10^{-1}
Silver		3.0×10^{-3}
Tetrachloroethylene	5.1×10^{-2}	2.0×10^{-2}
Tetrahydrofurans		
Toluene		3.0×10^{-1}
Trichlorobenzene, 1,2,4-		2.0×10^{-2}
Trichloroethane, 1,1,1-		2.9×10^{-2}
Trichloroethane, 1,1,2	5.7×10^{-2}	2.0×10^{-1}
Trichloroethylene		
Trichlorofluoromethane		3.0×10^{-1}
Trichlorophenol, 2,4,6-	2.0×10^{-2}	
Trimethylbenzene (mixed isomer)		
Xylenes		2.3

NOTE: ADI = acceptable daily intake, UCR = unit cancer risk.

and evaluated their potency in relation to what would likely be safe levels of exposure. The compounds were scrutinized for their ability to move offsite and contaminate water in the municipal well field and for the degree of difficulty in removing them from potable water.

The data base was adequate to perform all steps of the evaluation save one: it was not possible to estimate the maximum concentrations of contaminants in the well field. Despite that limitation, it was successfully argued that the future hazards would probably be sufficient to cause imminent danger to public health (by exceeding consistently the likely public health standards). The authorities met their burden of proof and received a favorable judgment to obtain full reimbursement for the costs of remediation.

DISCUSSION

Data Problems

Quantitative conclusions about the health risks associated with a site often appear precise and accurate. That appearance is not always correct, however. Estimates often do not explicitly represent the large variations in the quality of the underlying data. Some of the more glaring problems glossed over in numerical estimates include (1) extrapolation from brief durations of exposure to much longer exposure periods, even a lifetime; (2) reliance on studies of limited pathological observations and of narrow designs; and (3) sometimes, recourse to unverified information. Ordinarily, compensation can be made for poor-quality studies and major deviations between test data and environmental conditions through the judicious (and at times arbitrary) application of "safety" factors (perhaps as small as 10 or at times as great as 100,000) to define lower levels of acceptable exposure. Some degree of comfort may be generated by such practices, and major public injuries are not known to have occurred as a result of them. Nevertheless, the extent of safety inherent in the procedures remains indefinable without the undertaking of targeted research.

Additional Uncertainties

Other components of the analysis necessarily incorporate uncertainties for which control is often beyond the grasp of conventional and ethical research and testing. Some of the major unknowns include the need to apply information from labora-tory animals to humans. Although both test and target species are mammals, they differ in substantive ways that may produce errors—in either direction—in the application of toxicity data to humans. Even if one species is capable of closely reproducing a pathological lesion caused by a chemical in another species, the injury may appear at a totally different organ in the second species. That phenomenon, particularly prevalent in carcinogen-esis, may be related to differences either in metabolic pathways or in the distribution of binding sites. Quantitative differences in toxic potency also occur among species, which are related largely to quantitative differences in kinetics of absorption, distribution, biotransformation, and excretion of toxicants and to differences in the rate of repair of molecular and cellular lesions.

Many of these issues considered to be of concern for single substances are thought to be of even greater concern for complex mixtures. Activation and detoxication rates might be altered in the presence of other substances at toxic doses; reserve capacities or organs might be depleted significantly by toxic doses; and, finally, repair rates in pathologically affected organs might be changed as the result of multiple insults.

When such underlying biologic understanding exists, it serves as the basis for considering differences between the dose-response characteristics of test animals and humans. In turn, that basis provides the foundation for solidly based environmental standards of exposures to the waste products.

CONCLUSIONS AND RECOMMENDATIONS

Quantitative risk assessment is the only method currently available to estimate risks from waste sites. Both the underlying data about toxicity and methods for extrapolation have greater or lesser amounts of uncertainty. On a more positive note the de-mands of risk assessment are forcing the development of standard-ized data bases for health effects; they are also contributing to the development of extrapolation methods. Nevertheless, uncertain-ties must always be considered and conveyed to the decisionmaker so that the strengths and limitations of the risk estimates are ap-propriately considered in selecting risk management approaches.

The most pressing need is for more biologic information to guide extrapolation methods. In part, that information will come from standard toxicologic tests of substances present in waste sites, but more fundamental research is probably the real key to improvement. Research on biologic mechanisms, shared and unshared between test animals and humans, needs considerable emphasis.

Along with such data and information will come increasing opportunities for interactions among biologists, statisticians, risk assessors, and decisionmakers. The fostering of those interactions is important to the proper use of vital information and to direct research in obtaining that information.

REFERENCES

Bellin, J. S., and D. G. Barnes. 1986. Interim procedures for estimating risks associated with exposures to mixtures of chlorinated dibenzo-p-dioxins and -dibenzofurans (CDDs and CDFs). U.S. Environmental Protection Agency, Washington, D.C.

ENVIRON Corporation. 1986. Elements of Toxicology and Chemical Risk Assessment. Washington, D.C.

Gold, L. S., C. B. Sawyer, R. Magaw, and nine others. 1984. A carcinogenic potency database of the standardization results of animal bioassays. Environmental Health Perspectives 58:9–31.

National Research Council. 1983. Risk Assessment in the Federal Government. Washington, D.C.: National Academy Press.

U.S. EPA. 1986. Guidelines for the health risk assessment of chemical mixtures. Federal Register 51:34014–34025. September 24.

U.S. EPA, Carcinogen Assessment Group. 1985. Relative Carcinogenic Potencies Among 55 Chemicals Evaluated by the Carcinogen Assessment Group as Suspect Human Carcinogens. From Mutagenicity and Carcinogeneity Assessment of 1,3-Butadiene. EPA 600/8-85-004F. Washington, D.C. August.

PROVOCATEUR'S COMMENTS
William Cibulas

I found Dr. Tardiff's paper very interesting in that it touched upon several important issues that all of us involved in quantitative risk assessment of hazardous waste sites are concerned with. However, like many papers written in this field, it leaves us with many unanswered questions concerning the future of quantitative risk assessment. I hope this is not an overstatement, but in my opinion, the tone of the paper appears to be very pro quantitative risk assessment and numbers oriented. Scientists must be very careful and understand the limitations of risk assessment when making public health decisions.

One of the major questions that we at the Agency for Toxic Substances and Disease Registry (ATSDR) are continually faced with deals with the issue of inhalation exposures from volatile organic compounds in contaminated ground water. Often, this issue arises after an affected household has already been placed on an alternative water supply for consumption. The question then is, can my baby bathe in this water? Is it still okay to shower with this water? Based on some recent work by Julian Andelman at the University of Pittsburgh and some of our own estimates of risk, ATSDR often concludes that if water is unacceptable for drinking for any length of time, it may be unacceptable for all other indoor uses for this same period, including showering, bathing, and washing clothes and dishes. I have questions concerning the relative risk assumed from drinking 2 liters of water contaminated with volatile organic compounds compared to the risks that one assumes from exposure to all other indoor uses of this water.

My second question deals with those compounds that act by secondary mechanisms. Dr. Tardiff touched on this subject when he discussed TCDD and current scientific thought that it is acting as a promoter and not a direct-acting carcinogen. As you know, there is currently no practical method to derive any distinction of carcinogens based on any principles of carcinogenic action. All carcinogens, whether they are proven human carcinogens or suspected animal carcinogens, are treated the same way. My question would be, after hearing Dr. Tardiff's comment, are compounds that are proving to be promoters and not direct-acting carcinogens better treated as threshold compounds? I do not think we have done this yet.

The third issue deals with high-dose/low-dose effects. As many of you are aware, there is growing concern over the selection of the maximum tolerated dose, or the MTD, for use in the chronic bioassay. For those of you who will be attending the Society of Toxicology meeting next week, there will be a whole symposium devoted to the use of the MTD in the chronic bioassay. Although there are only 20 to 30 known or proven carcinogens, approximately one-half of the chemicals tested in chronic bioassays have been shown to produce some excess of tumors in at least one of the animal species tested. Frequently, the only statistically significant increase in tumors is in those animals that were treated at the MTD, or at a concentration at which we might expect some toxicity in those animals. Thus, this discussion becomes particularly relevant as we are now beginning to find that certain essential elements, such as estrogens, selenium, and tocopherols, are proving to be carcinogens at high doses. I wonder about the use of the MTD in the chronic bioassay and what appears to be a growing trend of treating high-dose carcinogens as noncarcinogens, or compounds that have thresholds, when we are looking at them in low-level concentrations.

The final question deals with one of the specific critiques, the Hyde Park landfill, for which you quantify both the carcinogenic and noncarcinogenic risks from dermal exposure to contaminated water. My guess is you would reference Dr. Brown's paper on dermal exposures from VOC-contaminated water in the quantitation step. I was wondering if there are any recent studies that deal with a dermal exposure that perhaps would be more relevant at low-level concentrations.

Rapporteurs' Reports

Much of the success of the colloquium must be credited to WSTB members Lester Lave, James Mercer, Richard Conway, and Gordon Robeck, who acted as rapporteurs for the workshops on risk assessment/toxicology, hydrogeology, engineering, and regulatory strategies, respectively. The colloquium steering committee provided them with the following list of questions for use in generating discussion, with an emphasis on technical and scientific issues, during the workshop session.

- What methods are available for setting goals or standards? How are they helpful?
- What are some strengths and concerns related to these methods from a scientific, technical, or regulatory perspective?
- What is the ability of existing methods to account for diverse conditions?
- What is the adequacy of the data base in applying the existing methods?
- What uncertainties are associated with the methods and their predictions?
- What are the most important issues the methods neglect?

The following summaries of the workshops' efforts present the wide diversity of opinion, vast breadth of expertise, and singular approaches to the resolution of the issues of concern that characterized the entire colloquium.

RISK ASSESSMENT/ TOXICOLOGY WORKSHOP
Rapporteur: Lester B. Lave

The workshop participants decided to focus on risk assessment techniques for health and, most particularly, for cancer. Tools exist to examine other health end points, trauma, and ecological damage, but the participants felt constrained to leave these to another time and place.

TOOLS FOR SETTING AMBIENT ENVIRONMENTAL STANDARDS

Four general approaches have been used to set ambient environmental standards.

1. Using political and other nonscientific approaches. These approaches do not attempt to use scientific data or criteria; nor do they attempt to specify risks or health outcomes. Rather, they grow out of political compromise or the imposition of one powerful group's goals.

2. Setting the standard at the background (or nondetectable level) plus some increment. For example, the standard for benzene in water could be nondetectability, or background—or twice the background level.

3. Basing the standard on control technology and costs. Examples include the various EPA air and water emissions standards such as Best Available Control Technology (BACT) and New Source Performance Standards (NSPS).

4. Setting the standards by risk analysis to quantify the magnitude of the hazards and then by setting risk goals.

The first three of these approaches involve the "implicit" balancing of costs and risks. For example, the engineers determining the best-available technology consider the costs and control efficiency of each technology and implicitly decide which technologies are too costly for incremental control. As long as industry and the public have confidence in those making the implicit trade-offs, this can be a good approach. If that confidence is lost, however, the balancing must be done explicitly, which requires risk analysis and goal setting.

Criteria for Evaluating the Approaches

The following criteria were deemed the most relevant in evaluating each of these approaches to setting standards: (1) efficiency/effectiveness, (2) equity, (3) administrative ease, (4) transparency, (5) the qualitative and quantitative uncertainty of the approach, and (6) a miscellaneous category consisting of defensibility, residual risk, and others. The first criterion refers to whether the goal is being accomplished and if so, whether it is being accomplished at the least cost. The second criterion refers to whether the various parties are being treated fairly. Note that sometimes equity is defined by process (having one's "day in court") rather than by outcome (those who benefit must pay). The third and fourth criteria are somewhat similar. The third looks at whether the solution can be implemented simply and at low cost. The fourth asks whether the approach is so simple that the public and other parties understand how it works and see it as addressing their concerns. The fifth criterion focuses on the extent to which scientists are confident that their answer is qualitatively correct, and then on the range of plausible quantitative estimates. The last category refers to the ability of Congress and administrators to defend the resulting goals and the risk after the process has been lowered sufficiently to be accepted.

The criteria are best illustrated by applying them to the various approaches. The first, political or arbitrary standard setting, is not efficient or effective; it may be equitable, although those who are unhappy are likely to complain that they had no chance to present their case. Standard setting is administratively simple, although implementation may be extremely difficult. The approach is not transparent because the public and other parties are simply asked to trust the person making the arbitrary decision. There is likely to be great qualitative and quantitative uncertainty associated with the standard. Because the basis of the decision is unknown, it is not likely to be defensible. Also, the residual risk might be too high. In particular, this approach is faced with the efficiency-residual risk dilemma. It is likely to impose too high a cost or leave too large a residual risk. The background plus an increment criterion scores well on administrative ease, equity, transparency, residual risk, defensibility, and uncertainty. Its principal problem is efficiency—it simply costs too much in most cases.

Technology-based standards depend on the quality of the decisionmakers and the information they have. If the process is performed extremely well, it is likely to be efficient and administratively simple, and have low residual risk and relatively low uncertainty. It will not be equitable, however, and so those who must bear the burden will view themselves as having been treated arbitrarily. Also, this approach is not likely to be transparent; thus the public can easily lose confidence.

In fact, by the 1980s the first three approaches no longer enjoyed the confidence of the public and other parties. Environmental controls were too expensive for arbitrary or other political judgments. Although background seems a wonderful goal, it is incompatible with an industrial or other high-consumption society. Engineering judgments have become more complicated as a greater array of alternatives has emerged and as the control technology has become more expensive. It is simply not feasible to rely on undocumented expert judgment in a highly emotional area with many different levels of control and cleanup available at very different cost levels. Thus, risk assessment and goal setting have emerged as the prime approach to standard setting by default rather than through an attractive display of the strong properties of this approach.

Setting Risk Goals

Estimating the risks of some hazard is only one step in a long process. Another necessary step is defining the safety goals: how safe is safe enough? Several approaches have been proposed for setting safety goals. In the 1980 "benzene" decision, the Supreme Court mentioned significant and trivial (de minimis) risks, without ever attempting to define either. A significant risk was one so high that it was worthy of attention and presumably of control. A de minimis risk was so small that it was not worthy of attention. Beyond this, the court gave few clues as to how to define these concepts, and there has been little success by the agencies in implementing the notions. The Food and Drug Administration has defined a risk of one cancer per million lifetimes to be de minimis. EPA has been somewhat less explicit in considering that risks on the order of one cancer per million lifetimes or per hundred thousand lifetimes are de minimis.

Some researchers have used the notion of comparative risks. They examine situations that we routinely encounter and accept in our activities to infer the safety goals. For example, in smoking cigarettes, someone is implicitly accepting high risks of lung cancer and heart disease. In eating peanut butter, one is implicitly accepting the risk of liver cancer from aflatoxin contaminating the peanut butter.

Finally, some researchers have attempted to examine the safety implications of decisions made by federal regulatory agencies. The agencies had no explicit safety goals and instead agonized over each decision individually. Despite the individual decisions, a pattern seems to emerge that gives some general guidance. Nevertheless, setting safety goals is one of the most difficult steps in the process.

Strengths and Weaknesses of Risk Assessment and Management

In focusing on risk assessment the greatest strength was seen as its internal consistency and its ability to make comparisons across chemicals and waste sites. Risk assessment is targeted to health outcomes, the area of greatest public concern. Furthermore, it gives quantitative estimates of the health risks. Finally, the method is able to deal with multiple chemicals and to offer an aggregate measure of risk for such chemicals "stews." In summary, risk assessment offers an intellectually appealing approach to a difficult problem.

Its basic weakness stems from the difficulty of implementing this approach, the method for which is complicated and difficult to understand. Thus, few people understand the basis for the estimates or the objections raised by injured parties. There are rarely adequate data to implement the method, particularly with regard to individual exposures. Indeed, exposure data were identified as the primary source of uncertainty in current estimates. The complexity of the method means that it is difficult to communicate results and uncertainty to the public and to decisionmakers, a major weakness in a democratic society. The models currently in use were developed on the basis of somewhat plausible assumptions rather than on the basis of the underlying biology. In the last year or two, however, great progress has been made in understanding the biology of carcinogenesis, and recent work in pharmacokinetics has developed the foundation for much better risk assessment models.

The group also discussed the extent to which the risk estimates had been validated. There has been some validation, but first, one must understand that all current risk assessment techniques are attempts to derive reasonable upper bounds to the risk level. They are somewhat analogous to "probable maximum floods." Thus, validation does not consist of asking whether the risk estimates are accurate indicators of what is found in epidemiological investigations. Because the risk estimates are reasonable upper bounds, one needs to ask whether the risk estimates have been found to understate the risks observed in the world. There have been a few cases in which this question could be answered, such as the bladder cancers from saccharin consumption; these cases find that the risk levels estimated by the models are upper bounds to what is measured in the world.

The Strengths and Weaknesses of Setting Risk Goals

Setting risk or safety goals requires public education and debate; as a result the strengths and weaknesses of the method are opposite sides of the same coin. Educating the public about safety issues and about tiny levels of risk is extremely difficult. Even statisticians have difficulty making decisions concerning small probabilities unless they do the calculations first. Yet because the United States is a democracy, there is no alternative to educating the public sufficiently to select a system for managing toxic waste hazards.

Equity also plays an important role in the debate because the public is concerned not only with the overall safety level but with how the risk is apportioned. If children are at high risk, for example, the public is concerned. Risk analysis has the ability to estimate risks to individual groups, and thus safety goals must be examined in detail.

CONCLUSION

The process of risk management and goal setting helps to focus the attention of analysts, scientists, decisionmakers, and the public on the issues of critical importance. Thus, in an emotional, complicated world, these tools help to push aside the secondary issues and ensure that the important ones are highlighted; as a result the tools help to ensure progress.

Risk assessment is still in its infancy, however, and there are large uncertainties, both qualitative and quantitative, associated with the estimates. Although advances in biology promise more certain estimates in the future, the primary reason for using risk assessment in setting standards is that nonscientific approaches, approaches that do not balance safety and costs, and approaches that do the balancing implicitly rather than explicitly are not accepted by the public and other interested parties.

EPA's effort to bring the public into setting standards for the ARSARCO smelter in Tacoma, Washington, is an example of how difficult it is to educate the public about risk assessment and to discuss safety goals. Yet whatever the difficulties, it is unclear that there is any alternative to using risk assessment and setting safety goals.

HYDROGEOLOGY WORKSHOP
Rapporteur: James W. Mercer

After discussing the colloquium papers the workshop group summarized the role of hydrogeologists in hazardous waste site management. That role is to use some methodology to estimate exposure from ground water contamination. Exposure calculations are subsequently used with effects data in estimating the associated risk. Such exposures may be estimated on a generic basis and the results used in setting policy, or the exposure may be estimated on a site-specific basis and the results used to implement policy. With this understanding as a foundation, the workshop addressed six questions presented to all workshops. Discussions of the questions are given below under the following headings: Methods Used in Exposure Estimation, Strengths and Weaknesses of the Methods, Methods' Effectiveness Under Diverse Conditions, Associated Data Base, Associated Uncertainties, and Important Issues.

METHODS USED IN EXPOSURE ESTIMATION

Hydrogeologists use a variety of methods to estimate exposure at hazardous waste sites. These methods help us to understand existing conditions and to evaluate remedial actions. They include direct measurement, ground water modeling, theoretical calculations, and expert opinion.

Direct measurement includes tools and techniques normally associated with site characterization such as siting, drilling, and installation of monitoring wells; sampling ground water; and chemical analysis of those samples. Ground water modeling refers to the use of numerical and/or analytical solutions to simulate flow and transport in the subsurface. Theoretical calculations include statistical analysis and other mathematical expressions that are not considered part of ground water modeling. Finally, expert opinion refers to best professional judgment.

STRENGTHS AND WEAKNESSES OF THE METHODS

Direct measurement or monitoring has the advantage of directly observing concentration distributions. This method should be included even if other methods are selected. The disadvantages of this method are its costs and the problems associated with proper monitoring well siting, well construction (making sure that a representative sample is obtained), and sample analysis. Also, this approach provides only a snapshot of the situation and not a prediction of the future.

Ground water modeling is a valuable tool that aids site conceptualization and the relative evaluation of various remedial alternatives. Modeling ground water flow is generally performed with confidence. Unfortunately, that confidence is greatly diminished when models are applied to organic transport. Such processes as sorption and degradation are not as well understood as flow, and rate constants describing these processes are generally unavailable. Thus, modeling organics has a great deal of uncertainty associated with it.

Statistical techniques, such as time series analysis, may be helpful in predicting trends. These tools, however, require significant data and do not aid in improving our physical/chemical understanding of solute transport. Other theoretical calculations— for example, geochemical relationships—may indicate possible reactions or transformations, but they cannot provide the reaction kinetics. Therefore, these methods also have uncertainty associated with them.

Expert opinion is used throughout these methods. It is used to help site wells and to form conceptual models for testing and analyzing. It is also used to estimate ranges of values for certain parameters. Expert opinion by itself, however, without the above methods, is of limited value.

METHODS' EFFECTIVENESS UNDER DIVERSE CONDITIONS

All of the above methods, given the limitations discussed, work for diverse conditions if there are sufficient data. The uncertainty introduced by a lack of sufficient data must be addressed when using any of the methods. For example, in a ground water modeling application, multiple simulations may be required in which both sensitivity analysis on uncertain parameters and scenario analysis on uncertain conditions are performed.

ASSOCIATED DATA BASE

As indicated throughout this discussion a major problem with all methods is the data—or rather, the lack of it. The data requirements may be divided into two groups: site-specific and chemical-specific data. Site-specific data include hydrologic units, intrinsic permeability distribution, source terms, hydrodynamic dispersion, and so forth. Chemical-specific data include solubility, wettability, volatilization, biodegradability, and others.

Participants in the workshop generally concurred in the belief that both kinds of data are lacking. The emphasis at hazardous waste sites is on chemical monitoring, and important hydrologic data, such as intrinsic permeability, are often overlooked. In addition, the time frames associated with remedial investigation/feasibility studies are generally less than 1 year. Thus, not even one annual cycle of hydrologic data will be available when the remedy is specified. Chemical-related data are also lacking, a circumstance that is particularly true for multiphase flow problems and chemical transformations.

ASSOCIATED UNCERTAINTIES

The uncertainties associated with the four methods noted earleir have been discussed throughout this report. More uncertainty is associated with transport than with ground water flow. The sources of this uncertainty are complex processes, data limitations, and site variability.

Because of these uncertainties, the prediction of future organic fates and their transport is very difficult. Although exact predictions cannot be made, our ability to predict is adequate enough to make many engineering decisions concerning remediation.

IMPORTANT ISSUES

The following important issues were identified by the workshop participants:

1. The methods discussed in this report must be used by qualified people. Misuse of the methods obviously negates any value that might be assigned to them.

2. The communication of results is critical. This process should include the dissemination of enough information to allow the results to be reproduced, the assumptions and methods used to obtain the results, and the limitations and uncertainties associated with the results.

3. It is important that these methods be validated and that performance measures associated with these methods be verifiable.

4. Public education is important. Ground water characterization and cleanup is a long-term process, with some cleanup standards exceedingly difficult to achieve.

ENGINEERING WORKSHOP
Rapporteur: Richard A. Conway

The formal presentations at the colloquium emphasized the aspects of toxicology, hydrogeology (transport/transformation), regulatory strategy, economics, and public concerns in setting cleanup levels at hazardous waste sites. The role of engineering was elucidated in a following workshop.

The first step was to define what was meant by "engineering." Webster's defines engineering as "the science by which the properties of matter and the sources of energy in nature are made useful to man in structures, machinery, and products." The operative word here is *useful*. Also encompassed by "products" presumably would be the categories of processes and operations.

Thus, engineering transforms the findings of scientists (e.g., hydrogeologists and toxicologists) into products useful to man. In terms of water quality issues the workshop participants recognized that engineers play a role in developing useful models of transport and transformation; they agreed to limit their discussion to mitigation processes and operations, however, because engineering plays a unique role in setting water quality goals.

DISCUSSION OF POSSIBLE CHANGES IN THE
ENGINEERING ROLE

With material from the formal presentations of the colloquium, a schematic of the process of setting cleanup goals was synthesized (Figure A). In this figure the cleanup goals—that is, the site-specific levels of acceptable exposure or risk—are established by comparing release concentrations with background levels; exposure concentrations with accepted concentration standards for chemicals in the various media; and the risk level with policy goals for acceptable risk. When discrepancies between any two of these inevitably are found, various mitigation strategies are applied until a level of risk is achieved *at a cost and degree of reliability acceptable to society*. As shown in Figure A, mitigation strategies can be applied to prevent releases, to contain releases, or to treat the contaminated medium at the exposure point (see Table A for some alternative mitigation strategies). This is an iterative process; that is, various strategies are tested until an acceptable risk level is achieved.

The process described above can take up to 4 years and cost several million dollars before remediation, a 2-year process itself, is even started. The workshop further explored a concept suggested by David Miller during the colloquium to the effect that the time and cost could be reduced markedly by starting studies of remediation alternatives immediately after release characterization and well before the full risk assessment is completed (Figure A).

Knowing what kind of remediation is feasible in terms of

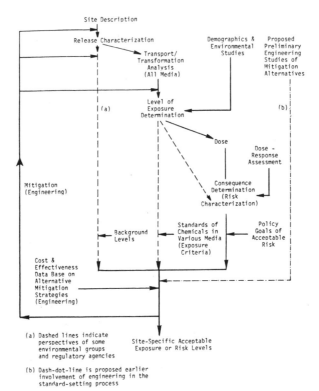

FIGURE A The role of engineering in establishing cleanup goals as discerned from colloquium presentations.

reliability to achieve goals (uncertainty), time to reach goals, permanency of goal attainment, and cost would provide direction for the risk assessment instead of its pursual in the abstract. The only factor keeping society from insisting on near-zero risk is the cost of attaining it. Hence, knowing something of the cost-effectiveness of engineered alternatives early in the process should markedly speed up the assessment and thus the final remediation. In addition, factors that are critical to design are identified early and can be resolved during the hydrogeologic studies and not later as an add-on study.

In a similar vein but from a different perspective, during the colloquium, Toby Page pointed out that factors like useful (cost-effective) engineering solutions should be more fully considered. When one tries to make an objective decision in this arena based on classic risk analysis (an inexact process with great uncertainty),

TABLE A Some Alternative Mitigation Technologies

Activity	Technology
Excavation and offsite disposal	
Containment	Physical barriers (e.g., slurry walls and caps, leachate collection)
Treatment of wastes and plumes near release point	Incineration and other thermal treatment
	Stabilization, solidification for leaching control
	Soil flushing with water treatment
	Soil biologic treatment
	Pumping, treating, and recharging of ground water
	In situ biologic treatment of soil and ground water
	Chemical treatment (chemical reactions)
	Physical separation of contaminants for treatment (e.g., volatilization)
Treatment of plumes at the drinking water wellhead	Air stripping and activated-carbon adsorption

Based in part on U.S. General Accounting Office, Hazardous Waste: EPA's Consideration of Permanent Treatment Remedies, GAO/RCED 86-178BR. Washington, D.C., July 1986.

paralysis (inaction) can result. Subjective decisions often are appropriate in cases in which uncertainties are great. Knowing the effectiveness and cost of solutions is a component that helps a subjective decision. But as David J. Leu pointed out the need for action should not be overemphasized; we should follow a policy of ready-aim-fire and not ready-fire-aim. (As Tom Hellman quipped, we should also avoid a policy of ready-aim . . ., ready-aim . . ., ready-aim . . ., ready-aim-fire.)

Another observation of participants in the engineering workshop was that remediation systems cannot be reliably designed for very low standards because design relationships are not proven down to those levels. Also, analytical methods with "practical detection limits"—that is, reasonable detection levels based on available analytical technology, considering economic and technical feasibility at or below the proposed cleanup standards—are needed for proper evaluation. Those individuals involved in risk assessment should keep this in mind as they debate goals in the low micrograms-per-liter range.

In addition, engineers have a responsibility to describe the usefulness of their design solutions in terms of effectiveness, reliability (uncertainty), the time it takes to accomplish them, permanency, and cost, in descriptions that are understandable to the public. Specific uncertainties with the flushing method of soil cleanup, the extraction/treat/recharge method of plume mitigation with its associated problem of hystoresis because of slow desorption, and the longevity of plastic covers were identified. Also, much less experience exists for in situ subsurface remediation compared to surface treatment; consequently, the former is less reliable at this time. Designs should be favored that fail in a safe way, that is, there is little risk to the community, and corrective action can easily be taken.

Finally, the public needs to be informed of constraints in the utility of remedial technology. Engineers need to get across to decisionmakers who are trusted by the public what can and cannot be done at a cost acceptable to society. For example, a qualitative term like exorbitant cost could be expressed quantitatively in terms of very low reductions in risk for the additional cost (Figure B). Public expectations need to be tempered by the ability to pay—which is what the public ultimately does, no matter from which pocket the funds originally came.

Also incumbent on engineers is the need to continue to seek more effective, lower cost solutions to this problem. Furthermore, additional arbitrary political barriers to the implementation of innovative options should be removed; in this manner, more field sites could serve as engineering "laboratories" and potential demonstration projects when risk to the public is minimal.

CONCLUSIONS

- Engineering solutions that are cost-effective should be discussed early in the process of setting water quality standards; that is, in selecting a method for dealing with a particular hazardous waste site, consideration should be given to achievable engineering solutions.
- Requiring a particular site to be rehabilitated to background or parts per billion levels often is not achievable with present-day engineering methods.

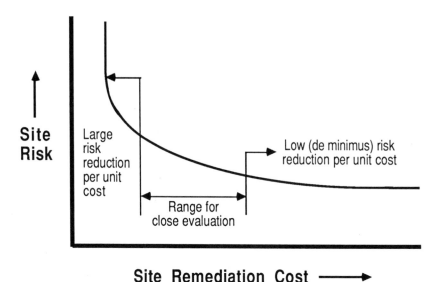

Site Remediation Cost ⟶

FIGURE B   Cost-effectiveness.

• Designs should be pointed toward rugged concepts that are of a safe/fail perspective rather than a fragile design in which failure can result in serious consequences.

• Engineers should take a leading role in helping to inform the public and in some cases regulatory staff of the reliable engineering aspects of hazardous waste site management and water quality issues.

• Engineers need to communicate with the public on the alternative solutions to a particular site cleanup: the cost versus the level of pollutant cleanup, the reliability and uncertainty involved, and the permanence of the alternatives.

REGULATORY STRATEGIES WORKSHOP
Rapporteur: Gordon Robeck

The methods used by some states and EPA to set water quality goals or standards rely heavily on a risk assessment that involves setting some numerical concentration limit at a water use point. Reducing carcinogens to a risk of 10^{-6} would be one example.

Several workshop participants contended that this method has not worked very well for federal cleanup cases and claimed that available money, the time to do the cleanup, and feasible technology were—and still are—the driving forces for action. These people seemed to prefer a goal based on future land and water use, in addition to one that gives more weight to anticipated exposures. Such a policy would give the local citizens more control over how much cleanup they wanted and how much money should be spent on a specific site. A third faction proposed that the most straightforward goal was simply to clean up the site to its original state.

One of the weaknesses of trying to calculate risk is that many toxicants—singly or in combination—have not been evaluated for their health effects; thus, the total exposure from air or water, or to the skin, for present or future users of the land and water is difficult to estimate. Consequently, many believe a negotiated technical solution to pump and treat ground water to the level of surface water resources is the most practical and the quickest way to confine the ground contamination. Although this approach has been conducted successfully at some locations with the help of predictive models and strategically placed wells for testing the movement and quality of water, there is still much to be learned about contaminant retardation and biotransformation in the anaerobic zone. Incidentally, the federal health program is making an effort to determine the health effects of 100 chemicals that may be involved in such contamination, with perhaps hundreds more to be considered in the distant future. Some estimate these evaluations may cost as much as $1 million–$4 million per chemical, and even when they are completed, many in the field doubt that the information will change the choice of technology for remedial action. Others realize that health effect determinations and risk assessment analysis must go forward and that with time and effort a stronger basis and understanding will support the remedial actions and promote public confidence.

To expedite the cleanup process, EPA has proposed classifying waters in three categories and thus guiding the decisionmaker as to where, when, and how much cleanup should be required at any one site. Some workshop participants thought that the system of permitting discharges, as allowed by the Clean Water Act, would be a fairer and more practical way of protecting a large aquifer from excessive contamination. One state representative maintained that the decision tree process was working in his state, but he also admitted that, initially, there was a lack of knowledgeable well drillers, consultants, and staff people to aggressively handle all the major cases. This individual stated, however, that there has been rapid improvement in technology and personnel so he is encouraged about future cleanup and source control. Other workshop participants were concerned about the lack of oversight and reliable statistics to help measure the rate of progress in the state or federal cleanup programs.

Many people feel a great frustration with the congressional mandate to clean up to background levels, and they believe that in 5 more years there will be great disappointment with the slow rate of such cleanups. They think much of the effort must be made by technical people to educate Congress and the public in general as to what can be done with the available funds; they also think it is necessary to convey how impossible it is going to be to achieve original or background levels at all major sites. In any event the workshop participants anticipated the need to be open and flexible because circumstances will undoubtedly cause other changes in legislation and in the availability of cleanup funds.

Appendix A
Biographical Sketches of Principal Contributors

Edwin F. Barth III is an environmental engineer with the Hazardous Site Control Division of Superfund. He is involved with the development of Superfund approaches to ground water contamination and alternative technology implementation. He has an M.S. degree in environmental engineering from the University of Notre Dame.

Halina S. Brown is an associate professor of environment, technology, and society at Clark University, Worcester, Massachusetts. She received a Ph.D. in 1975 from New York University. Her principal areas of interest are regulatory toxicology, environmental public health policy, and the management of environmental pollution. Trained as a chemist, for several years she pursued basic research on molecular mechanisms of cancer induction by polycyclic aromatic hydrocarbons. Prior to her affiliation with Clark University, she worked for the Massachusetts government as chief toxicologist and public health policymaker for the state environmental agency. Dr. Brown has served on numerous advisory committees, both on the state level and for the U.S. Environmental Protection Agency.

James M. Davidson received his Ph.D. in soil physics from the University of California at Davis. Currently, he is assistant dean

195

for research at the University of Florida. His area of expertise has encompassed the development of mathematical simulation models for describing the movement of nitrogen and organic pesticides in unsaturated soil–water systems. He is experienced in environmental sciences and hydraulics technology. Dr. Davidson is a member of the Water Science and Technology Board.

Richard M. Dowd, president and principal scientist of R. M. Dowd & Company, consultants in science and environmental policy, Washington, D.C., served from 1977 to 1981 as principal science advisor to the administrator of the U.S. Environmental Protection Agency. He served as EPA's acting administrator for research and development in 1980–1981. From 1981 to 1984 he headed the Washington, D.C., office of Environmental Research & Technology, Inc. Prior to joining EPA, he was one of the first principal analysts in the newly created Congressional Budget Office (CBO), where he helped design the policy and budget analysis programs for CBO's Division of Natural Resources and Commerce. He began his professional career as a professor of physics at Tufts University and has had 12 years of experience in directing federal and state environmental and policy research programs. Dr. Dowd has an active interest in issues concerning the quality and interpretation of environmental monitoring data and in the development of research protocols for hazardous chemicals; he maintains continuing contact with EPA decisionmakers in these areas. He holds a Ph.D. in physics from the University of Wisconsin, Madison, and a B.S. degree from Yale University.

Ronald R. Esau, assistant general manager for the Santa Clara Valley Water District, has a B.S. in Civil Engineering from Kansas State University and an M.S. in Civil Engineering (Water Resources) from San Jose State University. He is affiliated with the Bay Area Water Resources Council; State Water Contractors, Inc.; the Association of State Water Project Agencies; and the American Society of Civil Engineers. He has been president of the Santa Clara Valley Engineers Council and the Engineers Club of San Jose.

Linda E. Greer is a science associate with the Environmental Defense Fund, Washington, D.C. She received an M.S.P.H. in 1979 from the University of North Carolina. She has been an assistant environmental scientist at the Midwest Research Institute,

Raleigh, N.C.; a research assistant in the Department of Environmental Sciences and Engineering, University of North Carolina, Chapel Hill; and a limnologist at the University of Michigan Biological Station, Pellston. Currently, as a scientist in the toxic chemicals program at EDF, she is involved in promoting scientifically sound regulation and management of hazardous waste (RCRA and Superfund); analyzing federal regulatory efforts; providing technical information necessary for lawsuits; and explaining technical information to citizens with nontechnical backgrounds.

Thomas M. Hellman obtained a B.A. in chemistry from Williams College and a Ph.D. in organic chemistry from Pennsylvania State University. Dr. Hellman has 16 years of experience as an environmental scientist and manager in industry. From 1970 to 1973 he worked for Union Carbide and simultaneously taught at West Virginia University. In 1973 he joined Allied Corporation holding various positions in several geographical locations including manager for air and water programs and department head for health, safety, and environmental sciences. In July 1984 he moved to the position of director of Allied's legislative and regulatory affairs pertaining to environmental matters in Washington, D.C. In 1985 Dr. Hellman joined General Electric Company as corporate manager of health, safety, and environmental protection. Dr. Hellman is the past chairman of the Chemical Manufacturer Association's Environmental Management Committee (1984–1985). He also served for 4 years on the New Jersey Hazardous Wastes Advisory Council. Dr. Hellman served as a member of the National Research Council's Committee on Ground Water Quality Protection from 1984 to 1986.

David J. Leu is chief of California's Alternative Technology and Policy Development Section, Toxic Substances Control Division, Department of Health Services. He is responsible for managing the Environmental Science and Environmental Technology elements within California's Hazardous Waste Program. The Environmental Science element is responsible for developing geotechnical and toxicologic standards and cleanup criteria and for assessing alternative remedial technologies affiliated with site mitigation efforts. The Environmental Technology element is responsible for seeking out and encouraging new technological developments in the area of hazardous waste. Dr. Leu received his

B.S. degree from the University of Michigan's College of Engineering, his M.S. degree from the University of Michigan's Rackham School of Graduate Studies, and his Ph.D. from the University of Delaware's School of Marine Studies.

Robert G. Tardiff, a principal with ENVIRON Corporation since 1984, is a recognized expert in toxicology and health risk assessment, with a specialized focus on chronic intoxication from chemicals in drinking water. Dr. Tardiff received his A.B. in biology from Merrimack College in 1964 and his Ph.D. in pharmacology and toxicology from the University of Chicago in 1968. Before engaging in consultation, Dr. Tardiff served for more than 5 years as the executive director of the Board on Toxicology and Environmental Health Hazards of the National Research Council. Previously, he was chief of the Toxicologic Assessment Branch of EPA's Office of Research and Development and had served as research toxicologist in the Water Supply and Sea Resources Program. He is on the board of directors of the Academy of Toxicologic Sciences and is a founder of the Society of Risk Analysis.

Appendix B
Colloquium Attendees

MARY P. ANDERSON, University of Wisconsin-Madison
CHARLES ANDREWS, S. S. Papadopulos & Associates,
Rockville, Maryland
ROY ARNOLD, Bureau of Reclamation, Washington, D.C.
EDWIN F. BARTH III, U.S. Environmental Protection Agency,
Cincinnati, Ohio
MARLENE BERG, U.S. Environmental Protection Agency,
Washington, D.C.
JOAN BERKOWITZ, Risk Science International, Washington,
D.C.
WILLIAM BIVINS, Federal Emergency Management Agency,
Washington, D.C.
JOHN J. BOLAND, The Johns Hopkins University
EDWARD BOUWER, The Johns Hopkins University
HALINA SZEJNWALD BROWN, Clark University
EDWARD BRYAN, National Science Foundation, Washington,
D.C.
STEPHEN BURGES, University of Washington
PAUL BUSCH, Malcolm Pirnie, White Plains, New York
CAROLE B. CARSTATER, National Research Council,
Washington, D.C.

DONALD L. CHERY, JR., U.S. Nuclear Regulatory Commission, Washington, D.C.

WILLIAM CIBULAS, Agency for Toxic Substances and Disease Registry, Atlanta, Georgia

PHILIP COHEN, U.S. Geological Survey, Reston, Virginia

RICHARD A. CONWAY, Union Carbide Corporation, South Charleston, West Virginia

SHEILA D. DAVID, National Research Council, Washington, D.C.

JAMES DAVIDSON, University of Florida

RUTH S. DEFRIES, National Research Council, Washington, D.C.

NORBERT DEE, U.S. Environmental Protection Agency, Washington, D.C.

RICHARD DOWD, R. M. Dowd & Company, Washington, D.C.

LEO M. EISEL, Wright Water Engineers, Denver, Colorado

RONALD R. ESAU, Santa Clara Valley Water District, San Jose, California

MARY J. GEARHART, Colorado Department of Health, Denver

MICHAEL GOUGH, ENVIRON Corporation, Washington, D.C.

JASON GRAY, Virginia Water Project, Roanoke

LINDA E. GREER, Environmental Defense Fund, Washington, D.C.

MATTHEW HALE, U.S. Environmental Protection Agency, Washington, D.C.

HARRY HAMILTON, State University of New York, Albany

THOMAS M. HELLMAN, General Electric, Fairfield, Connecticut

R. KEITH HIGGINSON, Higginson-Barnett, Consultants, Bountiful, Utah

JOEL HIRSCHHORN, Office of Technology Assessment, Washington, D.C.

PATRICK W. HOLDEN, National Research Council, Washington, D.C.

MICHAEL KAVANAUGH, James M. Montgomery Consulting Engineers, Oakland, California

ARNOLD KUZMACK, Office of Drinking Water, U.S. Environmental Protection Agency, Washington, D.C.

LESTER B. LAVE, Carnegie-Mellon University

DAVID J. LEU, Department of Health Services, Sacramento, California

LUNA B. LEOPOLD, University of California, Berkeley
ORIE LOUCKS, Butler University
G. RICHARD MARZOLF, Kansas State University
JAMES W. MERCER, GeoTrans, Inc., Herndon, Virginia
DAVID W. MILLER, Geraghty & Miller, Inc., Plainview, New
    York
FRED MOSELEY, Northeast-Midwest Institute, Washington,
    D.C.
ISHWAR P. MURARKA, Electric Power Research Institute,
    Palo Alto, California
FRANK OSTERHOUDT, Office of Policy Analysis, Washington,
    D.C.
TOBY PAGE, Brown University
STEPHEN D. PARKER, National Reseach Council, Washington,
    D.C.
BRENT PAUL, Bureau of Reclamation, Washington, D.C.
RICHARD PIPER, Bureau of Reclamation, Washington, D.C.
GORDON ROBECK, Water Consultant, Laguna Hills, California
WILLIAM ROPER, Office, Chief of Engineers, Washington, D.C.
PHILIP J. STAPLETON, Dames and Moore, Bethesda,
    Maryland
ROBERT TARDIFF, ENVIRON Corporation, Washington, D.C.
FRANK H. THOMAS, Federal Emergency Management Agency,
    Washington, D.C.
J. DAVID THOMAS, Eastman Kodak, Washington, D.C.
JAMES THOMAS, Bureau of Reclamation, Denver, Colorado
LLOYD O. TIMBLIN, JR., Bureau of Reclamation, Denver,
    Colorado
RICHARD URBAN, Tennessee Valley Authority, Chattanooga,
    Tennessee
EDITH BROWN WEISS, Georgetown University Law Center
ERIC WOOD, Princeton University

Index

A

Acceptable daily intake (ADI)
acceptable soil contaminant level derived from, 52
for carcinogens, 52, 160
conversion to unit cancer risk, 156
definition, 36, 37, 154
derivation, 38, 49, 60–61
gassifier wastes, 160
heavy metals, 160
polynuclear aromatic hydrocarbons, 160
volatile inorganics, 160
see also Dose
Air quality, Washington State standards for, 54
Animal experiments
of carcinogenicity, 154
data base from, 16
extrapolation of toxicologic data from, 6, 38, 49–50
Applied action levels
application in site risk appraisal, 71–72, 96
arsenic, 80
chloroform, 83–84, 96
definition, 7, 44, 68, 71, 94, 96
derivation, 44, 46, 72
naphthylene and xylene, 74
uncertainties in, 96

Aquifers
biodegradation in, 143, 157
classification system for, 31
cleanup potential, 65–66, 89–90, 92–93, 103–104
major, risk assessment for, 169–170
vulnerability assessment, 141–142
Arizona Department of Health Services, numerical rating of priority pesticides, 142
Arsenic
ADI, 160, 162, 170
carcinogenic risk, 160, 162, 170
case study of contamination, 75–82

C

California
EPA regulatory role and responsibilities in, 125
hazardous materials storage ordinance, 123
Porter-Cologne Water Quality Control Act, 124
Regional Water Quality Control Board, 124, 131–132
regulatory agency roles and responsibilities, 123–125